A1.

from Kathleen

Oct 1938

THIS IS MR. FORTUNE

THIS IS MR. FORTUNE

by

H. C. BAILEY

LONDON
VICTOR GOLLANCZ LTD
1938

WARNING

All the persons and events in this book are entirely imaginary. Nothing in it is derived from anything which ever happened.

PRINTED IN GREAT BRITAIN BY PURNELL AND SONS, LTD. (T.U.)
PAULTON (SOMERSET) AND LONDON

CONTENTS

I

THE YELLOW CLOTH

THE YELLOW CLOTH

"Not one of your best corpses, Lomas," said Mr. Fortune.

"Sorry about that," the Chief of the Criminal Investigation Department was brusque. "Well?"

"Been in the water four weeks or more. However. Some of life's sad story still to be read in the remains. Male of sixty plus. Cause of death, drowning. Not a nice male. Drank too much. And other sins. He was limpin' paralytic. Poor beggar. Well out of this world."

The Hon. Sidney Lomas heard the beginning of this report with a grimace, and at the end made an angry noise.

"My dear old thing!" Mr. Fortune sympathized. "Sorry. Friend of yours?"

"You're a nuisance, Reginald."

"That's what I'm for. Compellin' the official mind to think. Grievous effort. Especially at ten a.m. Why did you bring me here so horrid early?"

"Quite sure of all this—dead a month—old drunkard?"

"Absolutely. What's the matter? Did you want him to be somebody else?"

"Confound you," Lomas scowled.

"Not me, no. Another tragedy of the police force.

Convenient theory slain by a fact or two. Tell me all. Who claimed to know him?"

"Nobody. He was too decayed. But we had reason to believe he was a fellow who disappeared, badly wanted."

"What for?"

"Information. The missing man is an old lag turned nark. We value him. Pet name, Chatty Brown. A fortnight ago he told Grice, the inspector in the Whitecross division, that he'd got on to some big stuff. He's never been heard from since, and they can't find a smell of him in any of his haunts. On Sunday, this body was picked out of the Regent's Canal, down Whitecross way. Grice and his men agreed the size and shape looked like Chatty Brown. So we passed it to you. And now you've made the time of death all wrong and the age and the type of man."

"Happy to oblige," Reggie murmured, and contemplated Lomas with dreamy eyes. "Yes. Your Mr. Brown was alive long after that body was dead. Deceased is one more irrelevant unfortunate. And the next thing, please? Was Mr. Brown's stuff very big?"

"Nobody knows what the devil it was," Lomas snapped.

"Oh, my Lomas! Why so curt? Why has the great mind gone jumpy over the death of an informer who didn't inform and hasn't been found dead?"

"I don't know that he isn't dead," Lomas spoke with cold fury. "You can only tell me we haven't found the body."

"Splendid!" Reggie smiled. "The official mind is now working. I have not been dragged out of bed in vain. Go and look for your Chatty one, if you want him."

"He's been looked for everywhere, I told you so. And now one of the men who was after him has disappeared too."

"Oh!" Reggie sat up. "When was that?"

"Last night. Cay, a detective-sergeant in the White-cross division, went out to work round Chatty Brown's pals. He didn't come back to report. They sent round for him this morning and couldn't make anyone hear. Cay's a widower, lived alone. They got the door open. His bed hadn't been slept in, but the rooms were all on end as if they'd been rummaged. There we are!"

"Well, well," Reggie murmured. "Not a nice place to be." He gazed at Lomas, and his round face was like a child's surprised by the weakness of the grown up. "I wonder."

Lomas stared hard and exploded. "Do you conceive yourself to see a line?"

"Not me. No. I haven't tried. But I should like to."

He was right. Not, as he loves to assure Lomas, that he had then the slightest idea of what had happened or what was going to. But the case of the yellow cloth is considered an exemplar of his work in pure detection. He calls it a triumph of the science of making objections. It also saved a life and a soul or two. To this he points as a queer proof of the uses of things. Only the unknown wastrel who fell drunk into the canal for his private purposes made the salvation of these others possible.

The Whitecross division is in the centre of London, half warehouse and factory, half slum. Between its roaring highways stretches a labyrinth of narrow streets which wind upon themselves and are pierced again by squalid courts. Glancing into the dingy maze at either side, as the police car sat on the tail of a tram, Reggie asked his companion, Inspector Underwood, "What do they do down here?"

"Everything you ever heard of, sir—and then some. Dry goods, soft goods, tobacco, leather, metal work. Nothing in particular."

"Much crime?"

"Quite enough. Warehouse and van robberies, the speciality. Used to be a regular rookery of thieves— that's thinned out now by rebuilding for business. But they get a bad break in the division every once in a while. And a good deal more is still put up down here. Some of these back alleys keep pretty tough. Crooks find it very central, and a fine clearing house for news. Lots of carmen and porters live round about. Easy to pick up where the goods are going. That's how Chatty Brown was so useful, he gave us the office who was after what. And Cay had done all his service here, he knew too much about most of the old hands, he'd jugged half of 'em in his time."

"Livin' dangerously. Yes. It is up to us, Underwood. 'We are not divided, all one body we.' Narks and all."

The car turned into a by-street, where children were playing football with a tin can between warehouses, turned again and stopped at a grey and yellow block

of workmen's flats, hideous and pathetically respectable. They climbed stone stairs and a door on the
second landing opened to them.

Inspector Grice received Mr. Fortune with the
patient endurance of a man who could be surprised
by nothing unpleasant. "Very good of you to come and
help us, sir. I don't know what you'd like to do."

"Nor do I. You're going to tell me."

Grice became still more dreary. "I have nothing for
a doctor in this, Mr. Fortune. There's no body, nor
trace of it."

"Not even a wrong one this time. Too bad. Are we
down-hearted? Yes. Any other results?"

"Cay's been made away with all right," said Grice,
a stubborn satisfaction obtruding in his gloom. "So
was Chatty Brown. And it took a brain to do those
two in. No flies on Chatty. Poor old Cay was one of my
best men. Safe and sure. A regular terrier, all eye and
nose. And they're both out—like that!" He snapped
bony fingers.

"As you say. Have they left a lot of little things
behind 'em?"

"Chatty? Not him. He had no people nor home.
His pals have gone to ground. Of course the word's
been passed. Cay was out night by night nosing
after 'em. He hadn't got anything up to yesterday.
You can bet he did get something last night. That's
why he hasn't come back."

"Yes, I think so," Reggie looked round the living
room. It had the neat, meagre furniture of an old-
maidish man who spent little on himself, but it was in a
mess, cupboards open, drawers open, half their contents

lying about, a tumble of freshly burnt paper on the hearth. "But somebody came here not long ago."

"Ah! Somebody who searched the place, good and well, Mr. Fortune. See that." Grice opened the door of the bedroom. There also drawers and cupboards were open, linen dragged out of them, clothes flung to the floor with pockets inside out. "Somebody who took pains, eh?"

"That is indicated, yes. How did somebody get in?"

Grice gave a joyless grin. "You saw that? The door wasn't forced. A key was used—a bunch of keys—Cay's own keys"—he thrust his lean face forward and directed Reggie's eyes to the table—"there they are—look at that smeary muck in the ring—that's a dollop o' blood."

Reggie looked close. "Yes, blood clot," he said slowly. "Any more?"

"Not a drop. It isn't here Cay bled. Couldn't be. Look now. The other people in this place, they're up and down all hours of the night. Lot of the men work on the railway, in the markets, carting and so on, and the women are about looking after them. Nobody saw Cay after he went out on duty, nobody heard any noise. Well, what's that mean? He struck big trouble out on the job last night."

"Oh yes. That also is indicated. He picked up the scent of the fellows who removed Chatty Brown, and he also has been removed. He'd run a scent hard, would he, your Mr. Cay?"

"He would so." Grice smacked his lips. "That's Jim Cay all over. Keen as mustard. Didn't know what fear was. He'd go down to hell to get his man."

"Model for us all. Well, well. It is up to us. What about it?"

"Well, here you are. He's been made away with, like Chatty Brown, and by the same crowd. Most likely he was laid for in one of the dark courts and finished there. There's the canal and the river handy— or a body can be dumped anywhere with a motor van these days, and never found till it's no ruddy use."

"As you say. And one of the operators thought Cay might have left something awkward on record, took his keys and came round to make sure. Yes. That is the provisional hypothesis." Reggie gazed dreamily round the rooms. "Any idea what has been oblite-rated?"

"I couldn't say at all, except the silver's gone."

"What? Much silver owned by our Sergeant Cay?"

"My Lord, no," Grice gave a dismal chuckle. "How much would he have? Just a few spoons and forks, and sure to be only plated. Of course they were taken to make it look like a straight burglary."

"Oh ah. I didn't get that."

"Common trick," said Grice with patient contempt. "But this kind of job isn't in your line, Mr. Fortune. Now here's what shows you." He gave Reggie a note-book from which some pages had been roughly torn. "You can handle it how you like. We've done all the finger-print work."

"Any good?" Underwood asked quickly.

"Nix. One set all over the place. That'll be Cay's. Rubbed here and there. That'll be the gloves of the beggar who did the job."

"Negative confirmation of our theory," Reggie murmured, inspecting what was left of the book. "Yes. And this is positive. There was something in Sergeant Cay's archives which the nocturnal visitor didn't want Inspector Grice to see. In a way it's a compliment. Any idea what Cay might have put on record?"

"How could I?" Grice spoke as a martyr. "He'd talked Chatty's case inside out with me, but we never got anything hard on anyone. I take it he'd made out a list, names of suspects, places to work and so on and the real goods was among 'em. But what it was, search me."

"My dear chap!" Reggie sighed. "I'm trying." He put the book down and wandered to the hearth and gazed down at the burnt paper there. "That's fairly thorough too." The paper had not only been burnt. Most of the heap was broken up into tiny fragments.

Underwood knelt down beside him and peered into the heap. "Not so good," he pronounced.

"No. As you say. Thoughtful fellow against us. However. Do your stuff."

While Underwood gathered the larger pieces of tinder, Reggie drifted about the room. He was at a shabby bureau when an exclamation recalled him.

Underwood had found under the ashes bits of a photograph which had not been burnt, but torn up with some violence. Pieced together, they made the head and shoulders of a man. "You have found something, Mr. Underwood," said Grice drearily satirical. "That's Jim Cay himself."

"Well, well," Reggie murmured, and studied the

photograph. The face, in spite of destruction, came out clear, a sharp-featured face underhung by a good deal of jaw, declaring discipline and stubborn zeal. Reggie looked up at Grice. "Anything else occur to you? No? Oh, my dear chap! Nothing to be concealed by tearing up the photograph of your Mr. Cay. And it was torn with some zeal. The obvious suggestion is hatred and malice."

"That helps a lot." Grice sneered. "Of course the fellow who was here hated Cay. There's nothing new in a crook messing up the portrait of a man he had a down on."

"Oh no. No. The natural savage, his way. Kill your enemy, kill his image. Before or after. Any suspicion of a woman in the case?"

"I have not," Grice was flustered. "What makes you say that?"

"There are points. You don't think women are different from men? No, you may be right."

"Of course they are," Grice scowled.

"I wouldn't say that. No. However. You didn't mention this." Reggie went to a shabby little pedestal desk and took the blotting pad from it. The blotting paper was clean but it bore pencil sketches such as a man might draw carelessly while he was thinking what he would write—the head of a fish and the head of a woman.

Both were satiric, but had some character. The woman was given a button of a nose and fat cheeks and chin under a mop of hair. The sloping brow and sliding chin of the fish's head unkindly suggested a man without brain.

Bf

"Human, all too human," Reggie murmured, as Grice gaped at them. "Anybody you know?"

"My God!" Grice exclaimed. "This is something, Mr. Fortune. There is a fellow we call Fishface. Young chap by name, Arthur Ellis. He was a carman, and Cay nailed him for a van robbery. He's in with a nasty crowd, never done an honest job since he came out of clink. I always had him in my eye for Chatty Brown's business, but neither Cay nor me could fix anything on him."

"And the lady?" Reggie watched him with dreamy curiosity. "She also looks like somebody. Had her in your eye, too?"

"I can't place her. But you wait. We can easy find out who is Fishface's best girl. See what this means. These were the two poor old Cay was thinking about just before he got done in."

"Yes. That is indicated. Why didn't the careful fellow who cleaned up the records of your Mr. Cay clean up their portraits too?"

"Why, he didn't notice 'em. Just pencil scribble on a clean blotting pad. He wouldn't."

"No. You didn't either. I wonder." Reggie wandered away into the dark little hall and turned a torch into every corner and on to the door mat. He grovelled. He picked up from the fibre of the mat some scraps and put them into a pill box. Then he turned into the bedroom. Grice followed him. "What's the idea, Mr. Fortune?"

"Any other little things you didn't notice." Reggie worked over washstand and toilet table. The usual articles of toilet apparatus were much worn but neat.

He took something from the clothes brush and shut
it into another pill box. Then he made an examination
of clothes and drawers and cupboards which was slow
but unceasing till he stood still contemplating a cupboard door. On the latch of it was a scrap of yellow
cloth.

He pored over it, he smelt it before he removed it
and put it in a third pill box. The cold curiosity of his
face was mellowed with satisfaction as he passed
Grice and went out to the little scullery. There he
inspected sink and roller towel and boot brushes.
"Well, well," he murmured. "Somebody had a wash
and brush up recently."

"Of course," Grice complained. "Cay would clean
himself before he went on duty. And I daresay the
other fellow did too."

"Quite likely, yes," Reggie returned to the living room.

"What have you got, Mr. Fortune?" Grice
demanded.

"Exhibit one: vegetable matter from door mat,"
Reggie showed him some small brown leaves. "Bits
of dried bracken frond."

"That's a lot of good," Grice sneered. "Anybody's
boots might pick up that round the market or a
market van, and no knowing how long it was on the
mat either."

"No. There isn't. Sorry you don't like it. Try again.
Your Mr. Cay kept his hair cut didn't he? And it
was going grey. Exhibit two. One longish red hair
from his clothes brush."

"Strike me!" Grice muttered and gloated over it.
"That's the stuff, Mr. Fortune. A red-headed girl in

it. And we had a girl before. The old, old story, eh? Find the woman."

"Yes. You had better. Yes. However. One moment. Exhibit three. Curious and interesting. Piece of yellow cloth torn from garment by cupboard latch."

Grice frowned over it. "You mean this job was done by somebody wearing yellow clothes."

"It could be. Yes." Reggie watched him with closing eyes. "Any other inference?"

"No man would wear clothes that yellow colour."

"Not likely. No. Even in these glad days. And your Mr. Cay had very sober tastes. Well."

"There must have been a woman! That's right. That goes with the rest. I'll be on to Fishface's girl good and quick. If you'll excuse me."

"Rather. Get on with it." As the door slammed behind him, Reggie turned to Underwood. "And what do you think of Inspector Grice?" he asked softly.

Underwood exhibited a proper surprise. "He's considered very sound, sir. Put through a lot of good work. One of the old school, you know; it's dogged as does it. He relies mostly on his knowledge of crooks."

"The more we are together, the happier we shall be," Reggie murmured. "Yes, I thought that."

"Are you suggesting there's something fishy about him?" Underwood frowned.

"My dear chap! Not me, no," Reggie smiled. "Most respectable force, the police force. Making England what she is."

"He isn't scientific, of course," Underwood admitted with some complacency.

"Not like us, no. Well, how are we doing?"

Underwood had a few pieces of burnt paper stuck with gum upon glass. One had carried a stamp with a postmark in which the last letters were A L E. A second had been ruled, and on it could be made out some figures, 393. The others bore scraps of writing which were unintelligible. "All the rest is practically dust," said Underwood. "Pretty well a wash out."

"I wouldn't say that," Reggie murmured. "Curious and interestin'." He reached for the notebook from which pages had been torn. "See anything there? Our Mr. Grice didn't." The first remaining page bore indentations from a pencil inscription on one of the pages destroyed.

"'T—O—T—S'," Underwood read out, "and then a gap and then a figure, looks like a 2."

"Yes. It could be. 'Tots 2.' Record of our Mr. Cay's offspring? Or what?"

"I don't know," Underwood frowned. "Might be an account of his drinks."

Reggie looked admiration. "You're so ingenious! Yes, it might be. Makin' our Mr. Cay a very careful fellow. Notin' all the little drinks that didn't do him any harm. 'Tots 2.' Of A—L—E perhaps. As per burnt postmark. Would you say he also had 393 tots?"

"I don't know why you're making fun of me." Underwood was hurt. "Can you put things together, Mr. Fortune?"

"Not yet, no. But not without hope. If we're lucky, which we have not been."

"I'll say we haven't!"

"No. Haven't deserved to be. Study to improve. What about this?" He pointed to a mass of tinder which was not all broken up.

"It's only a newspaper. *Daily Record* of April 17."

"As you say. Yes. Why burn it? Oh! A portion missing. Across two columns. Page 14. Well, well."

"That's a lot of use," said Underwood. "If you look, you'll see it's a magazine page, Mr. Fortune."

"I did. Interestin' and curious."

Both turned at the sound of talk with the policeman on guard outside. A breathless man was admitted. "Mr. Fortune, sir? Inspector Grice says would you come round at once to King's Head Court. I was to show you the way."

"Do," Reggie waved him out. "Come on, Underwood," and as they followed spoke to Underwood's ear. "Quick worker, Mr. Inspector Grice. Now we're behind him with a bradawl. Very quick. I wonder."

"You can bet he's got something, sir."

"I'm sure he has. Yes. A felt want by our Grice. However. So have we."

Underwood stared. "I haven't."

"My dear chap. Oh, my dear chap!" Over Reggie's face came a small, wistful smile. "You heard Sergeant Cay's spoons and forks were gone. You saw the scrap of yellow cloth torn off by the latch of his cupboard doors. Nature of case quite clear. We only want the people now."

Underwood looked at him with a mixture of distrust and awe. "You're telling me!" he said bitterly. "Only the people! Is that all? Only Chatty Brown and

Cay and the brutes who did 'em in! How are we any nearer because Cay's silver——"

"Oh, my Underwood!" Reggie reproached him. "Hush! Preserve the reputation of the police."

The detective, who had guided them through a street which was a cleft between tall warehouses and factories, paused at the turn to a narrow lane of older buildings, low and ramshackle, a squalid shop here and there, the rest of them let out to nondescript, dubious trades or inhabitants. He led on past a greasy eating house and stopped where a flight of steps led down to a court which was a dead end shut in by blank walls.

A policeman in uniform guarded the entry. Some men in bowler hats were busy below the steps. From them Inspector Grice detached himself as Reggie came delicately down. "This way, Mr. Fortune, if you'll be so good," his civility was satiric. "I ask you." He pointed to a dark splash on the flagstones. "Is that blood or is it not?"

"A felt want," Reggie murmured, and bent over it, knelt down by it. . . . "Yes," he sat back on his heels to look up at Grice like an enquiring child. "One dollop of blood in this particular lonely court."

"There's a bit more here," Grice went on to a drain pipe which ran down the wall. "Is this blood too?" There was a dark smear on the grey paint.

Reggie frowned at it. "Answer probably in affirmative," he mumbled. "Oh!" He came close to the pipe.

Grice gave a crow of triumph. "You see them, do you? You don't miss much, Mr. Fortune."

"Not often, no," Reggie extracted from between the pipe and the wall a broken set of false teeth. Upon them also were clots of blood. "Well, well." He looked up from them to Grice. "Cay didn't use nature's growth?"

"Sergeant Cay had a denture," said Grice with dignity. "Easy to identify."

"Oh yes," Reggie murmured. "It will be. And the inference is, he came here last night, he had a scrap, his teeth were knocked out of his head, after which he was abolished."

"That's right," Grice nodded; "all fits like we said. Strike me——" He dashed away up the steps.

Behind the guardian policeman a girl was loitering, a girl with a mop of red hair.

Two of Grice's men went after him. He caught her by the arm as she made off, he gave her to them, and they hustled her away, Grice marching in front.

"Well, well. Your Mr. Grice is swift," Reggie murmured. "'Follow after, follow after, for the harvest is sown. By the bones about the wayside shall you come to your own.' Come on, Underwood."

They followed, going hard through a labyrinth of byways to the Whitecross police station. Grice took the girl into his own room. Reggie and Underwood arrived before the door was shut. "I hope I don't intrude?" Reggie fanned himself with his hat.

"Waiting for you," Grice grinned triumph, and jerked a nod to the girl's red head. "What do you say now?"

"It could be," Reggie sighed. "Carry on."

The girl turned to look at him. She was panting, she was flushed, she showed fear and anger. Her face had a simple prettiness, but was plainly the original of the unkind sketch on Cay's blotting pad, something too full and with a nose too small for it.

Grice snarled at her. "Kitty Evans, aren't you? Waitress at Old Bill's eating house. Where were you last night?"

"Where would I be?" She had a low, husky voice, she spoke slowly with a sullen stare. "It wasn't my night out. I was in the kitchen till I went to bed. Sewing, I was."

"Sewing your trousseau," Grice sneered. "You're hopeful. When did you see your boy friend last?"

"I don't have boy friends."

"Oh, you've broke with sweetheart Fishface? He has left you to hold the baby, hasn't he?"

"You got no right to talk to me like that. I'm an honest girl."

"Show it, then. What made you come and spy round us in King's Head Court just now?"

"Spy yourself. Nor I wasn't spying. Just out for a breath of air after serving the dinners."

"You're fond of that court. You went there for a breather last night. It's a nice, quiet, dark place for sweethearting. Something else was done there last night, wasn't there? Look how you've been given away, my girl. You were in the court with Fishface, and Sergeant Cay came along and was set on. Now then. Let's have the truth. Give yourself a chance. How much was done to Cay before you quit? What do you say?"

She met his truculence without flinching. "That's all bunk," she answered. "I never went out last night at all. You ask the guv'nor. You ask missis."

Grice scowled at her. "Don't be silly. Where do you suppose Fishface is now? He's put it all on you."

"God's truth, you're a——" she cried and checked herself. "That lie don't go. You hound him out of every place he gets, and now you're working to plant something fresh on him. Not by me, you won't."

Reggie had been studying her intently. Now he rose and crossed the room behind her. She started round to face him, alarm and defiance in her tired eyes. "Did you know Sergeant Cay?" he asked gently.

She moistened her lips. "I've heard of him," she muttered. "I've seen him at our place."

"Ever had any dealings with him?"

"No, I haven't. I'm straight, I am." Her flush deepened.

"What were you doing in his rooms?" Grice barked at her.

She stammered in a fury. "You—you foul brute—I never did. I wouldn't."

Reggie beckoned to Grice, and Grice nodded and went out with him. "Nasty bit of stuff, ain't she, Mr. Fortune. I saw you had a good look at her hair. What do you say? Was that a bit of hers on Cay's brush?"

"Yes, I think so," Reggie murmured.

"Good. Lying like hell, wasn't she?"

"Not the whole truth, no. And some that wasn't the truth."

"I believe you," Grice nodded. "But what have we

got hard against her? Her hair in Cay's room. Not so good. Fishface might have brushed it off his coat cleaning up after he'd gone through Cay's things—got it on him by canoodling with her or both of 'em in the scrap with Cay. But Cay might have got it on himself in her eating house. Anyhow, not enough for a charge. And she's got her alibi for last night. Old Bill and his missis, they're hard cases, but there's nothing against 'em we could use in court. What they'd swear to would go with a jury. We've no right to hold her. My idea is, send round to old Bill's place and see if they back the girl—if they do, let her out and keep her under observation. That'll do, eh?" he winked. "Most likely she'll——" He broke off as a sergeant in uniform tapped his arm. "What's the matter with you?"

"Van robbery reported from Elm Lane, sir. A big thing. Railway van with bars of silver for Pillgroves, the manufacturing silversmiths, you know. Matter of four hundredweight of silver boxed. Driver was delivering a crate of goods at the shirt works in Elm Lane. Van boy helping him. When they came back the van was gone. Motor van. Happened half an hour ago. Might be out of London by now."

"Strike me!" Grice muttered.

Reggie gazed at him with closing eyes. "Is that surprise? Oh no. No. Not really."

"How do you mean?" Grice scowled. "It's been done before, of course it has."

"In your division?" Reggie murmured.

"Yes, and in every other blinkin' division," Grice retorted. "Wherever they have these vans with bullion.

It's a marvel to me the ruddy fools will go on delivering the stuff like it was ordinary goods."

"Very sad. As you say. Opportunity makes the thief. And a stitch in time saves nine and so forth. Opportunity here but no stitch. I wasn't thinking of that. At present. Only pointin' out this little incident was to be expected. Obvious connection with the elimination of our Sergeant Cay."

"You mean Cay had got on to the place of this robbery? Well, he may have, of course. What good is that to me? You say I could have expected it. How could I? You didn't think of it till it happened."

"Oh, my Grice! I pointed out that the removal of Cay's silver was curious and interestin'. I showed you the yellow cloth. Connection of Sergeant Cay, with operations in the silver plate trade quite clear."

"Yellow cloth!" Grice's mouth came open. "I don't get it. Oh, hell, I can't waste time like this." He strode away.

"Don't forget Miss Kitty Evans," said Reggie sharply.

"I don't forget anything," Grice flung over his shoulder. "I'll have her looked after."

"Mind you do," said Reggie.

"I know my job, thank you," Grice vanished.

Reggie turned to Underwood a face without expression. "Swifter and swifter yet," he murmured. "I wonder. Suppose we do a little work, young man."

Some time afterwards Reggie strolled into Lomas's room with a look of wistful patience on his round face. "One of your smaller cigars is indicated," he said sadly, took it and dropped into the easiest chair.

Lomas put up his eyeglass. "Very well. A last smoke before arrest may be allowed. I have long had my suspicions, Reginald. This case is conclusive. You go down to Whitecross, engage the attention of the police and get off with a van load of silver. Too blatant."

"Oh no. Very clever of me. I am."

"I take it you've come to give yourself up?"

"Not yet. No. I aim at larger crime, the crime of all the ages. I just looked in now to show up the police."

Lomas shook his head. "Unworthy of you. The usual trick of the crook when caught."

"Yes. But I'm not usual. I do it while still at large. Caught anybody who is usual?"

"Not yet. Your confederates are still at large. Better get in first by betraying them. I may tell you the van has been found abandoned—like you—and empty—I'm sure that isn't like you."

"No. There are things inside. I wonder. I've been in Fleet Street. A sad place. They don't lunch there. They only eat. It is the cause, it is the cause, my soul, of many of the throes of our great newspapers. However. Where was the van?"

"In Highgate. Below the cemetery."

"Well, well. Touch of grim humour. Hunt the buried treasure. I doubt if it was buried. Or Chatty Brown or Sergeant Cay. Just a nasty mind. Had many of these bullion van robberies?"

Lomas made a grimace. "More than I want. Especially this last year or so."

"Oh yes. Yes. Good organisation grown up to dispose of the stuff."

"There's a fence with a brain somewhere. A big man. We've never got near him."

"Someone with resources. Someone who doesn't stick at a trifle. And your Sergeant Cay was on to somebody in the silver plate trade. Curious and interestin'."

"How do you know that?" Lomas exclaimed.

Reggie smiled. "You didn't? Grice wouldn't. Curiouser and curiouser. However. No probable, possible shadow of doubt. Fellow who abolished Cay's records abolished also his spoons and forks. Grice says he was pretending to be a burglar, which is silly. These crimes aren't. Obvious purpose, to prevent recognition of maker's mark on Cay's bit of plate."

Lomas put up an eyebrow. "Rather fantastic, what? You have a great imagination, Reginald."

"Not me. No." Reggie squeaked. It is a charge which he always resents. "I only believe evidence. You ought to try that. Great change in police work. Further evidence. Yellow cloth—torn off on Cay's cupboard latch—you see? Quite conclusive."

"I do not," Lomas frowned at it.

"My dear chap! Oh, my dear chap. Smell it."

Lomas gave him a look of dislike and obeyed. "Faintly acid odour," he pronounced. "Well?"

"Senses not wholly inactive," Reggie murmured. "Nitrous odour. Nitric acid stain. Some fellow barged round Cay's bedroom wearing a dark tweed coat on which nitric acid had fallen, burnt a hole and made a stain. Hole caught on the latch, bit of the stain was torn off. Nitric acid is largely used in silver plate manufacture. You've been losing silver, large and frequent. Chatty Brown was abolished when promising big information. Your Sergeant Cay, told off to look for him, was abolished last night. To-day you lose another load of silver. Circumstances in abolition of Cay prove its connection with the electro plate industry. That's where your fence is—your fence with no scruples."

"Quite good, Reginald," Lomas nodded. "May even be right. We are not wholly futile ourselves. We had thought of the trade. But there's a lot of factories that use silver in England. This last haul may be half way to Birmingham by now. There's quite a few works in London. Did you happen to think you'd found a clue where it's gone?"

"Not yet. No. I'm not so swift as your Inspector Grice. I have to work for my results."

"That's why you went to lunch in Fleet Street."

"I didn't. I wouldn't," Reggie was shrill. "Sacrifice on duty's altar. I went to look over the files of the *Daily Record*." He shuddered. "What have I done for thee, England, my England! *Daily Record* of April 17 was burnt in Cay's rooms. Article on magazine page had previously been cut out. But I found it on the file. Simple as you see me. It was all about poultry." He lay back, blew a smoke ring and put out the cigar. "So that was that."

"Quite," Lomas chuckled. "You have my sympathy. I've tried to make meaning out of the meaningless myself. But you will keep young."

"Think again," Reggie rose slowly. "Everything means something. No effect without a cause. Why were the poultry cut out?"

"Do you conceive yourself to know?" Lomas scoffed. Reggie shook his head. "Quite. What on earth can it matter?"

Reggie looked down at him with narrowing eyes. "To your previous bullion robberies? I don't know. I don't care. There's been a lot of ignoring evidence, Lomas. Not any more, please. I'm thinking of a life or two."

"Damme, so are we all," Lomas was angry. "You don't suppose I've forgotten Chatty Brown and Cay?"

"Oh no. Proper professional interest. But I meant Kitty Evans and her Fishface." Reggie moved to the door. "Let me know all you hear from Grice. I shall be in Underwood's room. Doin' a little work, Lomas."

Underwood was bent over a paper of notes. "Well? Does it come out?"

"You've given me a teaser," Underwood pushed back his rumpled hair. "I don't say you're wrong, 'Tots' and the figures in Cay's book were a telephone number. If they are, 'Tots' must be Totsbury, you know, the suburb. No other exchange in England beginning 'Tots'. But Totsbury's all residential. No electro plate works there. No works at all to speak of. I've had a rare old time with the telephone people. You know those figures are pretty dim. Look like 2 and 393 but not to swear by. Well, Totsbury 2393 is a fishmonger's. The 2 was the most uncertain. I made 'em send me all the names to numbers ending 393. Not too good. I've been going through them with our local men. All known except one—Mrs. Redland-Smith 4393—newcomer in a block of new mansion flats."

"On with the dance. Who is Redland, what is she? What's Smith do when he isn't at home? I'll take up the burnt post mark."

"I don't know what you'll do with that, sir. It's only the end of the word. Host of places finish in A L E."

"Quite human. Yes. However. Other evidence converges. What was cut out of the burnt newspaper? Tips on poultry."

"I don't follow," Underwood stared at him.

"And there was the bracken too," Reggie murmured, and studied a gazetteer and a postal guide together and made notes, while Underwood again worried the Totsbury division over the telephone.

Lomas came in unheard, unseen, in the zeal of Underwood's exhortations and Reggie's devotion to geography. "How do the little busy bees improve each shining hour!" he interrupted them. "Found out why hens don't lay, Reginald?"

"Yes," Reggie glared at him. "Because they won't take things seriously. What are you going to tell me?"

"Grice has got the fellow who drove the van away."

"Oh my hat!" Reggie muttered. "Fishface!"

"What you expected?"

"One moment." Reggie wrote fast and passed the results to Underwood. "Take that next, young fellow." He stood up and took Lomas by the arm. "Yes, I did expect it. Not quite so quick. But he's very quick, your Grice. Now."

"You make a habit of expecting things after they've happened," Lomas's smile was unkind.

Cf

Reggie met it with a blank stare. "What? I showed Grice the sketch of Fishface on Cay's pad. He ought to have found it himself. Said he hadn't. My responsibility. I'll go down and see him."

"What for?"

"I'm afraid, Lomas."

Lomas put up an eyebrow. "You don't trust Grice?"

"I wonder." Reggie's round face was pale and drawn. "It's all on me," he shivered a little.

"I'll come with you," said Lomas.

A murky twilight darkened the dingy streets of Whitecross as they came to its police station. Grice received them with a mixture of complacency and surprise. "Very kind of you to come down, sir. There's no doubt I'm on to the real goods. I've had my eye on Fishface all the time. I set my chaps on to his pals good and quick. And we ran him down lying doggo in a doss house. He changed his lodging last night. That talks of itself, don't it? And there's a lot more. I've picked up two fellows who saw Fishface drive the van away, and a woman who thinks it was him. We could get him convicted for the robbery on that. But I reckon to do better. He's got a black eye and a rare old cut lip, done fresh. That links him with poor Cay's business good and well. If we can't prove it on him now, it's a wonder."

"What's his story?" Lomas asked.

"He hasn't got one," Grice grinned.

"Have you charged him?"

"Charged with the robbery, sir."

"No answer?"

"Only that he didn't know anything about it, and a bit of cursing. The usual."

"I'd like to see him," said Reggie, and Lomas nodded.

Grice looked injured. "Very good, sir."

He brought his capture shambling in, a sight unpleasant. The name of Fishface was justified by a countenance which might have been comical, but its injuries and its hopeless, embittered dejection made it repulsive. Its owner's clothes were shabby and dirty, and his body did not fill them.

"Now then," Grice barked at him, "you've been charged with robbery, Arthur Ellis. Anything you say may be used in evidence. And you don't have to say anything. Do you want to?"

The answer was an oath.

"There may be another charge, Ellis," said Lomas. "If you're innocent, your best course is to tell the truth: to make a statement of where you were all last night. I am thinking of what happened to Sergeant Cay."

"I dunno. So I don't say nothing. See? I know you busies. All ruddy liars. I don't care what you do. You can't do worse to me than what you done."

Reggie had come close to him, and was looking him over, bent down and looked close at his dirty hands.

"You ain't got no right to touch me," Fishface slunk away.

"Oh no. Don't want to. Thanks. That's all."

Lomas nodded and Grice thrust the man out.

"There you are, sir. He's not talking," Grice triumphed.

"Oh yes," Reggie murmured. "With his mouth, instructive. With the rest of him, decisive. Under nourished. Too weak for a hard scrap. And his knuckles haven't suffered. What about Miss Evans, Grice. Does she know you've arrested him?"

"You bet she does," Grice grinned. "She's hopped it."

"What?" Reggie's voice went up. "You—you let her out to see where she went. I told you to take care of her. You—— My God!" He snatched the telephone and rang up Underwood.

"How was it, Grice?" Lomas snapped.

"That's not fair, Mr. Fortune rounding on me, sir," Grice spoke as a resentful martyr. "I had a man kep' her under observation. She bolted down an alley way, and when he got there, there she wasn't. Nobody can help these things. We'll get her."

"As you got Chatty Brown," said Reggie over his shoulder. "Shut up. Is that Underwood? Speaking, yes. Go on. . . . God bless you. Hold the line." He turned. "Run away, Grice." Grice looked a passion of injury. Lomas waved him out. "Here you are," Reggie said. "Mrs. Redland Smith, 4393 Totsbury, in Cay's burnt memoirs, Mrs. Redland Smith is the wife of the managing partner of Efford and Efford, electro plate manufacturers. They had works in Whitecross till two years ago. Moved out then to Edmonton."

Lomas pulled his lip. "Two years. Period the robberies have grown. I'll buy it!" He took the telephone. . . . He rang off and called "Grice!" A melancholy resentment appeared. "What do you know about Efford and Efford?"

"I don't have the name in my mind." Grice was slow and sullen.

"Don't you? Cay had," said Reggie.

"Cay?" Grice stammered. "He—he never told me, Mr. Lomas. How——"

"Damme, don't you know your own division?"

"I beg pardon, sir. Efford——" Grice scratched his head. "There used to be a little firm of that name. But old Efford he died, leaving no son, only a daughter, and their works were shut down long ago."

"Is that all you're going to tell me?"

"It's all I know, sir. I don't understand what you said about Cay and them. Anything like that could only be for some old case, dead and cold. If you'll excuse me I want to go to a comb out of the place where that girl Kitty slipped us. It's a regular rabbit warren full of bolt holes but I——"

"No!" Reggie stopped him. "No! Come and see if you know the Efford daughter. Is her hair red, Grice?"

Grice's lantern jaw gaped. "You said yourself that hair was Kitty's. How——"

Lomas made an angry noise. "Get on to my car."

Driven furiously, it slowed in the Edmonton High road for directions from a policeman, and twisted away through side streets of dwarf houses to a region of darkness and waste land. A man walked out into the road and as the chauffeur stopped opened the door. "All ready, Mr. Lomas. Better leave your car here."

He took them down a rough by-way, "Nothing known against Effords. Employ about fifty men. Factory's inside a ring fence."

Not a gleam showed through the misty dark. With the odours of wet earth and decaying vegetation mingled a faint, chemical smell. Something loomed more solid and blacker than the darkness. They came to a fence of corrugated iron and a gate in it, all crowned with barbed wire. Several men closed on them. "Carry on, Wanford," said Lomas. A man bent to the lock, worked for a moment and the gate opened.

One window opposite let out a thin rod of light, enough to betray a range of buildings. Far to one side something shimmered.

The light from the window vanished. They found a door and rang and knocked. There was a faint sound of movement from within, then silence.

"Bolting for the back gate," Wanford muttered. "That's all right, sir. Open up."

Torches flashed into a hall, showed doors inscribed stockroom, office, private. Through the last they came to the room in which there had been a light. It was empty, but on the table were the remains of a game pie and a bottle of champagne. "Two people," said Wanford. "Did it *de luxe*."

"Nice people," Reggie murmured. He gazed at the wine disgust and horror. "Stayin' 'emselves with flagons." He shuddered. "Before or after? Come on."

He turned and ran out, ran on to the shimmer which could still be seen ten yards away. It came through frosted glass in a low building apart from the main factory. The locked door there gave more trouble than the others. Inside the air was thick with acid fumes. A row of earthenware tanks took most of the floor space.

Reggie shone a torch into yellow liquid, seething and bubbling. "Silver bars, begad," Lomas chuckled. "Good work, Reginald."

"Yes, here's your precious silver," Reggie passed from tank to tank. "Going gaily into solution." He stopped at the last tank. "Not here. Nothing solid." He bent over and smelt the still liquor. "Oh, my God! She couldn't be——" He looked wildly round the shed, and went on to a door at the far end. "Open this," he yelled.

It opened, not on the outer air, but a room equipped for a testing laboratory. He swept his torch light round it. Under the sink lay something tied in a sack. He cut the cords and drew out a head of red hair, a lifeless body.

"Strike me dead!" Grice gasped.

Reggie looked up at his livid dismay. "Yes. This is Kitty Evans." He bent over her. "And still alive. Dose of knock-out drops. One of you chaps jump to the 'phone. Ambulance with injections for chloral hydrate poisoning." He began to work on her with artificial respiration. "Anybody know this game? Give a hand."

．　　　．　　　．　　　．　　　．

There was trampling outside the shed. "Mr. Wanford in here?" a gruff voice called. "Right." A man and a woman were hustled in. He was a fat creature, gurgling in a sweat of terror, hardly kept up by the hands that gripped him. She stood erect, glaring hate from a face of shrunken, painted beauty.

Reggie thrust Grice in front of him. "Don't be shy. Do you know the lady?"

Grice scowled at her and she thrust back her tumbled hair, hair of a henna red, for her fierce eyes to see him plain.

"That hair's dyed, ain't it?" Grice muttered.

"Miss Efford's used to be red by nature?" Reggie asked. "Confusin' for you. However. What was going into the last tank, ma'am? The tank not required for the silver. Oh, won't you tell me? Traces of organic matter still present. Difficult to eliminate. Remains of Chatty Brown, what? Miss Evans won't join him now. Your error. Did you make sure Brown was dead before——"

The man gave a hoarse cry and collapsed. The woman laughed. "You stupid rat, Grice," she said quietly. "You won't get out by rounding on us. You've always had your share. You——"

"It's a lie!" Grice roared.

"You're fifty-fifty with us to the end."

"Take them off," Lomas said.

The man had to be carried. As the woman was led out she looked back. "And Mr. Inspector Grice," she called. "Where's Sergeant Cay, Grice?"

"Mr. Lomas, sir," Grice whined. "I——"

"Hold your tongue," Lomas snapped, and turned to Reggie. "These cursed tanks, they'd dissolve a body?"

"Oh yes. They did. There'll be chemical evidence."

"Cay!" Lomas muttered.

Reggie shrugged. "Kitty Evans first." He went back to her. . . .

Ambulance men hurried in with a stretcher. "This way," Reggie called. "Doctor with you? Good." They worked on the girl together. . . .

Lomas tapped his shoulder. He raised a damp and angry face. "What's the matter now?"

"Wireless to the police car on the road." Lomas gave him a sheet of paper. "Do you pretend to know what it means?"

The message was "Man thought like description bungalow poultry farm Black Heath, Theale. Going down. Underwood."

Reggie read it and spoke to the doctor of treatment for the girl. . . . He rose and drew Lomas away out of the shed. "Underwood believes evidence, Lomas. What was burnt in Cay's place—envelope with postmark ending A L E. What wasn't burnt—cutting about poultry farms, bits of dried bracken, also Cay's photograph. No point in burnin' photograph. We knew what he was like. Other omissions, errors of operator. Underwood's worked it all out, Theale, in Berkshire, has bracken and poultry farms around. He got on to the police there and heard of a man like Cay. We'll go down too. Takin' our Grice. To make sure."

With Grice between its chauffeur and Inspector Wanford their car bore them through the night at sixty an hour. "Not too bad. For a police car." Reggie murmured. "We're not bad as policemen go. When we get going." To the disgust of Lomas he slept. . . .

The station at Theale was wide awake to receive them, and gave them a guide. They caught up Underwood as his car, laden with local constabulary, climbed out of the valley. The light of a waning moon broke through thin clouds upon a common where bracken and gorse made a puny jungle. Little houses looked above it.

Headlights were put out, the cars pitched and rolled down a lane and stopped. Some way to the left was a bungalow, pale in the gloom. A cock waked and crowed.

The constabulary spread themselves. Underwood hammered at the door. "One moment," Reggie held his arm. "Grice! You call him. Whatever you do call him."

"Call who, sir?" Grice whined.

"Cay," said Reggie.

"Strike me," Grice gasped, and then his voice rose cracking "Cay! Here, Cay! Cay!"

Reggie stepped aside from the door and waved the others back.

It opened a little, a torch shone upon Grice's face and Reggie flashed his torch at the face within, the sharp-featured underhung face of Sergeant Cay. As Grice hurled himself forward two shots cracked. There was a yell of pain from Grice in the thud of falling bodies. "You devil!" he groaned. "Ugh, I've got you though."

Cay fired again in a mad struggle before they mastered him, but that shot went into his own side.

. . . . .

Reggie sat at lunch in the little restaurant which he loves best tasting a new fantasy on the theme of sole and crayfish. "Yes, joyful." He smiled benign.

"With the Montrachet," he filled Lomas's glass. "One of my best cases, what? In the simple style. Grice is doing nicely. Rather a mess of shoulder and collar bone. Sorry. The best way, though. It clears him clean, Cay's desperation to kill him."

"And to kill himself," said Lomas.

"Yes. Very successful experiment. I thought Cay was a realist. Wonder if he led the woman on or she him. Probably she. Female of the species is more dreadful than the male. Sometimes. But he has the better brain. When the wretched Chatty Brown had his mouth stopped in her infernal tanks, Cay knew the pace was getting too hot to last. Made his arrangements to vanish and let her stand the racket. Very neat arrangements. Got across Fishface and Kitty affectionate in the court to fix up a scrap. Left Fishface's blood and his own denture behind for evidence. Burnt his papers, providin' sketches of Fishface and Kitty as further clues. And retired to keep hens. No, that's not chicken I'm giving you. Veal in a cream sauce. Very able fellow, Cay. But underestimates the simple mind. My mind."

"Devilish good your work on that yellow cloth," said Lomas.

"You did notice that?" Reggie purred.

"I take it Cay was in at the death of Chatty Brown."

"You can, yes. He'd been where nitric acid splashed. Let him explain. I should say the woman's husband will break and blab. If handled."

"Don't worry," Lomas smiled.

"I'm not. Finished. Triumph of the art of makin' objections." There came a dish of peaches. "Not so bad." Reggie scanned them. "With a little of your brandy, Aristide." They sipped and ate and sipped. "One more objection though. You can't hold Fish-face."

"Why do you say that?"

"My dear old thing! Why did the Efford gang kidnap Kitty Evans to send her the way Chatty went? Because she knew some of 'em were in your silver robberies. Because they saw her coming from the police station. Worth anything to keep her out of the witness-box."

"Quite. That's clear enough. But it makes the case against Fishface stronger."

"Oh, my Lomas! No. Contrariwise. They hoped to abolish Kitty and they put up fellows to accuse Fish-face. Knowing our Grice would lap it up and go hard off the scent."

"You believe it wasn't Fishface drove the van away?"

"My dear chap!" Reggie lit a cigar and blew a smoke ring. "Now Cay and the Efford firm are caught, the witnesses against Fishface will die on you."

"Well, I don't mind," Lomas shrugged.

. . . . .

Reggie came into the hospital room where Kitty Evans lay in bed. She gave him a wan smile. "Is that the best you can do?" he sat down beside her, examined her. . . . "Not a very good girl, are you? You will worry. You shouldn't." Her eyes filled with tears.

"Oh no. No." He went to the door and let in a clean Fishface.

"Arty! Oh, Arty!" Kitty rose from her pillows, arms open.

"I'm out, kid," he flung himself on her.

"Steady. She's not strong." Reggie grasped his shoulder. "Plenty of time. You're both out. For good. I object to the deal you've had. Fresh deal now."

II

THE CHILDREN'S HOME

THE CHILDREN'S HOME

WHETHER THE CASE of the children's home was one of Mr. Fortune's failures or a shocking success, people differ. He maintains both opinions from time to time with equal fervour for the good, if possible, of his wife's soul: demonstrating that either way it was all her fault.

Beyond dispute, she brought him into the thing. On a dingy March evening he opened her drawing-room door with the one innocent purpose of persuasion that they should cut a visit to relations and do something festive.

A voice broke upon him, a loud, babbling voice. He blinked, his alarmed eyes saw a woman swelling out of a mink coat in crimson silk. The face above was also expansive, but much powder subdued its colour to shades of mauve. She shone and flashed, teeth, eyes, diamonds and red nails on the podgy hands which caught at Mrs. Fortune's.

"My dear, Jacob's good for ten thousand," she was saying. "I'm sure he is, when you talk to him, you just come and try, we'll manage him, you and me, bless you—well now, is this your husband, dear?"

"I think so," said Mrs. Fortune watching his timid approach from under her eyelashes. "He's very vague, you see."

"Oh, my dear! These clever, scientific men."

DF

"Reggie," Mrs. Fortune's voice had a thrill in it, "Mrs. Saunders doesn't know you."

"Mr. Fortune! Well now this is a pleasure." Her hand sank itself into his and shook it hard. She giggled and made eyes at him. "I thought I'd be sort of frightened to meet you, but you're not a bit like that."

"Not me. No. Sorry," Reggie sighed. "How do you do?"

"I'm splendid, thanks. I'm so glad I just caught you to-day, nice to meet you first. Your good wife's promised to come down to our little place." She giggled again; she made a movement of head and neck as if she were swallowing a pill. "Well, it's not so little as all that, you'll be very comfortable, I will say, and Jacob's so interested in all your doings, Mr. Fortune. But, my goodness, I must fly! Jacob can't bear me to be out when he comes home."

"Very natural," said Reggie. "Sorry."

She embraced Mrs. Fortune with vigour and he let her out.

He came back, stood over Mrs. Fortune and demanded in a voice of doom, "Woman! What have you done?"

"The greatest of these is charity," said she.

He collapsed into a chair, he gazed at her with reproachful horror. "Woman of no morals," he mourned.

"No, darling, none. The perfect woman, nobly planned, to warn, to comfort and command."

"Which is this?"

"All the three. Such a comfort to get the money for the children's home. Here's the way. Hannah says

Jacob can be brought to write me a big cheque. Forward, Reggie. The eternal womanly leads you aloft."

"Hannah?" Reggie was alarmed. His wife is not prone to sudden intimacies.

"She asked me to call her Hannah," said Mrs. Fortune. "You needn't, yet."

"Who are they?"

"She is Jacob's third wife. I think she said third. I don't know why. I haven't met him. But she's quite sure they're very rich. He makes cement or bricks or something. And she's fond of children. They haven't any. So you see."

"I do. Invitation by Hannah to come and rob Jacob. With the highest motives. 'Do you hear the children weeping, oh my brothers?' Or did you invite yourself?"

"No," said Mrs. Fortune thoughtfully. "I was quite shy. She wouldn't be denied."

"Always an artist, Joan," Reggie admired her.

"Do you notice that you're being horrid?" she answered. "You know you want the home enlarged. You said it must be."

This home by the western sea for children who need nursing in sunshine when the hospitals have finished with them is an enterprise which has had a good deal of service from him.

"Yes. Charity covers a lot of sins," he murmured and met his wife's smile with a plaintive gaze. "When did you mean to go to Hannah's little place?"

"On Wednesday."

His sad eyes opened wider. "Oh no. No. Going to Aunt Sophia."

"My dear child," Mrs. Fortune laughed. "You never meant to."

"Joan," said he, wistful and confidential, "I was thinking of a week in Paris."

"No." Mrs. Fortune remained firm. "Murpham."

Reggie shuddered. "Murpham? Down in the Midlands. Cold! Not now, Joan. Why the hurry?"

"I promised. Hannah said Jacob was in a good mood. He's just making a big deal or some such thing."

"Is he? Well, well. Was it his idea we should assist?"

"Of course not. He doesn't know we're coming."

"Unconscious of his doom the little victim plays. I wonder. Well. The woman tempted me and I did eat." He took the telephone and rang up Aunt Sophia and told her that he had been called away to a difficult case and conducted a duet of commiseration with her.

Reproachful, he turned upon his wife's amusement. "Yes, Auntie has a heart, Joan. Not like you. And I tell her naughty lies so I can shiver for your sake. Sinful institution, marriage. And Jacob's been married three times."

"Never despair, child," said she.

"I wasn't. I was wondering. Wonder how much he doesn't know," Reggie murmured.

"Who could know more than you?" she asked reverently, but he did not answer; he lay back gazing with wide eyes at nothing. . . .

"Reggie!" She called him to attention. "You're like a small dog, pretending there's a rat when there isn't."

"Oh, my dear girl! Not me. No. You have a bad conscience. So you ought."

In this manner they decided to go to Murpham Court.

It rose before them out of the east wind haze which blurred sodden plain and dumpy hills, a grey, sprawling mass of a house on a knoll in the flat of its park. By an avenue that wriggled tediously to make the most of a yellow pool, and patches of plantations they reached the terrace over which its sham classic front scowled.

A shriek like a jay's greeted them, the yap of a Pekingese. Mrs. Saunders rushed upon their car, the quadruped prancing at her ankles, a biped lagging behind. She gushed, she embraced, she wrung Reggie's hand, she babbled herself out of breath while the biped, a large, sleek man, contributed one fixed, silent smile.

"Well, now, dear," Mrs. Saunders recuperated for a fresh start. "Isn't it a pretty country? I was just having my constitutional, I was saying to Sir Harold —there now, what am I thinking of, do excuse me." The smiling man was introduced as Sir Harold Vine, and let it be seen that he was so kind as to admire Mrs. Fortune, but had some doubt of the reason for Reggie's existence.

Mrs. Saunders clattered on with exposition of how lovely the country was and what a view they had from the terrace, the vistas were wonderful, weren't they, the sight of the county, their vistas . . . through long-suffering minutes Reggie gazed into the murk at a formless landscape while Mrs. Fortune encouraged the woman . . . she would show them to-morrow, the sweetest places . . . at last she took them into the house.

A vast hall, in the style of an ancient temple, but as full of furniture as a store, surrounded them with close, fusty air. "Quite a palace, isn't it, dear?" Mrs. Saunders continued. "But Jacob put in central heating. We have all modern comfort you'll see. I just keep to an open fire in my drawing-room, that's all, I do like a fire to look at, this way now, isn't this a staircase?" It was of marble green and brown. As they climbed Reggie saw a woman flit across the landing above, smoothing her bob of chestnut hair. A door shut. A typewriter began to clack. Before they reached the landing a lank, dark man came down. He was stopped and presented—Mr. Nicholas Wadham. It gave him no gratification. His glance at them was an embarrassed scowl.

"Such a nice boy," Mrs. Saunders whispered too audibly as he swung away down.

She brought them to a room which had been of gracious design before radiators and plumbing broke its shape, and her demonstration of innumerable gadgets concluded by switching on red lights which made a sham fire in the comely eighteenth century grate.

Reggie stood still contemplating this, speechless. Some time after the door had closed behind her he found voice to gasp: "My only aunt!" He pointed a quivering finger at the futile glare.

"Isn't it pretty?" Mrs. Fortune smiled.

"Hannah and her Jacob—their ideal home—a little pretend hell for everyone." He plunged at the switch and snapped it off. "We shall have fun. Charity endureth all things. You wait, Joan. But why did Hannah and Jacob want us?"

"He didn't. He didn't know she'd asked us."

"Said she!"

Mrs. Fortune, passing him, rumpled his hair. "Not a nice mind."

"It is fear, oh, little huntress, it is fear." Reggie went to one of the windows. They looked out across the terrace and the park. "Hannah said there were vistas. Wonderful vistas," he murmured. "Begin to believe Hannah. Very distressin'."

Mrs. Fortune came to his side at the window. "Rather empty vistas. Rather a tame country. Poor Hannah."

"You think so? Look down. Hannah's returned to her Harold. Arm in arm. Close and confidential."

"An unpleasant mind." Mrs. Fortune frowned and turned away.

"Not mine, no," Reggie murmured. "Rational and natural. Reactions to the unpleasant wholly hostile. Queer house, Joan. Where's the man? Where's the house party? Why is Hannah concentrated on Sir Harold Vine? What was the sportsman up to who plunged downstairs not loving us, after the damsel fled with her chestnut hair rumpled to type like a fury? And why did Hannah call him a nice boy? He's rising forty."

"Such a clever child," said Mrs. Fortune. "It is a terrible world till you know something about it."

"My dear girl! Contrariwise. Jolly world—till you do know something. Afterwards—not so good."

Mrs. Fortune made a face at him. Mrs. Fortune said: "Bo."

They went down to dinner, and found that there was a house party, small but stodgy. In the thickets of Victorian bric-à-brac round the real fire in the drawing-room, several solemn people lurked who seemed to know each other too well to talk, women in a minority. Hannah Saunders, gorgeous in purple and many diamonds, condescended among them. But Reggie was unable to discover her husband. Sir Harold Vine, imposing and complacent, arrived. She paid him flattering attention before she consigned him to Mrs. Fortune. The sportsman of the staircase, Nicholas Wadham, swaggered in, looked lost, and was captured by Reggie.

"Do you know everybody? I don't."

"Saunders' business crowd," said Wadham. "Aren't you in business?"

"Not me. No. I haven't the intellect."

"For what?" A pert voice spoke at his elbow. He turned to see the chestnut hair of the woman who had fled across the landing.

"For big business," Reggie murmured. "Any business. Won't you introduce me, Mr. Wadham?" Like Wadham, she had passed the ingenuous age, but her complexion was a clear pink and white without art and her buxom figure not overblown.

"Poor you." Hazel eyes laughed at him. "It's great fun, business, believe me."

"I do," said Reggie.

"I'm Sally Hopkins, Mr. Saunders' private secretary."

"Tell me all," said Reggie.

"What?"

"Who is everybody? Why is everybody?"

"You're Mr. Fortune. This is Mr. Wadham, who makes cement. Or his grandfather did. There's Mr. Brown, who is Mr. Saunders' managing director. And Mrs. Brown. That's Mr. Gore—another director of National Materials. And—I don't know who the lovely woman is, but she's talking to Sir Harold Vine and he's high finance in the provinces."

"Thanks very much. She's my wife," said Reggie.

"Help!" Miss Hopkins laughed. "Sorry and all that. I always drop the biggest bricks, don't I, Mr. Wadham?"

"I don't know," said Wadham sulkily.

She made a face. "You know Vine hears himself as the big noise and then some."

A little man came strutting across the hall and announced himself in a strident voice. "Now then, Hannah, what's doing?"

He was ill-designed and badly-assembled, legs even shorter than became his small stature, head not big enough for the stocky body, he looked feeble and askew. But the face under an untidy thatch of white hair did not suffer from an inferiority complex. It had a lot of bone for its size and no flesh to speak of, sharp features assertive of power and cunning and contempt.

Reggie had only time to decide that this Jacob Saunders would fit in to his worst expectations when the butler announced dinner and, hardly waiting to be introduced to her, Jacob pattered off with Mrs. Fortune.

It was a meal of vast, Victorian length and solidity, but all good in its overwhelming kind. Labouring through it, Reggie admitted that, though the wine was insignificant and his mind flinched and failed from conversation with Hannah's vivacity. She retired upon Sir Harold Vine at her other side, who was confidentially intimate and made her shake with archness. Reggie started his other neighbour, a dowdy matron, upon children, and made a good listener while he watched his wife's fortunes with Jacob at the other end of the table.

Method number one. Royally gracious. Triumphant as usual. The nasty little man was a squirming, ogling captive. Like a terrier after sweets. Yes, very like a terrier. Not wholly concentrated on the kind lady. An eye on everybody. Wicked look at Vine and his Hannah. And one for the secretary wench when she started cross-table talk with Wadham. Made her cut that short. Wadham was not pleased. Sulky animal. Didn't care who knew it. Deaf and dumb to his neighbours.

Hannah took the women away. Jacob ordered the men to close up, and praised his port and set it going. The port was good and Reggie mourned the cursed spite which made the only drinkable wine a wine he does not drink. He dreamed hopeless dreams while Jacob told them all about the shooting last season and how many pheasants he was going to rear for the next. . . .

"Had your whack, Harold?" Jacob called, with some difficulty over the aspirates. "Everybody had enough? Come on then."

They went back to the drawing-room; they were distributed by Jacob round bridge tables. That fate

Reggie was awake enough to anticipate and shun. He loitered in the hall; he effaced himself till they had settled down without him.

The green frock, the chestnut head of Miss Hopkins, glimmered in the shadows. "Where's that doctor fellow got to, Sal?" said the voice of Jacob Saunders.

"Ask me another."

"You had a go at him. How does he feel?"

"He doesn't. He had a go at me. Just wanting to know, you know."

"Was he?" Jacob sniggered. "You'd teach him. Run away."

Reggie moved into the light examining a terrible knick-knack of onyx and lapis lazuli.

"Here, Fortune," Jacob called. "Don't you play bridge?"

"Oh no. No. Never. Too dangerous. Provokes others to murder and me to suicide. Brain can't understand cards. And you?"

"That's a pity. You've got a rare card face. You look like a sleepy baby, you know."

"Thanks very much. Face is poor but honest."

"You mean you're here for what you can get out of me? I don't mind. Sit down here." Jacob pushed him into a settee by a radiator. "Now let's have it straight." He spread his little legs to the ungenial warmth and took snuff. "Go ahead." Reggie gave him a curt account of the deserts and the needs of the children's home. . . .

"Good prospectus," Jacob chuckled. "I won't say you've put it up to the wrong man, Mr. Fortune. I believe in paying fire insurance. A lump of a dole now and then makes a man hopeful he's not booked for hell. Anyhow, you can't take the stuff with you and it'd melt if you did. I know what you're thinking. I'll have to come down handsome to get clear—big premiums for my risks. I don't deny it." He laughed and took snuff again. "But get this. I take care to see I'm paying to a sound concern. My Hannah's fallen for your good lady's talk about the poor little children. That's no use to me. No offence, sir. Your wife's a queen. But you're not a business man, eh? I have to make sure there isn't any ramp to this home before I part. Give you my answer before you go—and final." He jumped up. "How's that?"

"Thanks," said Reggie.

"Don't sour on it. Come and have a drink now." He took Reggie's arm and led him to the drawing-room. "I may tell you," he whispered, "you've caught me at a good time. I'm just pulling off the deal I've worked for quite a bit." He nudged Reggie and looked at Vine playing with Hannah as his partner. "See that fellow? He don't know."

Jacob grinned malicious self-satisfaction over the array of fluids, but only the malice remained when Reggie declined to put any whisky in the glass which he filled with soda water.

"What's the matter? Mine's real good stuff."

"Oh yes. Yes. It would be," Reggie yawned. "Not for me though. Keep me awake."

"Careful of yourself," Jacob sneered, and abandoned him and pried about watching the play.

Reggie went to bed disliking him and all that was his, but was not thereby kept awake. One drowsy eye opened to the arrival of Mrs. Fortune. "Coward," said she.

"Same like Jacob said," Reggie murmured. "Bold bad people, you and Jacob. Did Jacob tell you I was funkin'?"

"He made fun of you. Do you wonder?"

"Yes. All a wonder and a wild surmise. Vistas, lots of vistas. Good night."

He is not an early riser if he can help it. When he came down to breakfast only his wife and Hannah and Sir Harold Vine remained at table. Hannah was naughtily facetious about lying in bed, Hannah babbled on to a programme of showing them the country, and Vine told Mrs. Fortune tales of more things she must see, and Reggie blenched over his eggs and bacon. Then he was surprised by some consolation. Vine was not coming. Vine departed to golf.

Even without him Reggie suffered. It was another bleak, dark, east-wind day. They drove over interminable miles of flat land, dreary, unkind, in drab uniformity, to behold from bumps in it, prospects of dim wood and muddy water. They lunched late and vilely in a great, bare Elizabethan manor, the mistress of which patronized them with unhidden contempt. And always Hannah babbled till, on the homeward journey, material ran out at last and she subsided into yawning regrets Jacob hadn't been able to come— he knew everything—but he was so busy—a big conference with his people—such a bother.

Cars met them leaving Murpham Court as they approached, and Hannah renewed her energy to call and wave at the occupants. It appeared that Jacob had ended his conference and dissolved his house party. When they entered the house not a creature but servants was to be spoken to or seen.

Numb in body and mind, Reggie huddled over the drawing-room fire, the only real fire which burnt. He had the room to himself while the twilight dwindled. . . . His aggrieved eyes opened on a blaze of light and Hannah in a tawny tea gown. The raucous voice of Jacob penetrated his ears. "You're a glutton for sleep, aren't you? Do you have any time to be awake?"

"As and when required," Reggie mumbled. "Am I?"

"That's right, Mr. Fortune," Hannah applauded. "Don't you stand any nonsense from him. He's behaved very bad, shutting himself up all day."

"I have to work for my living," said Jacob. "Where's the tea, Hannah?"

"Hark at him! He don't know how to live except driving people to work. He's always a bear till he's had his tea. You just wait, Jacob. There's others besides you."

Reggie started up. Some shrill sound had come from outside. He crossed to a French window and opened it. There was no mistaking the louder sound which entered—a woman's scream. He went out of the window and ran down from the terrace into the shadows of the park. Another, wilder scream rose and quavered into silence.

"Whatever is it, Jacob?" Hannah whispered.

Jacob had crossed to the window and stood ineffectually peering out of the light into the gloom which gave forth no more sound. "How the hell should I know?" he snarled.

Mrs. Fortune came into the room. "Oh my dear!" Hannah swept upon her. "Such a dreadful thing. There was a woman screaming and your poor husband's gone out to her."

"He would," said Mrs. Fortune, and looked at Jacob. "Won't you, Mr. Saunders?"

Jacob made an inarticulate exclamation; Jacob vanished through the window. Mrs. Fortune followed. "Ah, don't you do that, dear," Hannah wailed.

"Please ring and send some of your people," said Mrs. Fortune.

Reggie was not built for speed, and his habit of life is adverse to it. But he can move fast to an emergency. He ran in the direction of the screams, and found himself on a path which led straight across the park. By the edge of a plantation he trod on a woman's hat and saw a woman's body.

She lay upon her face, arms outstretched, one glove half off. A moment Reggie stood listening to hear footsteps behind and at the side. But they all approached. He knelt down by the woman . . . she neither spoke nor stirred as he dealt with her, her face was covered with dirt and blood.

Jacob and Mrs. Fortune arrived together. "Here, what ha' you got, Fortune?" Jacob barked. "God, it's Sal!"

"As you say," Reggie murmured. "Your Miss Hopkins." He stood up and, to his wife's look, answered· "All right, Joan," and turned round. "Who else is comin'?" From the corner of the plantation a lean, long man moved at a run. "Mr. Wadham, I presume."

"Is that you, Fortune?" Wadham panted. "What the devil's happened?"

"I haven't the slightest idea," said Reggie. "Where have you come from?"

"From the house, of course. I heard somebody screaming. Who was it? Who is it?" He pushed past Reggie to bend over her. "Sally! Is she—Fortune— is she——?"

"No. Not dead, no," Reggie murmured. "What was she doin' here?"

"How should I know?" Wadham cried.

"See anyone about?"

"No, I've just come from the house, I told you."

"Well, well. Better get her back." Reggie turned to menservants coming up at a trot, and directed them how to carry her. Jacob prowled around them. "Oh, Saunders," he called. "What about it? Any notion why she came walkin' here in the dark?"

"She'd be taking letters down to catch the night post. It's a short cut to the village."

"Is that so? No letters visible."

"I can't make it out," Saunders answered.

"Nor can I."

"Is she hurt bad, Fortune?"

"Difficult case. She may help us."

"You expect she'll come round soon?"

"Oh yes. Yes. Get on." He marshalled Saunders and Wadham in front of him and urged them back to the house. . . .

Sally Hopkins lay in bed, her face clean, only a bruise on the brow with some broken skin declaring her injuries, but her eyes were closed and she gave no sign of life but slow breath. "Most of the blood was from her nose, Joan," said Reggie. He painted iodine on the cut brow. Sally moved, gave a little cry. "Well, well. Feeling more yourself, Miss Hopkins?" he asked.

She opened her eyes. "Who is it?" she said faintly. "Oh, where am I?"

"Look!" Reggie smiled.

"How did I get here? What are you doing?"

"Just necessary repairs. That wound won't leave a scar."

"Wound?" she repeated. She put her hand to her head. "Oh! my head aches."

"Too bad," Reggie murmured. "Who did it?"

"You—you're Mr. Fortune." She looked at him with puzzled, frightened eyes. "It wasn't you?"

"Oh no. No. I have a fair alibi. Didn't you see the brute?"

"The brute—you mean the man that hit me?"

"It was a man?"

"Yes, I think so. Yes, of course it was. I was taking Mr. Saunders' letters to the post. A man came round the trees and snatched my bag with the letters, and I called out and he hit me. It was all dark, I couldn't see anything. I tried to hold him, and he hit me." Her voice failed.

"Well, well. Do you always take the letters to the post?"

"No. Only when they're late and when they're

Ef

important and have to be registered. Then I go myself. I wish I hadn't had to."

"Would anybody know you had to to-night?"

"No, of course not. How could they? It was only settled this afternoon. The horrid man snatched my bag." She drew a sharp breath and shuddered. "Ah, my head!"

"Yes. Nasty knock, wasn't it?" Reggie sympathized. "Now you're going to be quiet and sleep it away. Just drink this first. . . ."

As he came out of the telephone box in the hall Jacob confronted him and demanded, "Here, what about her?"

"Were you worryin'? Sorry. I had to tell the police."

"What do you want the police for? She isn't hurt dangerous, is she?"

"Police obviously required. Didn't you notice that? Case of robbery with violence."

"Sal says she was robbed, does she?"

"Oh yes. Yes. Miss Hopkins' statement—she was going to post registered letters for you, man came out of the dark, snatched her bag, knocked her on the head."

"Blast him!" said Jacob. "Poor little Sal. That's right, Fortune, you want the police on it. I was thinking of her. How is she?"

"No serious injury. Common type of bag snatchin'. With some differences. You might tell me about that."

"I get you, don't I?" Jacob took his arm and spoke confidentially. "You mean what's a common bag snatcher doing in my park. Come along upstairs."

Reggie was taken to his study. "Funny, ain't it, a rogue lays for my secretary and goes off with my letters?" He took snuff and exhibited a cunning grin.

"As you say," Reggie murmured. "Indicates peculiar interest in your secretary and you."

"That's right. You want to know why."

"The police will," said Reggie.

"I can tell you. Look here. You know my line— building materials, cement and so on. I've had a conference of my people here about buying Wadham's cement works. It's a big old business, family concern since Adam. Wadham's had enough. Between you and me, he's a back number, not up to modern conditions, hasn't got the guts, hasn't got the capital. But he's sticky proud and that makes him shifty. We couldn't fix him to terms that would suit me, but we worked out the basis of my final offer. What was in those letters Sal had to register was instructions to my lawyers and experts to draw a contract on that figure so I could put it to him, take it or leave it. So you see—anybody who got hold of the letters would know just how far I was going."

"Oh yes. Meaning Mr. Wadham," Reggie murmured.

"That's right. He'd find out for sure where he had to get off." Jacob gave a raucous laugh. "If you ask me he had no need to steal the letters. I gave him my limit straight and he ought to know I don't bluff nor be bluffed. But some fellows will be silly tricky. If it was him, he's the hell of a lot the wiser. He only has what he had before and what he'd have got over again next week."

"Well, well. Loss of letters not a serious loss to you."

"I should worry! Only for the girl being hurt, poor lass. Blasted brute of a fellow."

"Wanton damage, yes. Confusin' case. Wadham is indicated. But you think no real gain to Wadham. However. Some people are silly people. Any ideas about Miss Hopkins?"

"How do you mean?" Jacob asked sharply.

"Relations with Wadham. Relations with anybody else."

"I'd trust Sally Hopkins with anything. I do." Jacob glared.

"Oh yes. Anybody else interested in buying the cement works of Wadham & Co.?"

"Not to my knowledge," Jacob exclaimed. "No. I don't believe it. There's not much in this game I don't know, believe me."

"I do. Yes. Makes a curious case. Interestin' case. Thanks very much." He rose and gazed at Jacob with sad reproach. "I haven't had my tea," he moaned and wandered out.

It was already near dinner time, but he went down to the drawing-room. The lights were out, no one was there, the fire was burning low. Ashes of burnt paper deadened it. He squatted on a pouffe by the hearth, he removed grey films which crumbled to powder, but some pieces were uncharred, a bit of an envelope, pieces of stiff paper, typewriting paper. He made out the embossed heading of Murpham Court and some scraps of typing:

"Lys . . .

Loth . . ."

With all the lights on he wandered about the room, poring over carpet and furniture, but his round face remained plaintive. On a little table he found a bag of gold brocade, beyond a doubt Hannah's bag. Beside it was a glass tube which, according to the label, held tablets of phenacetin. "Oh, another feminine headache," he murmured, looked into the bag and found nothing but a handkerchief and a gold vanity case.

A footman came in to make up the fire.

"Large party to-night?" Reggie asked.

"No, sir. Most of the party have left. Only Sir Harold Vine and Mr. Wadham remaining."

Reggie went back to the telephone box and consulted the London directory. Lys—yes, Lyson, Lyson & Lyson were solicitors in Lothbury. Letter burnt, letter to them—Jacob's letter to his solicitors about his contract for Wadham. . . .

Mrs. Fortune, sitting before the mirror in their bedroom, saw her husband reflected.

"Curiouser and curiouser." He kissed the back of her neck, he turned away and switched on the sham fire in the old basket grate.

"My child!" she protested.

"Yes. Horrid and futile. However. Same for all. Jacob's kindly humour. But there is one open fire. Thanks to Hannah. On with the dance. Let joy be unconfined."

He can change with incredible speed. He did. He was back in the drawing-room before anyone else had come down. He went back to the hall and loitered there.

Wadham appeared first, strode at him and demanded, "How is she, Fortune?"

"Sleepin' it off."

"She's going to be all right?"

"Oh yes. Pretty as ever."

"Foul business. I can't understand it."

"Nor me. No. Job for the police."

Vine came downstairs with Hannah babbling to him. "Yes, I've just looked in to see her, she's sleeping like a baby, but what a dreadful thing, isn't it? I feel I shan't dare to go out alone, and I do so love my walks; I'm all hot and cold still, and, oh, when Mr. Fortune rushed out, when she screamed——"

Jacob called out from the landing: "Here, Hannah," he put his hand to his head, he lurched and reeled and fell bumping down the stairs till the marble balustrade checked him and he lay in a heap.

Hannah had turned, she shrieked, she stumbled and tumbled, clutching at Vine, who found enough to do in lifting her. Reggie pushed past them to Jacob.

Hannah became hysterical, struggling with Vine and Wadham to fling herself upon him, screeching: "Jacob! Jacob! Ah, he's dead! Don't you hold me, let me go, I want him."

Mrs. Fortune swept down the stairs to her, and was clutched, embraced, engulfed by her spasmodic, wailing bulk. Servants arrived from above and below.

"Who's his man?" Reggie looked round. "Give me a hand with him."

Jacob's body, sagging between them, was carried upstairs while Hannah lifted up her voice with new power and wept. . . .

"That'll do." Reggie drew away from the bed in which Jacob lay.

"Thank you, sir." Jacob's valet, a smug, lugubrious fellow, stood back. "I hope not hopeless."

Jacob's sharp face was of a bluish tinge. He gave no sign of breathing.

"You helped him dress, what? Notice anything unusual?"

"As you're asking me, I must say I thought Mr. Saunders wasn't quite himself, sir. He'll often be a bit short and hasty while dressing, not meaning anything unpleasant, and I don't take notice of it. But tonight he was all of a twitter, as you might put it, breaking himself off and jerking about. Excited like. If I may mention it, I was with a gentleman once who was that way before he had a stroke."

"Thanks. Observant fellow. Yes. Did Mr. Saunders say anything about feelin' queer?"

"Not to signify, sir. He sort of had everything go wrong, being so violent in changing, and talked a lot about it."

"Oh yes. Had he been takin' anything, do you know? Drink—medicine?"

"Mr. Saunders only drinks regular, sir. And I never knew him use medicine. If you'll excuse me, he doesn't believe in doctors."

"Pity. However. Uses a good deal of snuff, doesn't he? What's in his snuff?"

"I couldn't say, sir. I'm no judge, not caring for it myself. Now you mention it, I picked up his snuff box on the stairs."

"Yes, I noticed that." Reggie held out his hand.

"Mr. Saunders must have dropped it when he fell."

"It is indicated," Reggie murmured. He was examining the snuff. He rang the bell and opened the door. The butler himself bustled up. "Send somebody to help watch your master till a nurse comes."

"Very good, sir. There is an Inspector of police asking for you. I have put him into the morning-room."

Inspector Ince had no shoulders to speak of, and was otherwise gauntly puny, but his hatchet face looked alert.

"Sorry to trouble you," Reggie sighed. "Two cases now. Number one as stated—Mr. Jacob Saunders' woman secretary robbed and assaulted in the park. Number two—Mr. Saunders subsequently took a toss down the stairs with circumstances suspicious. Neither dangerously injured. But you won't get anything out of 'em to-night. Too bad. Have to work on my evidence."

"I shall be happy, Mr. Fortune. It seems kind of providential you were here."

"Yes. One of the things that worry me," Reggie murmured. "I was invited by Mrs. Saunders. However. Case of Miss Hopkins——" He related what he knew. "There you are. Snatchin' her bag put into somebody's hands intentions of Saunders over purchase of Wadham's business. Which suggests that the snatcher knew there was stuff in the letters useful to him. Which points at Wadham. But Saunders said Wadham knew all the letters would tell him. Not wholly convincin'. Nor is Miss Hopkins' injury. Something did make her nose bleed. Something did break the skin on her forehead. Don't understand the blows. Not like the usual fist,

stick or what not. Don't understand her being so long
unconscious. However. Hit somehow. Bag removed.
If she had a bag. None near her when found. Further
to that—some papers were burnt later in the drawing-
room. Only place here with an open fire. That's why
the drawing-room. And among the papers was a letter
to Saunders' solicitors as stated."

"All very fishy," said Ince. "If I take your meaning,
Mr. Fortune, the young woman may have faked the
whole thing, and it was somebody of the house party
what got the letters."

"Yes, I think so. Passing to Jacob Saunders. He fell
from the landing down the stairs all by himself, having
shown signs of distress and dizziness. His valet says he
was cross and convulsive just before, while changin'.
Symptoms of slight concussion. Also other symptoms—
blue face, weak, quick pulse, shallow respiration.
Probably from an anti-pyretic drug. Say phenacetin.
He takes a lot of snuff. Mixed with the snuff in his box
I found some white powder which is provisionally
phenacetin. And phenacetin is used by Mrs. Saunders.
That's all the evidence up to date. Two nice little cases
for you, Inspector."

"I'll say they are," Ince grinned. "Especially number two. As you put it, Mr. Fortune, there is reason to
believe that Mrs. Saunders has attempted to poison
her husband."

"One of the possibilities. Yes. But poison used not
likely to kill by direct action. Very hard to kill with
phenacetin. Especially in the presence of a medical
man. My presence was obvious. And it's known these
little games are in my line. On the other hand. Some

people are much affected by phenacetin. Go queer in the head with a small dose. Anybody knowin' Jacob was like that could calculate on puttin' him out of action by a fall or otherwise."

"We have intent to murder then," said Ince.

"Yes. As he did fall, any jury would say so. Whose intent? Somebody with phenacetin, somebody with access to his snuff box, probably somebody who knew phenacetin upset him. Mrs. Saunders is indicated. However. Not conclusive. Valet would know his constitution. Valet could get at his snuff box. Tube of Mrs. Saunders' phenacetin was lyin' about in the drawin'-room after somebody went there to burn the letters. Might have been used by the somebody."

"You mean the valet is the chap who stole the letters from Miss Hopkins?"

"One of the possibilities, yes. Valet picked up snuff box when Jacob dropped it on the stairs. Didn't mention that till I asked about snuff. Though he handed it over quick then. Valet may be the man you want, or connected. However. Other possibilities. Mrs. Saunders is particularly attentive to a fellow called Sir Harold Vine, who is still with us, though everybody else except Wadham went away before these little things happened. Miss Hopkins has received attentions from Wadham. Do you know anything about anybody?"

"I've heard of Mr. Wadham," said Ince slowly. "Wadham & Co. have had cement works over in Camfordshire since the year dot. They do say this Nicholas Wadham is a plunger. If he's got round the secretary woman, there you are."

"Where? Our Wadham found out from Sally Hopkins she was postin' letters from Jacob which gave the limit Jacob would pay him. She knew what it was. If she's all for Wadham she could have told him. Why should he steal the letters and knock her on the head?"

"That's an easy one," Ince chuckled. "He just knew from her Mr. Saunders had made his decision and was posting it. She wouldn't tell him any more, so he laid for her."

"Quite good," Reggie murmured. "Yes. It could be."

"Besides, sir," Ince went on briskly, "you were saying the assault on her might be all a fake. Very well. Suppose she just handed the letters to Wadham and then the stuff about being robbed and knocked out was put up to cover her."

"My dear chap!" Reggie purred smiling approval. "Pleasure to work with you. You take all the points. However. Conspiracy between Wadham and Sally for transferrin' the letters don't explain the dopin' of Jacob's snuff. Why should Wadham want to eliminate the old boy he wanted to sell to? Temper? Revenge? Because the old boy wouldn't bid high enough? Not likely, what?"

"I grant you," Ince frowned.

Reggie contemplated him with closing eyes. "I was askin' do you know anything about anybody. You haven't told me about our Vine?"

"Sir Harold Vine?" Ince gave the title with respect. "I thought you'd know of him. He's a very rich man, director of a lot of companies in Merringham."

"Is that so?" Reggie gave a little twisted smile

Merringham is the largest town of those parts. A town very impressive to Inspector Ince and the police of Mershire. "Well, well. You notice our Vine is one of the few with a chance of these little crimes. And the dopin' of Saunders links with Mrs. Saunders and Mrs. Saunders links up to Vine."

"You're putting it to me the wife and Sir Harold conspired to attempt her husband's murder," said Ince slowly. "That would be a case." His hatchet face softened to an expression of hopeful satisfaction. "A crime of passion—those two being lovers. Vine's a fine figure of a man and likes the ladies. I don't know Mrs. Saunders. Would she—eh?"

"Catch him? Or fall for him? It could be. Either. No limit to what can be in that way."

"I believe you." Ince chuckled.

"Mrs. Saunders has spread herself on Vine and him on her. Shouldn't have said she was passionate. Or commandin' passion. Full blown. However. Take it another way. She's Saunders' third wife. Saunders is rather intimate with the pretty secretary."

"Hullo, hullo!" Ince exclaimed. "Not so much another way, Mr. Fortune. Pretty secretary—jealous wife—and another gentleman gets going."

"Yes, I think that's all the possibilities. At present. And all theoretical. But the facts stand as reported. Robbery with violence. Doping with evil intent. Investigation required, what?"

"I'll say there is." Ince was enthusiastic. "Big stuff, Mr. Fortune."

"Full of interest, yes. But we do want evidence. First problem, where was Wadham, where was Vine, when

Sally Hopkins lost her bag. You might be able to work that out to-night. Servants and so on. Second problem, what really happened to Sally. Want to go over the place where she was found. Can't do that till the morning. They ought to put you up here, Inspector."

"Don't you worry about me," said Ince. "Look here, Mr. Fortune. What about Saunders? You say he's been poisoned. Somebody might play more tricks with him in the night."

"Oh no. No." Reggie stood up. "I'm not clever, but I am careful. I've got nurses for him. By the way—had any dinner?"

"That's all right, sir."

"Not with me," Reggie moaned. "I haven't. The body is empty. Quite empty. Same like the mind. Well, well. If you're waking, call me early. Do the painful right. Good-bye."

As he ate an overdone dinner of remains, Mrs. Saunders rustled in to fuss and babble. "You poor man, you must be starving——" That was the first theme. "Tell me, what do you really think about Jacob, is he really bad, this nurse you've got to him says he mustn't be disturbed——" This second theme Reggie cut short.

"He mustn't. Hence the nurse. Leave him alone please. Then he'll tell you about it."

"What's that, I don't understand, I——"

"No, nor do I. However. He will. If you don't mind I'll go to bed. Tryin' day. Short night indicated. Good night, Mrs. Saunders."

"Whatever is this policeman doing?" she cried.

"Doin' his job, I hope. There's been a crime or

so." Reggie went out and on the way to bed looked in at the two victims. Neither, he was told, had waked.

Mrs. Fortune was already in their room. "Well?" she asked.

"Oh yes. Patients quite comfortable. And with you?"

"It's weird. Those two men, Vine and Wadham, they're dumb as death. But Hannah talks all the time, and seems to be in wild spirits."

"Well, well. Vistas, Joan. Rum vistas."

"Reggie, do you think——"

"My dear girl! Don't be sympathetic. Except with ourselves. Poor us! Not bein' treated fair. I shall have to get up early."

Through the drizzle of a raw morning he trudged out with Inspector Ince. "The way I have it, sir," Ince announced, "either Wadham or Vine might have done the trick with Miss Hopkins. Wadham was in the house or round about all day long. Vine went off in the morning in his own car golfing, he didn't get back till half-past five, well after the girl was knocked out, but none of the lodge-keepers remember seeing him come into the park. So we haven't really got a fixed time for him at all. He might have stopped his car in the park anywhere. On the whole my money's on Vine. His game of golf looks like a try for an alibi."

"Yes. The point is well taken. You're very good. No reason yet before us why Vine should steal papers about Wadham. But I thought Vine's alibi too obvious."

"About the reason," said Ince eagerly. "Vine's big

business, you know. There's no saying where his interests stop. We've got it Vine was working on Mrs. Saunders, and the two of 'em are suspected of doping Saunders. How about Vine's working a business ramp through a love affair?"

"My dear chap!" Reggie purred. "Splendid. That would work out."

They came to the plantation by which Sally Hopkins had been found. Path and turf were trampled into a mess disintegrating from night frost and morning thaw. Ince picked his way around and about. "Fine old scrum you had over her," he grumbled. "Nothing doing, Mr. Fortune. Not one footprint I'd trust."

But Reggie had already turned away to the corner of the plantation nearest the house. "Not there, no," he said. "But here's one. Look. Ribbed rubber sole, man's, middle size foot. Provisionally Wadham's foot. Wadham came from round here after I'd found her. Said he'd come from the house. Had he?" They moved that way, saw another print and another by the plantation but none beyond. "Well, well," Reggie murmured and turned back.

"Not so good for Mr. Wadham," Ince chuckled. "Looks like he was on the spot when the girl was attacked."

"Yes. May have been. However. More evidence required." Reggie reached the plantation again and went round it in the opposite direction. On the further side from the house, the bare ground which the trees shadowed bore footprints of a studded sole. "Also fresh. Golf shoe, man's, rather big foot. Provisionally Vine's foot. You see? The owner stood there under the trees. He'd be out of sight of the house with the path in sight. But then we lose him. Pity."

"I'll say it is," Ince exclaimed. "Where are we now? Either of 'em laid for the girl and attacked her, or both together, which puts both under strong suspicion. We had that before."

"My dear chap! Oh, my dear chap! More now. Suspicion confirmed. Suspicion now certainty."

"How's that? Which do you mean did it?"

"I don't mean," Reggie murmured. "No evidence. But certainly things are not what they seem, not what we've been told. I wouldn't say either of 'em hit her." He wandered on.

"Good Lord! What is the idea then?"

"If you remember"—Reggie was peering at the trees—"I said I didn't think she'd been hit by the human fist." They were again near the place where Sally Hopkins had lain. "No. She wasn't. You see? Woman's footprint in the moss there——Something not vegetable on that sycamore trunk. Dark and sticky. Blood. Sally was just inside the plantation and banged her head on a tree."

"That's clever," said Ince without enthusiasm. "Suppose she did, though—just means she was assaulted and tried to get away and knocked herself out. That's no good to us—nor to the fellow that attacked her. It's robbery with violence just the same. The letters were taken by somebody. You got that yourself. She couldn't have burnt 'em in the drawing-room fire, her being in bed. And her bag was taken."

"As you say," Reggie murmured. "Case still alive. And kickin'. Quite a lot of kicks. I resent that. Not respectful. Strive and thrive. Better verify the bag. Probably somewhere handy. Bag wouldn't burn. Bag dangerous to keep."

They did find it, not in that plantation but the next, which was nearer the winding drive to the house. It was empty but for a handkerchief and a flapjack. "And that's a lot of good," Ince complained. "Just what you'd get with ordinary bag snatching—fellow takes all the stuff and chucks it away as quick as he can."

"Yes. Quite neat. Lot of neat work in this case. However. Fellow who flung the bag into this covert was going towards the drive, which is where our Vine would leave his car. Well. All this bein' thus, finish with outdoors, thank heaven. Come on. Bath and breakfast. Hot and large."

These operations had taken much time, adequate seething in a hot bath took so much more that everyone else had finished breakfast before he began. He was still eating when Hannah's voice penetrated the door. "Well then, I am so sorry losing you, I do believe there's really no need, but I won't press you, I understand how you feel, it's very kind of you——" He went out, to find her taking an affectionate leave of Sir Harold Vine.

"Oh. Are you going?" His voice was plaintive, his eyes were round.

"In the circumstances, Fortune," said Vine brusquely.

"Victims doin' quite well. Might like to see you."

"There, that's what I told him." Hannah took over the conversation again. "But of course it will be a dull house for a while, I couldn't really press him." She

Ff

made eyes at Vine. "You'll be coming back soon, won't you, Sir Harold?"

"Dear lady, you're most kind. Whenever I'm asked. Pray tell Saunders how sorry I am, and let me hear how he gets on." Vine was affectionate over her hand. She went out on the terrace with him and waved her handkerchief after his car.

Reggie found Inspector Ince at his elbow. Ince jerked a nod after Vine and whispered, "This is a queer game. He's quit quick and Wadham quit quicker; Wadham went before ever we got back."

"Well, well." Reggie drew him away into the breakfast room. "Quite correct, to leave when your host goes sick. However. They are swift. And our hostess didn't strain herself to keep Vine. Curiouser and curiouser." He resumed eating with gusto.

"That's right, it is. I've got some more out of the servants about the footprints. Vine did wear shoes with studs on yesterday. So he was on the job. And Wadham, he used a pair with grooved rubber, as we thought. But now what?"

"I wonder. Very interestin' case. Nothing more for you here. I'll let you know what emerges from Sally and Jacob. If anything. You might look after our Wadham and our Vine. What they're up to. If they meet. Where do they live?"

"Vine has a big house outside Merringham. Office in the town. I don't know about Wadham. He used to live in Camfordshire, near his works."

"Have 'em taped, will you? Keep touch with me. I——"

Hannah swept into the room. "Oh, there you are,

Mr. Fortune, I want to see Jacob, you know, of course I do, and that nurse says not to disturb him. I can't have that, really I can't, I must talk to him, I——"

"You would want to, yes." Reggie rose. "I'll go up. The Inspector's just departin'. I'm afraid we have nothing to tell you."

"Haven't you? It is a dreadful thing, isn't it? I suppose it was some horrible tramp, wasn't it?"

"We're looking into everything, madam," said Ince. "Good morning."

The nurse informed Reggie that Mr. Saunders had shown no sign of coming to. Reggie was thorough with him. His face had changed from blue to a paler tone of its normal muddy red. But the careful examination which showed both heart and respiration stronger did not wake his consciousness.

Reggie found Hannah waiting at the door, told her that she could come and see, and she did. "Oh dear, he does look bad, poor dear," she gulped and wept. The frozen composure of the sharp face on the pillow was undisturbed.

Outside the room again, "Not too bad," said Reggie.

"How can you say so?" she sobbed.

"I do. Would you like another opinion?"

She shook her head vehemently. "No, that's no use. Jacob never has a doctor. He hates them. And there isn't anyone. Don't be so unkind. I'm trusting to you. But it's dreadful. Poor Jacob. It'll be ever so long before he's all right, won't it?"

"It shouldn't be. No."

"Oh, you are nice to me," Hannah gasped, and hurried away.

Reggie went on to the other patient. Sally was completely conscious and very sorry for herself. She beset him with incoherence. Her head did so throb, and she felt like death. Whatever was it? She couldn't remember whatever had happened. The most ghastly dreams, Mr. Fortune. What was it? But couldn't he do something for the pain? Her head was splitting. . . .

Reggie found his wife alone by the drawing-room fire. "Oh charity, all patiently endurin' wrack and scaith!" he groaned at her.

"How are they?"

"They're all right. And givin' out they're not. And I'm the only doctor Jacob ever had. And Hannah trusts to me. Can you beat it? I hope not. Don't try, Joan."

"My poor child. What are you going to do?"

"Stay. In this fusty tomb." He dropped down opposite her and lit a cigar. "The greatest of these is charity," he mumbled and blew smoke rings and watched them with somnolent eyes. . . .

After lunch he startled her by recommending that they should take the air. He never walks for exercise. He does not care to drive unless the weather is amiable. Though the rain had stopped, the air was of a woolly texture. "Are you well, Reggie?" she asked anxiously.

"No. Vitality at low ebb. Havin' no use for same. Take another look round this jolly country."

He drove her away across the steaming flats and, again contrary to his habit, the driving was sedate. "An inferiority complex?" she asked with tender sympathy. "This is very unusual, dear."

"Yes. All repressions and inhibitions and frustrations."

"Something will come of this," she smiled. "I hope it won't be human gore."

"I don't. No," Reggie mumbled.

The car passed from the clay levels to a region of low chalk hills, and made for a white scar upon them by which two chimneys towered smokeless. A range of buildings below proclaimed itself by dingy boards the works of Wadham & Co., cement makers. "Rather under-vitalized," Reggie sighed. "Same like me." He got out and went into the office and emerged to remark: "Our Mr. Wadham not there. Nor at his house, which is adjacent but shut up. However. The village might give us tea."

It did, of a sort. Reggie made conversation with the ancient landlord of the least forbidding inn, and heard that things were not what they used to be when Wadham's had five hundred men on full time, nor didn't look like looking up.

He drove back to Murpham Court without any inhibition, and there shut himself into the telephone box.

When he emerged Hannah swept upon him. Wouldn't he go up and see Jacob at once, the nurse said he was better, was he really, she did so want to know.

Reggie went up. Jacob had recovered consciousness. Jacob's sunken little eyes flickered at him, in a faint, hoarse voice Jacob asked: "Here, Fortune, what do you think you're doing with me?"

"Hush! All for your good," said Reggie, and again examined him. "Must keep quiet."

"I'm as weak as a cat. I'm starving."

"Oh no, no. Live on your tissues for a long time. But you might have something." He left the nurse with orders to keep him on a diet of slops.

Sally Hopkins was also better and noisy. She declared that her pains had ceased to trouble; with vehemence she demanded food. But continued bed and slops were prescribed for her too.

"Doin' quite well Mrs. Saunders. Not fit for any talk yet," Reggie reported. "They'll be much better in the morning. Won't know themselves."

He exerted himself to be genial at dinner, but Hannah was incoherent, with flashes of silence, and, having turned over the papers, went early to bed.

"Well, well," Reggie smiled as he shut the drawing-room door behind her. "By high education brought pressure to bear. They don't like goin' hungry, Joan. They hadn't thought of that. Moral lessons. Much required. Work of charity."

"Pig," said Mrs. Fortune.

"Not me. No. On the side of the angels. Truth, for truth is truth, he worshipped."

"What do you think you can do with them?"

"Difficult question." Reggie took up the London evening paper which Hannah had dropped. "Interestin' question. Might make 'em see goodness in her shape, how awful. My shape, Joan."

"You are showing off", she spoke maternal contempt.

"Me?" Reggie looked up over the paper with round, aggrieved eyes. "My dear girl. Oh, my dear girl! Not me. Others. Playin' the deuce and all. I'm the common man as ever. Listen to 'em." He read from the paper. "'Accident to financier: Mr. Jacob Saunders chairman of National Materials, sustained a severe fall at his country house, Murpham Park, yesterday. It is understood that he will be unable to attend to business for some time. His condition is serious.' How do these things get into the papers? Who sent that? Condition not serious. No reason he shouldn't do business to-morrow. Why publish this fiction? Somebody is showin' off."

Mrs. Fortune frowned. "It's all hateful," she said. "I'm sorry, Reggie."

"My dear girl. Not worth while," Reggie murmured. "Interestin' experiment in morals."

He made up for his early rising that day by a late breakfast in bed the next. When he did come down he beheld Sally Hopkins smoking a cigarette in the hall.

"Well, well. Very improper, aren't you?" he remarked.

"Voice of the sluggard," she jeered at him. "You don't do your job, Mr. Fortune. I'm finished with the hunger cure. I couldn't stick it another hour."

"Too bad. No faith. No self-control."

"I should worry," she laughed, and the telephone bell rang and she ran to the box.

"Expectin' a call?" Reggie asked.

She slammed the door, she was some moments inside, she came out so flushed that the powder which hid the bruised cut on her brow showed dead white. "Someone for you," she said sharply.

"Fancy that," Reggie smiled. He let her hear him say: "Fortune here. Who is that? Merringham police station? Right——" Then he shut the door.

When he came out she had vanished. He went up to Jacob's room and was not well received.

Jacob had sat himself up in bed; the head of Jacob, shaggy and unshaven, was like that of a cross Cairn terrier, except that it had too much jaw, far too much, and he gave tongue: "Here, you're devilish casual, Fortune——"

"Oh no. Strenuous and careful. All for your good."

"Why didn't you come and see me before? I'm all right this morning and that cursed wench of a nurse won't let me have a square meal."

Reggie felt his pulse. "You don't know how bad you are. Condition serious. Unable to attend to business for some time. It's in the papers. By the way, how did that get into the papers? I didn't put it there." Saunders swore at the papers. "Well, well. Curious and suggestive. Seen your Miss Hopkins lately?" Saunders retorted that he hadn't seen anyone but that pie-faced nurse. "Feel confidence in Miss Hopkins?" Saunders asked with contempt what he thought. "Me?"

Reggie smiled. "Oh, I haven't. The police haven't." Saunders cursed him and the police. "Let's send for Miss Hopkins," said Reggie, and rang the bell and did so. "We know this was a put up job, Saunders. Miss Hopkins wasn't hit. She made her nose bleed bumping her head on a tree. She hadn't a genuine concussion. And Sir Harold Vine was on the spot."

"What do you mean?" Saunders snarled.

"Passed to you."

Sally Hopkins came in, brisk and beaming. "Oh, Mr. Saunders, you do look all in," she told him. "Is

Mr. Fortune bothering you?" Her hazel eyes flashed mocking defiance at Reggie.

"What do you think he's worked out?" said Saunders. "He's telling me you put up this business with Vine— handed him my letters and faked being hit, breaking your own head to pretend it was a robbery."

Sally laughed. "Isn't he clever?"

"Too clever by half, Sally. You're all right. I don't believe a word of it. I know you."

She flung round on Reggie. "That was slander, Mr. Fortune."

"You think so? Better sue Mr. Saunders. He's told you more than I told him. But less than I know."

"Oh, you know a lot," she flushed.

"All that matters, yes," Reggie murmured. "Expect Vine to admit he hit you? Your mistake. However. Finished with you. And now, Saunders——" he stopped.

"Now what?" Saunders answered, and his gaze fought against Reggie's. He turned on the pillow. "Run away, girl. You're all right." She hesitated. "Get away, I tell you," he rasped, and she fled. "Well?"

"Who put phenacetin in your snuff?" said Reggie.

Saunders swore at him. "It's nothing to do with you if I take phenacetin."

"Oh no. Lawful drug. But I object to being used by people like you. You notice that? Feelin' nasty empty? Yes. You are. You brought me here to certify the tricks weren't your tricks and you really were ill. Well, you have been. We're all happy. You thought I shouldn't see through you. Your mistake. You never meant to buy Wadham's cement works. Not worth your while, are they? You meant to plant them on the wretched Vine. Led him on to think you were buying, put up your secretary to sell him papers with your contract in 'em. Was it her idea or yours to cover the sale by a faked robbery? Doesn't matter. Vine got the papers, read 'em and burnt 'em and thought he had you on toast, and you staged a sham stroke with your wife's phenacetin. Very delicate. With me to certify you really were ill. Thus giving Vine time to bid higher than you for the dud works and fix up a deal with Wadham. Very neat, Saunders. But you misjudged me. I don't like it. Good-bye." He turned away.

"Here!" Saunders started up in the bed. "Wait a minute. Vine's a thief, ain't he? I didn't ask him to steal my contract. He did that on his own, the swine. He wanted to do me down."

"And you?" Reggie murmured.

"You're not going to tell Vine! Look here, I give it you, you're smart! I like a smart man, Fortune. Now listen, the truth is I wanted to try you out. And you've come through well. I'll do something handsome for that children's home of yours."

"I'm sorry I can't knock you down," said Reggie sadly.

"Same here," Saunders grinned. "All right, be a snuffling prig. But you won't stop the game, my lad. I know Vine. He won't believe a word you say. He'll think you're bluffing to catch him. If you want to know, I fixed it to do Wadham a bit o' good without hurting myself. Sal's fallen for him and been a nuisance about him. But the main thing was to knock Harold Vine. He's sweet on the wife. I've waited ten years to hit the swine so he'd feel it. Praise God, I've done him down now. Run away and play with your children."

"Yes. They are clean," said Reggie and departed. For Inspector Ince had already told him over the telephone that Vine was n.b.g. Vine was in no way grateful for a warning from information received to distrust the papers in Sally Hopkins' bag. Vine denied with violence any knowledge of them. But Wadham was with him in Merringham.

In a day or two it was announced that Sir Harold Vine had acquired for his combine the works of Wadham & Co. Rumour put the price at £200,000 and talked of a nasty knock for the Saunders' National Materials Company.

A week later an exultant children's home wrote to Mrs. Fortune that it had received a cheque for £10,000 from Mr. Jacob Saunders.

"Oh my hat," Reggie moaned. "Fire insurance for Jacob, his soul. Same like he said. Hopeful animal. You're an awful woman, Joan."

III

THE LIZARD'S TAIL

THE LIZARD'S TAIL

I₁ IS AT times disputed between Mr. Fortune and his wife whether he has more success with old ladies or the very young ones.

She was not surprised when she found Wendy Mardale consulting him, and heard him ask, "What do you want with a honeymoon at your time of life?"

"No weakness, Reggie," said Mrs. Fortune severely. "I am here."

Wendy gurgled at her. Wendy made eyes at him. "He would be a perfect lamb. Wasn't he, Joan?"

"He is very like a lamb," Mrs. Fortune admitted. "That haunts me."

"Lambs are possessive," Wendy winked a naughty eye. "Nice? Now, dears. You've been everywhere. You know everything." She returned to her subject. She wanted to go to Tyrol. Pongo dithered. Tyrol would be heavenly in June, wouldn't it? Tell places. Nog threw fits about the Traumsthal.

Reggie showed no sign of seeing a look from his wife. "Tyrol could give you a good honeymoon. Even without me. If you deserve it. Traumsthal—don't know." He discoursed fully of other places.

When she was gone. "Did it hit you, Joan?" he smiled. "What the children forget! However. Don't worry. Wendy wouldn't get a jolt if she did run into the old stuff. Bless her."

"Mormon," said Mrs. Fortune, and ruffled his hair. . . .

Some years before Reggie had assisted at a honeymoon which did end in the Traumsthal.

He was not invited. He was not welcomed. Nor had he any wish to join its revels. No purpose was more remote from his guileless mind. He says his wife compelled him. Her love of needlework shapes men's ends, rough-hew them how they will. There is some stern truth in that. Mrs. Fortune brought him into it. But what led him on was a memory of horrid accuracy and a ruthless sense of duty.

They were in Tyrol to comfort him after the exhausting case of the Cardinal's measles—the worst miscarriage of justice in Reggie's time. From his third ice in the Hof-Garten at Innsbruck Mrs. Fortune took him, protesting, to see the town. He blinked at the Golden Roof, he lifted his eyes to the consolation of the mountains, and discovered that he was alone. She had gone on purposeful. He toiled after her. "The cry goes up, how long?" he moaned. "Where is it, woman?"

She stopped, and her amber eyes were beautifully innocent. "What, dear?"

"Humbug," said Reggie.

"Look, isn't that quaint?" She crossed the street to a narrow lane of overhanging houses and stopped at windows which darkly displayed embroidery and silver. She gazed at the embroidery.

"I knew it," Reggie sighed. "Go on. Go in. The sooner it's over the sooner to sleep." He lit a cigar, but she kept him waiting so long that he went in after her. There was no hope. She was talking needlework to an ancient witch in ecstasies of expertise. Reggie drifted away to the less emotional curiosities, came to glass-topped cabinets of odds and ends: some lovely, some valuable, many of them genuine. He loitered, he stopped, he went on, he recurred. A grey beard with a man behind it attached itself and plied temptation. Reggie was coy to old silver and baroque jewellery, but kept the man hoping.

So Mrs. Fortune finished first. When she crossed the shop she found Reggie's hands caressing the sea green lucidity of a jade bracelet. "My dear child!" she protested.

"Pretty, what?" Reggie drawled, turning it this way and that.

"Wonderful, beautiful," the man ogled him and her amber hair. "Most beautiful on madame."

Reggie smiled sideways. "No, I wouldn't say that. What's your figure?"

"For madame, I ask you only twenty thousand schilling."

"Reggie!" Mrs. Fortune whispered.

"Yes. Eight hundred pounds. Rather a price. Where did it come from, my friend?"

"Ach, sir, it is from China, the best Chinese jade and the finest Chinese carving."

"Oh ah. You imported it?"

"No, I buy it from a gentleman, a traveller. I give you myself guarantee it is true old Chinese."

"Well," Reggie examined it again. "Pay you a thousand schillings for a week's option on it. What?" The man agreed readily.

Gғ

Outside the shop Mrs. Fortune took his arm. "My child, it's exquisite, but you don't mean——"

"Oh no. Not for you. Not really your colour. Not your style. You never made the flesh creep, Joan."

"Who is she?" said Mrs. Fortune tragically.

"Nobody I know. When I saw that bracelet last old Gampound had just bought it for his collection. Paid Lazarus £2,000. And a fair price too. Yet Methuselah here got it from a gentleman, so cheap he can sell at less than half. Bargain days in Innsbruck."

"Do you mean to buy it?"

"What a chance!" Reggie sighed. "Honesty not the best policy, no. But I'm timid. That's always kept me down."

"I'm sure those old people are honest!"

"Bless you!" Reggie smiled affection. "Of course you are. But you may be right. Methuselah didn't know what the thing was worth. Ignorance makes for honesty. Same like fear."

"Why did you take an option on it?"

"My civic virtue, darling. To make the world safe for collectors. What nobler aim has man?" He stopped outside the palace which is the post office. "Pray for me, I'm going to make a long distance call." He was plaintive. "And Gordon does atmospherics even on a local line."

Their hotel is a good hotel. It often has papers of the current year. When Reggie reached the lounge he found his wife looking at an English illustrated weekly only three weeks old. "Well, dear?"

"Oh no. No. A dem'd, damp, moist, unpleasant body," he fanned himself. "Donald Gordon more than usually Wagnerian."

"Why Donald Gordon?"

"Duty, stern daughter of the voice of God. He's Gampound's solicitor."

"What did he say?"

"He didn't. Like a seagull and a crow throwin' an oracular duet."

Mrs. Fortune's brow puckered. She turned the pages of her paper. "Gampound—that Sir Samuel Gampound, the grocer man?"

"Yes, one of our largest grocers. Recreation, collecting. Married Loftus's widow to collect Loftus's collection."

"Ann Loftus is just married," said Mrs. Fortune, and showed him pictures on a page headed "June's Brides." Miss Ann Loftus was portrayed, slight and gracious, with a head so faint she looked a demure ghost beside Mr. Lawrence Caval, her bridegroom. Nothing of the ghost about him. He asserted full-blooded vigour, a big fellow whose dark face knew very well that he was handsome and had no doubt of his right to own the earth.

"Chatter of a Châtelaine" opposite explained that Miss Loftus would be married on June 3, at Rule, very quietly, owing to the recent illness of her mother, Lady Gampound. Such a pity! Sir Samuel Gampound's place, Rule Manor, was a fairy palace. A knowing little bird chirped to the Châtelaine the well kept secret of the bride's honeymoon. The happy pair were going to Tyrol.

"Well, well," Reggie murmured. "Caval. The last new painter. You know, Joan. Landscape like geometry, with light that never was on sea or land. Him takin' old Gampound's step-daughter to wife! And on June 3. Last week. And bringin' her out here. And here's Gampound's museum piece of jade for sale half price. Curiouser and curiouser."

Mrs. Fortune frowned at him. "But Lawrence Caval's had a great success."

"Of esteem, yes. Shocked 'em and knocked 'em. But he was on his uppers not long ago."

"The girl's wealthy, isn't she?"

"Father Loftus was. Stepfather Gampound is. Yes. Compare photograph. Caval does look as if he'd made a kill. I wonder."

Reggie rose in sections and sought London newspapers. He found a report of the wedding. Sir Samuel Gampound had given his step-daughter away. Few people were mentioned. He knew none. Not even the best man, Mr. Robert Campbell, "the well known painter". Reggie went to his bath.

He had been some time immersed when Mrs. Fortune opened the door and gave him a telegram.

"'Hold it stop Reach you Thursday stop Gordon'"

It was then Tuesday.

"He is interested, isn't he?" Reggie slid down into the water and wallowed.

Mrs. Fortune gave him an imitation of a cock crowing. "Oh, the cleverness of you!"

"Not clever, no," Reggie smiled. "But so good.

Sorry, Joan. You shouldn't have married virtue."
She turned on the cold tap.

When she came down to dinner he was talking to
the porter, a painful struggle, for the porter would
only speak English, which he couldn't, to Reggie's
German, which is costive.

"Otto thinks well of the Traumsthal," Reggie
explained to her. "Give it a day, what?" He took
her away to sherry.

"The day before Donald Gordon comes," she
looked at him gravely. "Why?"

"Caval's taken an old place in the Traumsthal."
Mrs. Fortune drew a long breath.

"Sorry. Do you hate me?"

"No." Her hand touched his. "Are you afraid,
Reggie?"

He shook his head and smiled. "Bless you.
Don't worry. The mind is blank. I'd rather try.
That's all." He took her to dinner and made love to
her.

The Traumsthal is one of the loveliest of the valleys
which climb southward from maize and flax and vines
to the glaciers and the snow. They found it full of
sunshine till they drove into a ravine upon which
cascades roared down from towering cliffs on either
side. Out of the gloom and the spray they came again
to a blaze of sunlight over fragrant, flowery meadows
framed in circling slopes of larch and pine which rose
to the scarp of the high mountains. A cool wind
broke upon them from the snow peaks and the pale
green glacier tongues, glittering in the crystal air
as if close above the trees and the hot, jewelled grass.

Through the shadows of the woodland gleamed, turquoise blue, the still water of a little lake and close by that a mass of silvery rock stood out, crowned by the sullen tower of an ancient castle.

Reggie stopped the car. "Worth a day, Joan?"

"Fairyland." She looked all round. "And this is where Lawrence Caval's bringing his wife?"

"Yes. Fairies makin' rainbows in the grass. Fantastic geometry of crags scowlin' at 'em, and hobgoblins of the ice world up above. Just like his pictures. Now he puts in a human element. Quite new for him. I wonder."

"You can't believe——"

"My dear girl! I could believe anything in a place like this. But I don't. The perfect infidel. Till there's evidence."

She shook her head. "You go by feeling. You're uncanny."

"Not me, no." Reggie let in the clutch with emotion. "The common man. Only know facts."

They reached the scattered white houses of the village of Kreuz. A garland of alpine roses and pine boughs hung across the street from tree to tree. The landlord of the balconied inn came out to meet them in embroidered shorts and a velvet coat and with manners not less festive but beautifully ordered to suggest that Mrs. Fortune was a queen and Reggie her king consort.

He attended them after lunch to the garden; he was easily persuaded to smoke a cigar and talk.

"Very good of you to decorate the village for us, Herr Moritz."

"We would wish to honour madame," he bowed. "But I must be true. It was a welcome to Mr. Caval. He brings home his bride. You know him, perhaps?"

"Caval?" Reggie showed surprise. "Not me. Why, is he English?"

"But yes. A painter, a great painter."

"Caval?" Reggie repeated. "Oh, ah. I have seen some of his pictures. Lives here, does he?"

Moritz was happy to explain. Mr. Caval had come to Traumsthal years and years, alone, with a friend. Poor, a student, he would tramp, sleep anywhere and paint and paint. He was like one of themselves and— a check came, a look at Mrs. Fortune—he had friends everywhere. Always he used to swear that he would come back to them great. And now he had his fortune made, he bought the old castle Kreuzstein, there—a finger was pointed to the tower on the rock. See, that was once the castle of the lords of the Traumsthal, then a shooting box, then, since the war, ruin. Mr. Caval he bought it last year, he had it built up, electric, baths—a fine house.

"His castle in the air," said Mrs. Fortune. "But he has it real."

"And fairyland all round."

"So. You like?" Moritz beamed at her. "Gracious lady."

"Lovely place for a honeymoon," Reggie murmured. "They haven't arrived though?"

"Not yet. Mr. and Mrs. Caval, they make a tour of Tyrol first to show her."

"Oh, yes. I see," Reggie said slowly. "And the enchanted castle to end with."

Moritz looked arch. "The end? No, sir, the beginning." He turned to Mrs. Fortune. "A new life then, is it not true, madame?"

"I have heard men say so," she smiled, contemplating Reggie.

"Not noticin' any change yourself," Reggie sighed. "Well, well."

Moritz thought he had better change the subject. Did Mr. Fortune wish to climb? Reggie shuddered. Or sport, the fishing was good, there was shooting. "Oh, no. No. Never kill anything. Except in my trade. I'm a doctor. Only want to exist beautifully." Moritz said that it was most easy there in Kreuz—with madame—and bowed himself away.

Reggie closed his eyes and woke up to music— guitars, accordions, the human voice. A little band of the village folk arrayed in their costumes of festival, a lot of white and embroidery on buxom women, a lot of useful male leg revealed, gathered under the garland. A car was coming up the valley. Reggie gave his wife an arm and strolled towards the populace. "Easy to look at, these damsels."

The music stopped. The car stopped. A big car with two people in it. The driver leaned out, showing black hair that shone, a handsome dark face split in a gleaming smile of triumph, he talked loudly, thrust out a hand to be shaken.

"Full of it, isn't he, our Mr. Caval?" Reggie drawled. "Photo didn't tell us half."

Caval drew back into the car and his bride had a chance. They saw curls of light gold hair about a fragile face which was pale in the sunlight, a tired

face which would be gay. She bowed to bows and
curtsies. Way was made for a little girl who held up
a posy of mountain flowers, cyclamen, gentians,
anemones. Ann Caval reached down a bare arm of
more strength than her face promised; took the posy,
hid her face in it, put it to her bosom and threw the
child kisses. As Caval drove her away the village
music sped them on.

"Wish them joy, Reggie," said Mrs. Fortune.

"Yes, I do," Reggie murmured, but his tone was
without expression, like his face, as he watched their
car climb the hair-pin bends up the track to the
castle. A golden flag broke from the tower. "Well,
well. So they are come to their kingdom. On the gold
standard." He turned away.

That night after dinner he deserted his wife. The
midsummer dusk was falling when he appeared again
from the back of the inn, to find her still in the garden.
"Sorry. Just been social with the village folks. Good
folks. Not so good, the wine."

"Well?"

"Oh, they like Caval all right. Quite sure he's a
man. Not so sure he's a brother. But much admired.
And they know him well. And he had many contacts,
him and his pals. When he was poor. They don't mind
his having their castle. Good and right. The strong
man. His is the earth and everything that's in it. No
complaints."

"What a pity! We don't like success, do we?"

"Not as such. We like to see fair, Joan."

"Yes, I know," she took his hand. "But look."

A light silvery mist was gathering in the valley.

The meadows were hidden, the rock of Kreuzstein was lost, but high in air lights shone from the unseen castle. "That's wonderful," said Mrs. Fortune.

"The enchanted tower, yes. Come in. It's cold."

Some hours later knocking beat upon their door. "Please, please, Mr. Fortune!" Moritz called. Reggie rolled out of bed and blinked at him. "Pardon. But you said you were a doctor, sir. Climbers coming down from the Hirschspitze they have found a woman lying hurt on the track beyond Kreuzstein. She is like dead. They are not sure. Could you go to her, please?"

"All right. Who is she?"

"I do not know. They do not know. I have the guides to go with you, please. I go myself."

Reggie shut the door and crossed to the window. The pall of mist lay thicker over the valley. Lights still shone from the castle of Kreuzstein. "How late is it, Joan?"

"Just after midnight."

"Oh my hat!" Reggie moaned. "You poor child."

"Do you think——"

He stopped dressing a moment to kiss her. "Don't think. It's futile. Go to sleep."

Lanterns of long-striding guides swayed before him in the mist. He plodded on through their aroma of acrid tobacco, Moritz at his elbow pouring forth grateful apologies and encouragement. It was most kind of Mr. Fortune, it would not be far, nor steep at all, only just across the valley, and Mr. Fortune was so strong a walker he would make nothing of it.

"Thanks very much," Reggie panted, his eyes on the castle lights. A line of trees hid them for a moment. When he looked up again they had gone out.

"Only further a little, sir," Moritz exhorted him as he flagged.

"I wonder," Reggie moaned.

"Ach, it is so. Just up the first zigzags here beyond."

They passed into the pungent gloom of a pinewood, out to clearer, colder air. The lanterns shone on the glittering dew of pasture and a wall of rock beyond and stopped in a cluster. "Here! She is here," a man called.

Reggie came to her. Flickering lantern light showed him fair hair dark with blood, a young face torn and crushed.

He switched a torch upon her. She was dressed in a bodice of many colours over a white blouse, and a short, tucked, black skirt with light apron, the festal dress of the village. She had too full a form, too round a face for Ann Caval. He drew in his breath, he knelt down and turned the torch light to her wounded head.

"Gerechter Herrgott!" deep voices joined in oaths. "It is Amalie."

Reggie studied her close and long. "Well!" He stood up. "She is alive, Moritz." He shook his head. "Bad fracture. Brain injury, I'm afraid. Yes. I am afraid. Can't do anything here. Stretcher, please. Gentle as you go." He turned to Moritz. "Who is she? How would she get here?"

"She is Amalie Schöpf, sir. Her family are up on the mountain pasture with the cows. She came down to the fête of Mr. Caval to-day. She would be going back up the mountain again. And then, you see——" He directed Reggie's torch to the wall of rock above the pasture. "That cliff, the path goes round there. She must have slipped on the edge, poor child, and fallen—to the rock of the path here, so." He made a dramatic gesture.

"Yes, it could be," said Reggie slowly. "Someone must go up and tell her people."

"Johan is gone already."

"God help him," said Reggie. "God help them."

Moritz bent his head and crossed himself. "You are kind with us, sir."

"No. Useless," said Reggie drearily.

They tramped back to the wakeful village. The girl was put to bed in the house of kinsfolk and lay still as death. Reggie worked upon her wounds and turned to the helping women. "There. Just watch and wait. That's all." The priest of the village met him as he came out. Reggie bowed. "For you, sir." . . .

The sun was over the eastern mountains, the mist seethed up the valley, rising thin, pierced by shafts of light which discovered meadow and lake. Reggie trudged away from the inn with the faithful Moritz, both of them unkempt, unshaven and silent.

They came again to the patch of pasture above the first belt of pines where Amalie had been found. "That is the place, see you," Moritz pointed. "There is her blood." It was dark on the grey stones of the path.

"As you say." Reggie looked up at the overhanging wall of cliff. "Eighty feet of a drop."

"It is enough," Moritz shrugged. "I have seen no more than that kill before."

"Oh yes. Easy. However." Reggie beat about the pasture like a dog after scent. He returned to the path. "Come on." They climbed round a bend to the top of the cliff, a little plateau of rock jutting bare from steep, wooded slopes. Some scraps of paper lay on it. "People come here much?"

"It is a view point. It is favourite."

"Oh yes, beautiful view." Reggie looked across the valley over which the mist was no more than a lace veil, looked down at the turquoise lake, glowing to the sunshine, reflecting in its depths dark woodland and white mountain peaks, looked to the tower of the castle beyond and its golden flag. "Would you say Amalie was gazin' at the view?"

"I do not know," Moritz was hurt by the sarcastic tone. "The poor child! She might well. We folk of the valley, we love its beauty also, sir. She sees the view in evening glow, she does not see where she is going and then——"

Reggie wandered away from him to the cliff edge, lay down and bent over, scanning the face of the rock. He rose with a twist of a joyless smile on his lips and moved about, stooping to stare close at the ground. The smile vanished in a frown which grew heavier as he worked farther and farther away from the cliff. He stopped, he knelt down.

"No. It wasn't like that, Moritz," he said. "Come here." He pointed to dark splashes on dust and stone.

"This is blood, too, and not only blood, specks of fair skin and yellow hair."

"God be with us!" Moritz groaned.

"Yes. A felt want. Yes. Amalie didn't fall. She was hit here. Then she was thrown from the cliff. To pretend a fall."

Moritz shook his fists in the air and thundered oaths.

"As you say. Not a nice job. Any idea who would do it?"

"There is no one. Not of our folk. I would swear it. But, sir, perhaps a stone fell on her."

"Where's the stone? No. Wasn't a stone. Something to give a piercing blow; I knew that before."

"My God! An ice axe," Moritz exclaimed.

"It could be," Reggie looked up at him with closing eyes. "Suggest anybody to you?"

"No, no, sir!"

"I wonder. Well. Matter for your police. However. Collect the evidence. Might be obliterated." He gathered fragments from the ground and Moritz turned shuddering away.

Reggie stood up and surveyed the valley once more. "What's the nearest house to this place?"

"Sir?" Moritz was startled. "Alois Egger lives on the road. There is also the castle."

"Oh ah." Reggie's eyes narrowed to look at it. "How far?"

"Alois' house, half hour. To the castle less, perhaps."

Reggie gazed at the castle rock for a moment more, then made off down into the wood. "Someone coming this way from the castle, wasn't there?"

"Not this way, sir. That path she was on is to the lake. It was Mrs. Caval."

"Good eyes you have." Through the trees the castle rock came into sight again and the lake below. "Yes, she is trendin' there. Can we get round?"

"If you wish, sir," Moritz gave him a puzzled, troubled stare. "You wish to speak to her?"

"I might."

Moritz turned half right and struck across a shoulder of the wood. Castle and lake were hidden. Then below a steep slope from which the pines grew sparse amid boulders Reggie saw the lake, a turquoise mirror in a setting of pebbled beach and rocky headlands.

On one of these promontories of rock Ann Caval stood, every curve of a slight, gracious form clear against the sunlight in the sapphire blue of a bathing dress.

"God in heaven!" Moritz gasped. "She is going to swim there."

"Yes. That is indicated. Any objection?"

"But it is death cold. It is glacier water."

Reggie plunged on aslant down the slope, with Moritz thudding after him.

Ann Caval looked down into the water, raised her arms above her head and dived. Her sapphire cap rose from the eddies, she swam out into the lake, going hard, turned and came back. They lost sight of her. A white arm rose to the rock and grasped it. Out of the trees above a boulder rolled down, they saw it splash, they heard a cry. When the spray fell, her arm was gone.

Reggie shouted. As he reached the rock, beyond it, some way off, a man broke out of the wood and ran along the shore towards him. Reggie tore off his coat, peered down into the turbulent, clouded water and dived for the dark shadow in it. He rose breathless, from failure. He was diving again when the other man plunged in upon him.

They came to the surface with Ann Caval's body between them, swam back with it and Moritz hauled it on to the rock, while they dragged themselves out on either side.

"Mr. Lawrence Caval, I presume?" Reggie spluttered. "Thanks very much."

Caval dashed the water out of his eyes. "Who the devil are you?"

"I'm a doctor. Lucky, isn't it?" Reggie turned the body face downwards, feet above head. "Moritz— fetch help—blankets—brandy." Moritz made off at a loping trot. Reggie put the body on its back and propped up the shoulders. The flesh was of a pallid blue. The head lolled to one side. A pitted bruise showed on the brow. The backs of the hands were torn.

Reggie worked the arms up and down in rhythmic movement.

Caval's teeth chattered as he tried to speak. "Is she—will you—what do you think? Hit her head diving?"

"Head was hit. Shock from cold. And so nearly drowned. You're cold too, Mr. Caval. Shock for you also. You'd better run home."

"See you damned first."

"No. I don't think so."

"I'm not going to leave her to you."

Reggie laboured on. . . .

Moritz came back with men bearing blankets and feather quilts. "Good work," Reggie panted. "Her breath's coming. Brandy? Thanks." He poured drops through the white lips. "Now." Blankets and quilts were wrapped round her. "Where's the nearest house?"

"Alois Egger's," said Moritz. "They make a bed warm for her."

"What the devil do you mean?" Caval roared. "Take her up to the castle."

"Oh no. I want to save her life, Mr. Caval."

"Do as I tell you, Moritz!" Caval thrust forward.

Moritz stood against him. "It is nearer to Egger's, sir. We take her there." The men marched off with her.

Caval scowled at Reggie. "Thanks for your trouble. I'll get my own doctor. Send me your bill."

"A pleasure, Mr. Caval," Reggie drawled, and as he put on his coat Caval pushed past him and hurried away.

.   .   .   .   .

From the house of Alois Egger, Reggie emerged limp, his round face shrunken and drawn. Moritz strode from a group of smoking, debating men to meet him. "Not too bad," said Reggie. "She should come through."

"God be thanked!" Moritz breathed deep. "But you, sir." He looked at Reggie anxiously and took his

HF

arm. "You come back to the inn, please. You are worn out."

"Not yet, no. Come on. Want to look over that lake-side."

"What is to do there now?"

"Want you to protect me."

"So. You think that!" Moritz muttered. "Yes, I go with you."

But Caval did not interfere with them; Caval was not to be seen as they made their way back through the wood.

Reggie stopped. "About here our Mr. Caval appeared. Would this be his straight way from the castle to bathe with her?"

"A straight way to the lake, yes. But he had no bathing clothes. Nobody comes here to bathe. The water is too cold."

"Yes. As you were sayin'. I believe you." Reggie shuddered. "Caval would know that. But he didn't stop her coming to bathe bright and early. He only followed. Only made haste to assist when I shouted for him."

"That is true," Moritz nodded. "That is not good."

"Not nice, no. She was bathing two hundred yards further on. He came out of the wood here. Some moments after the boulder had rolled down and crashed on her." Reggie went on across the steep, stony slope of the wood, looking all round.

"There are no tracks of him, sir," Moritz said.

"No. Wouldn't be. He was wearin' rubber shoes,"

Reggie answered, but went on, "Why did the boulder roll?"

Moritz cleared his throat. "The stones fall of themselves sometimes."

"Yes. That would be the idea," Reggie murmured.

"It does happen, sir," said Moritz. "See, a big stone has just gone from there." He pointed to raw earth between the pine trunks.

"Yes. I had noticed that," Reggie looked down to the lake. "Straight above where she was bathing. Clear run. To hit her as she came out. You think it just happened?"

"Who can say not?" Moritz growled.

"I wonder." Reggie pored over the place, wandered higher. He glanced back. The promontory from which Ann Caval had bathed was still full in sight. He gazed at the ground again. "Well, well," he murmured, and the yellow stubble on his wan, tired face was twisted in a smile. He sat down.

"What is it?" Moritz exclaimed.

"Little lizard," Reggie mumbled. "Poor little lizard without a tail." He pointed to the creature, a shining green body which moved feebly on the pine needles. "And there is his tail."

"Pfui!" Moritz puffed. "What of it? They do that, the lizards. They shed their tails easily. And their legs too sometimes. Then they grow new ones. You could see it often, sir."

"Thanks, I have. Enterprisin' creatures."

"This makes nothing then," Moritz said sharply.

"Think again," Reggie drawled. "Lizards only act on stimulus. Same like you and me, comin' here.

Your lizard don't abandon his tail without cause. Only when caught, when handled, what?"

"So!" Moritz frowned at him.

"And this chap's tail has only just come off. Which makes quite a lot. Some fellow was here recently. The lizard fussed him and was reproved. What was the fellow doing? Watchin' the bride bathe. Not a nice fellow. No. That boulder didn't fall of itself, Moritz. He pushed it on her."

"Ach, you are clever," Moritz rumbled, glowering trouble and awe.

"Yes, I think so." Reggie smiled and picked up the tail of the lizard and the lizard itself in his handkerchief. "Poor little beggar. Exhibit A: One murdered girl. Exhibit B: One bride saved. Exhibit C: One lizard's tail, with lizard. Which should be conclusive. Up to your police. Take me back. I'm empty. Oh, my hat, I am empty." . . .

Late in the afternoon he came out to the inn garden, neat and pink again but with a sleep-walking manner. He made for Mrs. Fortune's chair and blinked to her. "Sorry, Joan."

"My dear! You." She put her hand on him a moment.

"I'm all right. Any reactions?"

"I went to see Ann Caval."

"Of course you did," Reggie smiled drowsily. "Well?"

"Mr. Caval had brought a doctor to her. He wanted to move her to the castle. She told him to go away. The people of the house said she wouldn't let him touch her. She turned her face to the wall.

The people made him go. They're good people.
When I saw her she was sleeping like the dead, poor
thing."

"That's all right. Thanks."

Moritz strode up to them, a spruce, alert man at
his elbow. "Please, you permit, madame?" He introduced Herr Gratl, of the police from Innsbruck, and
Gratl clicked his heels and bowed low.

In a frowsty, little room furnished with Moritz's
desk and his guns and his fishing tackle Reggie and
Gratl sat down together. "You're very quick on it,
Herr Gratl," Reggie smiled.

"I thank you. I hope we are always. But when I
had the telephone message from here that Mr. Fortune
asked for us I threw all to the winds and came myself.
I am most happy that I have the chance to do a case
with you."

"My dear chap! Oh, my dear chap!" Reggie shook
his head. "I'm nowhere in it. All on your shoulders.
I've just blundered on the raw material. Well. Moritz
has told you what there is?"

"Yes, sir. Now, I take it in order. The poor girl
Amalie Schöpf. There is a history. She was pretty,
you have seen that, also she was gay. Lawrence Caval
has an eye for the girls. Amalie had been with him and
his friends when he was here before many times.
These people say nothing wrong. But she came down
from the mountain to see him bring his bride. She
did not go back at once, not till night. There is a
young man went up that way to the Hirschspitze hut
just after dark. He heard two peoples talking in the
wood where she was found and they talked English.

What they say he does not know, he did not see anybody at all. But that looks like it was an Englishman met Amalie. Very well so. Now where was Lawrence Caval then? I have not asked him yet. I wait. But I have talked to Anton Immer, the old man who keeps the castle for him. And I hear a strange story, Mr. Fortune."

"Yes. There might be," Reggie murmured. "I thought that. Before Amalie was found."

"Aha. You have your reasons?"

"One strikin' reason. The lights in Caval's castle were still on long after midnight. Late for a honeymoon couple. They didn't go out till we'd started to look for Amalie."

Gratl nodded satisfaction. "So. Now hear Anton. You can believe him. He does not love Lawrence Caval. To him Caval is an upstart, a new rich. He had care of the castle in the old days. Caval took him over with it. But he is honest, he is faithful. Very well. Caval has had the castle made modern inside. There is an old room that was the chapel. Caval has turned it into a studio. He will not have anyone touch things there. When Caval brought Mrs. Caval to the castle yesterday, he showed her all over, then he went to the studio by himself and was there alone till he dressed for dinner. He came and found Mrs. Caval in the studio. Anton hears the woman cry out, then angry talk. At dinner they are dumb, she is white and he is red, they eat little. After dinner she leaves him alone, goes back to her room, locks herself in. Caval, he sits drinking and smoking a little, then he goes out. Anton does not know when he comes back. But he went out a little after nine. That would be the twilight, the gloaming, you say, is it not?"

"Yes. Roaming in the gloaming by our Mr. Caval. Just on the time Amalie was roaming up the hill. Speakin' without a post mortem, I should say she was struck around ten. It does fit. What does Anton say about this morning?"

Gratl smiled. "That also is strange. Mrs. Caval, she slept in a room by herself. She got up at seven hours. Caval came out of his room then also, but he was not dressed. He stopped her on the stair. There was more angry talk. Anton did not hear. Then she went out alone. In a very little while Caval goes after her. Anton sees no more till Caval comes back all wet, and curses him when he asks how and where, and goes to the telephone and talks, then changes and drives away."

"Who did he talk to?"

"Anton heard him try for the doctor in Grunfeld, he could not get the number. Then he was calling Innsbruck. Then somewhere else."

"Well, well," Reggie murmured. "Very full and good, I should say you have the real lines of the case already. Like to congratulate you, if I may."

Gratl bowed. "You are very kind. I am honoured, Mr. Fortune. But in fact you gave me all."

"Not me. No. Only a little raw material. Did Moritz tell you how Amalie was killed?"

"Oh yes! By a blow from a sharp weapon like an ice axe. A little raw material! It is the foundation."

"I wouldn't say that."

Gratl laughed. "You are too modest, sir. But the lizard's tail, that was brilliant. Without that, the stone fell on Mrs. Caval by accident. Now for sure a man rolled it on her, and Caval was there. There is very much for him to explain."

"Yes. That is so. I shouldn't ask him just yet, if I were you."

"No? I am happy for your advice. You would wait till Mrs. Caval can talk to us?"

"I should, yes. She won't be fit to-day."

Gratl nodded. "She has much shock. You would not let Caval take her home. And she would not speak to him. But you expect she can tell us her story to-morrow?"

"Yes. She may not tell the truth."

"So. You think she may defend her husband still? In spite of all? Women are like that sometimes, is it not? They will suffer anythings to be loyal."

"Some of 'em. However. Unknown quantity, Mrs. Caval. We do want to know what happened in Caval's very private studio—why they quarrelled—why she went to a separate room."

"Suppose in that so private studio there was something of other women—of Amalie Schöpf?"

"Oh yes. Quite possible. Other possibilities. Possibly involvin' Mrs. Caval's family. I——"

"What do you say?" Gratl broke out.

"I'm not sure the case began here. I didn't." Reggie told him of the jade bracelet in Innsbruck and the telegrams. . . .

"But, but this is more than ever strange!" Gratl stammered.

"You think so? I wonder."

"The girl Amalie murdered, Mrs. Caval almost murdered because some jewel is stolen from her stepfather. It is not sense!"

"Not obviously. No. However. Your framework's all right. But we haven't enough material. I should wait till to-morrow, Gratl. You notice the strong reaction from the stepfather end. Something queer happened there. Well, the stepfather's solicitor was to be in Innsbruck to-morrow morning. I wired him to come up here. He's quite good, Donald Gordon. I was thinkin' he'd give us some more stuff." Reggie contemplated Gratl with dreamy eyes. "Other ways worth tryin'. Somebody might have seen somebody about last night or this morning."

Gratl laughed. "Have no fear, there is a man or two enquiring everywhere of that."

"Good work," Reggie murmured. "And I could bear to know who Caval was 'phoning to, besides his doctor."

"Ah that!" Gratl frowned. "You miss nothing, sir. That also!" . . .

In the morning Reggie was spread in the lowest of the garden's deck chairs, a pipe in his mouth, his eyes shut, while Gratl sat stiffly and explained at length how he had failed to find anyone who had seen anyone where Amalie roamed, where Ann Caval bathed. "Life is like that," Reggie mumbled. "Takin' useless pains. However. What about Caval's telephone work?"

"There I have something," said Gratl. "For what it is. He made a call to Innsbruck. They do not know the number."

"Oh. Too bad."

"You think he called the shop which had the jade bracelet? I thought of that also. The shop people deny. But Innsbruck will, how do you say, shake them up. And then Caval rang up the Hôtel Krone, in the Planthal. It is only a little high inn by the Italian frontier. The man of the house is out climbing. The woman does not know of Caval."

"I wonder," Reggie murmured.

"You think Caval plans to go across the frontier? I also. But he will not. Not now. He is watched, be sure."

"That's all right. You won't let him get at his wife either, will you? She's doing quite well. Up this afternoon."

"She also is watched," said Gratl.

"Watch and wait. Yes. A hard life. The mind is practically impotent. No stuff." . . .

A car drove up to the inn and out of it came a plump little Jew, spick and span as if he had been just bathed and dressed, not plucked from twenty hours in the train to a jolting up a mountain road.

Reggie met him with admiration. "You're full of zeal, Donald."

"I want your blood. What is the great idea of leading me up this rock garden?"

"Herr Gratl, of the Austrian police. Mr. Donald Gordon, the solicitor in question."

Gratl clicked heels and bowed. Gordon's beady eyes twinkled. "Question is right. This Fortune fellow is the widow's cruse of trouble, Herr Gratl. All the worst, believe me. A spot of vermouth, and I'm with you."

He sat down between them. "Now what's your end of it, Fortune?" he demanded, and Reggie told him. He smacked his lips and compressed them. "Caval's going big."

"Surprise to you?"

"I don't know the fellow to know him. They do say he's full of sex appeal. Speaking for myself, I should class him with the bold, bad men. The get-theres. My instructions are Mr. Lawrence Caval is n.b.g. There's the personal angle for you. Now I'll hand you the cold facts. My client, old Sam Gampound, took a widow to wife, complete with money and daughter. He didn't want the daughter, I don't know that he wanted the widow, but she had an Arabian Night's collection of jewels and bric-à-brac and you know what Gampound is. Then Lawrence Caval made his big noise and daughter Ann fell for him. Gampound soured on that, but Lady G. is a sentimental old dame and she backed love's young dream. Some row. Lady G. went sick and won. She had the happy pair married from Gampound's place in the country. One in the eye for him. Very quietly, owing to illness of bride's mother. He thought he took a point with that. Saved him a little packet. But! The house is miles from anywhere. Everybody who came had to be put up, including bridegroom. Lady G. was carried down to give a mother's blessing, and Mr. and Mrs. Lawrence

Caval left to live happy ever after. When Gampound began to come to, he consoled himself with his collection. He's made that way. Takes out pearls to give 'em sun on the lawn and gloat. He had a go at Lady G.'s stuff. And then hell's bells rang out. The jade bracelet he'd given her, one of his best bits of jade, where was it? It was not! Where was the rig-out of diamonds she had from husband number one on producing her precious daughter? Gampound threw fits till she had him beat at that. Then he got me down. Poor me! Nobody but Lady G. could tell when she saw the things last, and she set up she was too ill to talk. Gampound swore blue Caval and the girl had scoffed the lot. Between cursing, he couldn't make up his mind whether Lady G. handed 'em to the girl or Caval pinched 'em, and how was he to set the police going on that, and couldn't I make Lady G. see reason? I tried, and she told me she was dying and it was all Gampound's fault, and go away, oh go away. I went."

"With any ideas?" Reggie drawled.

Gordon's face was a comic mask. "Natty little case, dear boy. Even before you cut in."

"Several possibilities, yes," Reggie watched him under drooping eyelids. "Lady Gampound might have given her daughter the things for love or for spite at Gampound. You noticed that? Ever thought of Gampound removing the things himself to get the Cavals into trouble?"

Gratl exclaimed amazement.

Gordon laughed. "He's only being clever, old man. Pretty Fanny's way. He knows that won't go now.

Not since he found the bracelet on sale at Innsbruck and Caval took to killing."

Gratl nodded approval, but with a frowning, puzzled brow.

"Not now, not since——" Reggie murmured. "Did you happen to think the vanishin' of the jewels gave Caval a reason to kill Amalie and try to kill his wife?"

"Come down," Gordon scoffed. "That's an easy one. Caval's girl friend blew in on the honeymoon. He wiped her out. Mrs. Caval spotted something wrong and threatened him over the jewels. So he went for her too."

"That would fit, yes. Assumin' the jewels were stolen, not given. Who had the best chance? They were in Lady Gampound's room, and she kept her room except when carried down to the wedding breakfast. Is that right?"

"On my instructions," Gordon nodded.

"Gampound's instructions. Yes. Gampound could have gone to her room at all times. Or her daughter. Who might take Caval. Durin' the fuss of the weddin' breakfast, anybody. Made enquiries of the servants and the wedding guests?"

"How could I? The theft wasn't discovered till days after. Nothing to go on with Lady G. dumb. What's the use of labouring that end? All the evidence on Caval is here. Let's go to it. His wife will talk now."

"Yes, I think so," Reggie murmured. "I wonder."

"You believe she was in it?" Gordon said sharply.

"It could be," Reggie answered. His round face was plaintive. "Not a nice case, Gordon. However." He rose with weary movements. "Take Caval first."

"Spot of lunch first," Gordon demanded: which made some difference. . . .

Reggie drove his car rocking and surging in a cloud of dust round the hairpin bends of the track up the castle rock. A high wall circled its summit. From within that rose the tower, still flaunting its golden standard, windows blazing blank at the sunshine.

"Weird place," said Gordon.

"Yes. Mr. Caval, his castle in the air. Ogre's castle. Feel like the fairy prince?"

The oak, iron-studded gates in the wall were locked. After some time a little door in them opened and Anton, a bearded ancient, looked out, saw Gratl and whispered that there was a gentleman come, and led them across the courtyard to the tower.

In a room of stone floor and bare stone walls on which old weapons hung, he left them to wait, but not for long. A lank, swarthy man with a shock of black hair strode in. "Good day, gentlemen," he said in German. "You are of the Austrian police, I understand?"

Gratl bowed and gave him a card. "I wish to see Mr. Caval, sir."

"My name is Campbell, I am an old friend of Mr. Caval's. He 'phoned for me to come over yesterday afternoon. You will understand he has had a nasty shock, Herr Gratl. He wants me to act for him."

"So," Gratl frowned. "That cannot be."

"Mr. Robert Campbell, I presume," Reggie asked in English. "You were at Caval's wedding, his best man?"

"I was, sir," Campbell gave him a sardonic smile, looked from him to Gordon. "You're not Austrian policemen?"

"No. This is Mr. Donald Gordon, Gampound's solicitor. I'm Reginald Fortune."

"The deuce and all," Campbell's smile had more amusement in it. "Does that mean the English police have been called on to act against Caval?"

"Why should you think so?" Reggie's eyes opened wide.

"I have heard of Mr. Fortune," Campbell laughed.

"Thanks very much. And was there anything at Caval's wedding which made you think the police might be called on?"

"What?" Campbell stared back derisive surprise. "I'm not a wedding fan. But his wedding was just like any other to me."

"Then you can't help us," said Reggie. "We must see Caval."

"I'll tell him. He's not fit." Campbell strode out, but they followed close.

Up winding stone stairs they went, and he opened the door of a room full of light but without sunshine. It had plainly been built for a chapel, a stone altar still stood on a dais, but the northern side had been made one big window, the other windows filled up, to turn it into a studio. Modernist divans and cabinets were all the furniture, but for the apparatus of painting, which spread in disorder everywhere, even upon the altar.

"These fellows would come and talk to you, Lawrence," Campbell said, and Caval started up from one of the divans and stumbled forward. His full face was sallow and distorted in a scowl of miserable defiance. A shrill, snarling cry came from him. Campbell took his arm. "Go easy, old man. Here they are, Herr Gratl, Mr. Fortune, Mr. Donald Gordon."

"You, damn you!" Caval's sunken red eyes glared at Gordon.

"Pleased to meet you, Mr. Caval," Gordon said.

Reggie was wandering round the studio to a corner in which stood a portable easel and camp stool, a stick or two and a sketching umbrella.

"There's no ice axe, Caval," he murmured, and Gratl swung round.

"What? Ice axe?" Caval said thickly. "I haven't got one. I don't climb."

Reggie gazed at the sketching umbrella which had a long steel-shod point to fix it in the ground. He turned away. "Glad to meet you in your studio, Caval. I want to know what happened here the night you brought your wife to the castle—the night Amalie was murdered—the night before the attempt to murder your wife."

Caval swore at him. "There wasn't any attempt to murder her. She fainted with the cold of the water."

"Oh no. A boulder was rolled down on her."

"I saw nothing. I didn't see her at all, till I heard you shout."

"Really? But you went there. Knowin' the water was too cold to bathe in. Knowin' she meant to bathe. Yet not stoppin' her."

"She would go. I couldn't stop her. As soon as I was dressed I went after her."

"Couldn't stop her? She wouldn't listen to you? Too bad, on the honeymoon. What did you quarrel about in here the night before she bathed? Something to do with Amalie?"

"No!" Caval roared and cursed him. "The wretched girl was nothing to me. Nothing, I tell you."

"Oh. Are Gampound's jewels anything?"

Caval glowered at him in sullen silence.

"Did you sell Gampound's jade bracelet in Innsbruck?"

Caval flinched as if he had been hit, and shrank away.

"Steady old man," Campbell put an arm round him. "They're doing their job. They have to. Better give 'em what you know. It's the only way now, Lawrence."

Caval groaned, looked up at him in despair, and stumbled round to face Reggie's cold eyes again. "I know nothing about the blasted bracelet," he growled. "I can tell you where the blasted jewels are." He went to one of the cabinets and took out a paint box and opened it and thrust it into Reggie's hands. Diamonds flashed from it.

IF

"Well, well," Reggie murmured. Gordon came to look. "Passed to you, Donald," said Reggie. "Are these the goods?"

"Collar, bandeau, pendant," Gordon handled them. "Speaking off hand, I think they are."

"And Caval thinks so too. How do you happen to have 'em, Caval?"

"I was telling you, wasn't I? The night we got here, just before dinner, I couldn't find my wife, I came into the studio and here she was. She had that paint box open; it's a paint box I brought out with me; she had the diamonds in her hands. I never saw the cursed things before. She said they were her mother's. I asked her where she got 'em from; she said she found 'em in the paint box. Then there was a row. That's what the row was about."

Reggie's eyes narrowed. "About who stole 'em. And you're telling me it was your wife."

"I don't know how the devil they got here," Caval snarled.

"Oh. But they were stolen. And you say it wasn't by you. Now we'll hear what your wife says. Come and listen, Caval."

"She's too ill to talk," Caval scowled at him. "They wouldn't let me talk to her."

"Not you alone. No. Come on."

"You'd better be there, Lawrence," said Campbell. "I'll see you through."

Caval made off in a stumbling hurry and Gratl followed close, with Campbell behind him.

"Campbell," Reggie called. "One moment." He

crossed to the corner where the sketching umbrella stood, picked it up and looked at the spike again. "Caval said he hadn't an ice axe. Ever seen this thing before?" He put the umbrella into Campbell's hands.

Campbell held it a moment and thrust it back on him with a look of distrust. "It's Lawrence's, of course."

"Thanks very much," Reggie murmured, and took the umbrella with him.

Caval was already in his own car. Campbell joined him and he drove off furiously. "My God! All necks for sale," Gordon gasped as Reggie swirled round the hairpin bends after him. But the two cars came safely and together to the house of Alois Egger.

A garden bounded by a low wall surrounded it. There, under the shade of an old apple tree, Ann Caval lay in a deck chair. She raised herself a little as they came. The fragile pale face was shrunken small. It flushed as she saw them and she trembled.

"Ann!" Caval cried. "About your mother's——"

"No, no, don't," she gasped.

"I say, Ann," Campbell came between them. "This is too bad."

"Bob!" She put out a shaking hand, she smiled pitifully. "How ever did you come?"

Campbell kissed her hand. "Lawrence 'phoned for me. Wouldn't I come. You know."

"What did he tell you?" she panted.

"Why, all the trouble. About the girl being

found dead. About you. About your mother's jewels."

She shuddered. "What did he tell you, Bob?" she cried.

"Just that, my dear. And these police fellows bothering him. So I'm with him and you."

"Police?" she sank back, staring horror at Reggie. "Mr. Fortune?"

"Yes. The police do have to look into murders and things, Mrs. Caval. There was a girl murdered. You were nearly murdered. And——"

"I wasn't."

"And your mother's diamonds and her jade bracelet came out here somehow without leave. Caval told me he found you with them. What did he tell you?" She turned her face away. She choked sobs. "I'm sorry," Reggie said gently. "There's no help but the truth now. What did happen in the studio that night before Amalie was killed; before you were nearly killed? Why did you break with him?"

"I didn't," she said faintly. "It is true. He did find me with the diamonds. I—I'd taken them. He was angry. He said it was like stealing. It was of course. Only mother wouldn't mind. I was so ashamed, I—I——"

"Ann!" Caval shouted, and flung himself on his knees to her and buried his face in her bosom and she put her arms about him and cried.

"Well, well," Reggie turned with a sideways smile to Gordon. "That bein' thus, that ends your natty little case, Donald."

Gordon's beady eyes consulted his. "I stand down," he said.

"So!" Gratl exclaimed. "There is a little something else, Mr. Fortune?"

"Yes. As you say. The lizard's tail," Reggie murmured. He swung round on Campbell, who stood, hands in his jacket pockets, watching the Cavals' embrace with the sardonic smile which he had given Reggie on their meeting. "You can give 'em joy, Campbell. You have seen him through. Congratulations. About the lizard's tail. Remember the lizard above the lake? Finger-prints on him and his tail. There'll be finger-prints on Caval's sketchin' umbrella now. Thanks very much. And your sketchin' umbrella with spike, somewhere between here and the Planthal."

Campbell took a stride forward and laughed. "Hear that, Ann?" he called. She looked up and he took his right hand from his pocket. As he raised his arm, Reggie struck it up. Liquid spattered through the air, drops splashed in his face and he yelled obscenities.

Gratl shouted, Gratl sprang at him. "Vitriol. Keep his arm back," Reggie cried. Together they brought him backwards to the ground and men ran up and he was dragged away.

Ann Caval lay still, her head fallen back, her arms dropped lifeless from Caval. He was shielding her, while he looked back at Campbell's groaning struggle. He turned to her again whispering, but she did not answer nor move. He raised her head and it lolled away. Reggie came to them. "Fortune!" Caval gasped. "Is she——"

Reggie bent over her. "No. Didn't reach her." He drew a long breath. "This is only a faint from shock. Sorry, Caval. It's been hard."

"Ghastly," Caval's teeth chattered. "Bob!"

Reggie made a gesture of obliteration. "No. Not any more. Carry your wife in. She'll want you." He put his hand on Caval's shoulder. "My dear chap!"

.   .   .   .   .

The shadows of the mountains were looming across the valley. He sat in the garden of the inn eating tarts of wild strawberries with cream, benign but pensive, because the tea tasted of nothing in particular.

Gratl and Gordon arrived in a bustle of importance. "Your busy day, what?" he gazed at them dreamily.

Gratl called for beer and drew up chairs. "In fact, I have enough to do," he said with dignity. "That wolf Campbell he will say nothing, he glares through his bandages like a trapped beast."

"'Henceforth I never will speak word'," Reggie murmured. "Same like Iago."

Gratl drank deep. "It is not easy yet altogether. The shop people in Innsbruck, they say they bought the jade bracelet from a dark man who spoke German like English. That would describe Campbell, yes, but also Caval, is it not? They would not know him again."

"Doesn't matter," Reggie mumbled. "Wasn't Caval."

"He can prove an alibi?"

"Haven't asked him. No need now."

"Isn't there?" Gordon grinned. "Where are you, Fortune? The lady said she lifted the diamonds. Have you fallen for her?"

"No. Don't believe her. She said that to save Caval."

"Yes, dear boy. I'm with you. But then you haven't exactly got Caval clear."

"My dear Donald!" Reggie contemplated him with plaintive wonder. "Caval's quite clear. Everything's clear. Campbell lifted jewels and bracelet. Actin' as Caval's best man. Opportunity while the mother was down blessin' bride and bridegroom. Motive, to smash up the marriage. Bein' bitter jealous of Caval. Both painters. Caval a success. Campbell not. Both wild to possess Ann. Caval got her. Campbell didn't. Campbell took the things. Put the diamonds in Caval's paint box, which he wouldn't open before he settled down here to paint. Calculatin' that durin' the interval old Gampound would discover the theft and raise hell. And it was so. Clever fellow, Campbell. Only he didn't work right. He doesn't understand women. Omitted to notice that Lady Gampound wouldn't allow the marriage to be smashed. To resume. Campbell was short of money, took the bracelet himself and sold it in Innsbruck. Quite neat. Leavin' a clue about pointin' straight to the Cavals. But as the days went by and nothing happened it looked to him the theft was bein' hushed up. He came over the pass from the Planthal to have another shot at the Cavals. That poor girl, Amalie, saw him, knew him, he used to be everywhere with Caval. Didn't suit Campbell at all. He was there to do in Caval's wife and leave Caval to take the blame. Amalie had to be wiped out. You'll find he had a sketching umbrella in the Planthal and it's missing. And there he was with a free hand in the morning for Ann Caval. Then things did go right for him. Ann found the diamonds, as Caval stated. Each asked the other who put 'em there. Both have tempers. A big row. Each furious and suspicious. And Ann shut herself up and didn't sleep and rushed off to bathe. Think of Campbell, gloatin', as he watched the castle rock that morning and saw her come alone. Not a nice man. Only my little lizard intervened. There you are. Finger-prints on lizard and tail are Campbell's. As on handle of Caval's sketching umbrella, which I gave him. He knew the game was up then. He was afraid before, when Caval 'phoned for him and said I was takin' action about his wife and Amalie. But he meant to be sure of Ann anyway. So he came. With vitriol. There you are. You'll get him all right, Gratl. You should find his umbrella. Anyway you can trace his movements. Just do a little work. Quite simple."

"I have him anyway," said Gratl. "We do not like the vitriol here."

"Very proper. But I want you to get him for Amalie, please," Reggie was plaintive. "Much rather he was dead."

* * * * *

Mrs. Fortune drove up. He met her and they went in together. "How was it, Joan?"

"Well. It's all well between them"; her eyes were dark as she smiled. "He's sitting by her bed holding her hand. And what do you suppose they're talking about, Reggie? Bob Campbell. Poor Bob Campbell. They're so sorry."

IV

THE COWSLIP BALL

THE COWSLIP BALL

THERE IS A famous, faded picture of Wyburn Park. Turner did it. Whatever he put on the canvas, it shows you now billows of iridescent steam from which grow trees like giants frozen in frenzy and an Arabian Night's palace of contorted fantasies.

But on this April morning Aaron Smith, trudging across the park, saw nothing like that. The waves of its grey green turf, full bosomed or rising steep, were defined in a cheerful solidity. Their slopes shone with primroses. From the hollows, cowslips swayed in golden groups. Here and there boughs of the great beech trees had broken into their first bright green. Beneath the grey trunks spread dark, glowing floods of blue bells. Aaron did not see the oriental palace of the picture. It never existed. The painter dreamed it out of a summer-house put up to look Asiatic when few people knew better. And the summer house is on the far side of the Pavon Pool.

That is as old as the hills, a stretch of shallow blue opal water fed by springs from their base. For two hundred years the owners of Wyburn Park have cherished swans upon it and all the other decorative fowl the earth could furnish.

Aaron had the care of them. He was going to their nurseries with a mind full of the matrimonial troubles of a Mandarin duck. But he did not reach her that morning. He had come near enough to hear a screeching of the peacocks who live above the Pool, when a bunch of the park's fallow deer rushed down hill towards him. He stopped, he scratched his head and as they shied away struck off up the slope to find out what had scared them. For Wyburn Park is severely private.

When he reached a terrace of higher ground he saw a woman with a child in her arms going towards the house. "Ay, ay, ay," he muttered, an expression of surprise; again his head was scratched and he strode after her.

She made a shambling hurry, a thick-set, short-legged woman. He knew her for sure. It was Miss Courtenay, the mistress's cousin, and then the kid must be Miss Peggy, the only child of the house.

The woman looked over her shoulder as he thudded near, showed him a heavy face purple and greasy and eyes which stared fear. "What is it? What do you want?" she cried.

"Beg your pardon, Miss. Is little missy hurt?" Aaron came up with her. She held the child clutched in a bundle which gave neither movement nor sound. The little head drooping from her arm had dirt on the hair and the brow was scratched and bruised. "Eh, dear. She be hurt bad. How ever was that, Miss?"

"She fell down running down that steep place there." The woman nodded to the slope just beyond where Aaron had climbed.

"Ay, ay, ay. Do'e let me have her, Miss. I'll carry her easier'n what you will."

"No, I don't want you," the woman hurried on.

"She's like dead," said Aaron. "I'll go to the house and tell 'em."

"Tell them Miss Peggy's had a fall," she cried. He strode away with many a backward glance. . . .

Mr. Fortune was in his shirt-sleeves, a condition which he finds necessary to the enjoyment of the greatest dramatic art, the performances in his marionette theatre. He had a still unfinished masterpiece, Faust by himself, to produce. Squeaks and clatter after Berlioz went well with Faust's mountain climb roped to the eternal womanly of Gretchen but the aspect of Mephistopheles lacked satanic dignity. "Lounge lizard in decay," Mr. Fortune rebuked him and withdrew him for transformation.

Mephistopheles was becoming a smug, fashionable physician, when the parlour-maid interrupted. Dr. Netherby, of Ranchester, had rung up, wanted to speak to Mr. Fortune. She told him Mr. Fortune was in consultation—her eyes dwelt with demure humour on Mephistopheles in a black tail coat—but he said he couldn't give a message, it was very urgent.

Reggie groaned and went down to the telephone. "Fortune speaking. Well?" Dr. Netherby was sorry to trouble Mr. Fortune. He had in Ranchester Hospital the daughter of Geoffrey Barham, of Wyburn Park— the rubber millionaire—Mr. Fortune might know——"

"I don't," Reggie snapped. "Not interested."

Dr. Netherby tried again. It was a perplexing

case. He felt it necessary to take Mr. Fortune's opinion. Could Mr. Fortune come down at once?

"Don't want to," Reggie said sullenly. "You said necessary. Why?"

Frankly, Dr. Netherby did not understand the child's injuries.

"Oh, Child." Reggie's tone changed. "What's worryin' you?"

"A girl of six, Mr. Fortune. I had rather not discuss my difficulties over the telephone. I told Mr. Geoffrey Barham that I must ask you to see her, and he agreed."

"Did he? Knowin' suspicion of crime comes up to me?"

"He is aware of your position, Mr. Fortune."

"All right. How far is Ranchester? Ninety miles? Expect me in two hours."

His chauffeur, Sam, was told to average sixty or he would drive himself and protested, "Anything but that, sir," and made the pace hot enough to keep him asleep most of the way. But he was restive before they slowed to the raw, red brick of Ranchester Hospital. "Twenty minutes late," he complained. "You have no conscience, Sam."

Dr. Netherby, a weighty man with a farmer's complexion and solemn, shrewd eyes, made much of him. "Deeply obliged to you for coming down, Mr. Fortune."

"My dear chap! If it's like that, needn't thank me. What is it?"

"I would rather you formed your own opinion."

"Thanks very much," Reggie gave a twisted smile.

Netherby took him to the room in which Peggy Barham lay. She was alive. Her breathing could be heard. But she lay quite still. Her face was white except for the scratches and the stain of a swollen bruise on her brow. Reggie sat down and examined the head, gently bared the little body. She neither stirred nor woke. The right leg was bruised too. His hands moved upon it and he frowned. The skin of her left arm was torn, the palms of her hands scratched. He drew the clothes over her again.

"Well, well." He turned to Netherby and met an intent gaze with half shut eyes. "Deep concussion. Double fracture of the leg. Thigh might be nasty. Had an X-ray of head and leg?"

"Certainly. I will show you," Netherby took him to a staff room and exhibited the photographs.

"Yes. I thought so. No skull fracture. Leg must be set at once."

"I was about to do that, Mr. Fortune; I only wished you to see her first. Would you give me your opinion how the injuries were caused?"

"Haven't an opinion. Not enough material. How was she found?"

"I was called to Wyburn Park. Miss Courtenay, her mother's cousin, had brought the child in unconscious. She told me that Peggy fell while running down a slope in the Park and stunned herself."

Reggie smiled awry. "Oh no. No. Wasn't like that, however it was. What did father say?"

"Mr. Barham knew nothing but what Miss Courtenay told him. He had been in the house all the morning, Mrs. Barham in the garden. Miss

KF

Courtenay took Peggy to play in the park alone. I am bound to say that when she told her story she was much agitated and alarmed, and became almost hysterical, though she repeated it again and again in the same words."

"They do, yes," Reggie murmured.

"Exactly," Netherby fixed him with a worried stare. "I may take it, then, your opinion justifies my doubt whether she was telling the truth?"

"Oh yes. Absolutely. She wasn't. Quite right to bring me down."

"I am glad to hear you say so," said Netherby in a tone of deepest gloom.

"My dear chap! Not a nice case, no. However. The child is alive. She ought to come through."

"I hope so, indeed. Then she may tell us what really happened."

"Yes. She may. No certainty. Even if she knows. Well. You put your doubts of Miss Courtenay to father and mother?"

Netherby coughed. "I advised Mr. Barham that the child could be treated more safely in hospital and I should like your opinion, and he agreed."

"Reluctantly or how?"

"Mr. Barham was distressed. But he is a strong character. He did not hesitate. Mrs. Barham showed a good deal of emotion. She has been very kind to her cousin."

"Both quite natural, what? Well, well. First things first. Must put that leg right." . . .

Thereafter Reggie sat in the staff room poring over the clothes which Peggy had worn. The shoes showed scraping, with greyish green marks. One stocking had a long rent. The left sleeve of the frock was torn below the elbow.

He turned to Netherby, and his round face was set in cold curiosity. "When you saw her"—he spoke sharply—"stockings up or down?" Netherby frowned. Netherby thought her stockings were down, but couldn't be sure. "Notice any dirt on her?"

"Her hands were dirty, of course."

"Did you look at her head?"

Netherby was both puzzled and annoyed. "Naturally I did. There was some dust in her hair. I remember it showed brown, because her hair is so fair. That's all I can say."

"Pity." Reggie gave a little contemptuous smile. "However." He rose slowly. "Let's talk to the family. By the way—none of 'em here to see how the child's doing?"

"Mrs. Barham has been in twice this afternoon," Netherby told him. "I advised her not to come again. I promised that she should be rung up if there was any change."

"Not father. Well, well. Come on."

In Mr. Fortune's estimate of human nature, which has been called unkind, Dr. Netherby is put in the first class of the third class. Like most people. He had some brains and he meant to be honest. But he didn't take pains, he was afraid of responsibility. These are not the weaknesses of Mr. Fortune, and he dislikes them. Yet to Dr. Netherby he allows the fundamental virtue of the common man, a stolid love of fair play. Without that force in action the devil would have won the case hands down. But it soon flagged and fell out. A sad, familiar flop.

As they drove out to Wyburn Park, Netherby was not helpful. Whatever he knew of the family, he would say little. The importance of Geoffrey Barham dominated him. It was obvious that he disliked Miss Courtenay, but he professed only the slightest acquaintance with her. He believed that she] was often a guest. He could form no opinion [of her position in the house. Mr. Barham was so occupied with large affairs.

"Like that?" Reggie murmured. Netherby said severely that he failed to follow. "Not occupied with Mrs. Barham?"

"You are quite mistaken," Netherby frowned. "Mrs. Barham is a charming woman. They are devoted to each other."

"And the child?"

"Certainly, Mr. Fortune. And to the child."

"Well, well. Bafflin' case. However. It happened." Reggie gave him up.

Wyburn House is a sprawling pile of reddish stone in the classic style. They were taken to the library and saw a vista of arches and alcoves ended by a blaze of light. In the dim middle distance a man sat alone.

To Reggie, who is without reverence for men of large affairs, the great Mr. Barham looked as dreary as they are made. He was a big, bull-necked creature of forty or more, with a lot of chin and a low brow and fishlike eyes. In his reception of them arrogance fought with shaken nerves.

"Quite wise to call me in, Mr. Barham," Reggie drawled, and sat down.

"It's a matter for Netherby who he consults. How is the child, Netherby?"

"Why, sir, I believe Mr. Fortune will agree that she is doing as well as can be expected."

"Oh yes. Yes. That is so. Or better. But——"

The door opened and a woman fluttered along to them, a lithe, vivid creature with big eyes, crying "Geoffrey, what is the news of her?"

Barham jerked in his chair. "It's all right, May. She's better."

"Oh, thank God!" She clasped her hands. "Is this Mr. Fortune, Geoffrey?" Barham nodded. "How kind of you to come," she ran to Reggie holding a hand out.

"Needn't say that, Mrs. Barham," Reggie bowed over it.

"Has Peggy come round?" Barham said brusquely. "Has she said anything?"

"She is still unconscious, sir," Netherby answered. "But I do not consider that need alarm you." He turned to Reggie for confirmation.

"Oh no. It shouldn't," Reggie murmured, watching Barham with half shut eyes. "She won't say anything for some time. But her condition says a lot. Would you be surprised to hear we haven't been told the truth about her?"

Mrs. Barham cried out "Geoffrey!" and shrank back upon the big man, looking up at him with a piteous, wild alarm. "What is it?"

Barham was flushed. He swallowed and his bulky

jaw set. "You've been told all we know," he growled.

"All you know is Miss Courtenay's statement?"

"Of course it is."

"She said the child fell running down a slope in your park. And then she picked her up as she brought her in—deep concussion, double fracture of the right leg. It didn't happen, Mr. Barham. None of it. Not like that. Suggest anything to you?"

Barham was sweating. "No. I only know what Miss Courtenay said. How do you say it happened?"

"I haven't the slightest idea," Reggie drawled, and Barham's eyes swelled.

"But Fanny!" Mrs. Barham cried. "Geoffrey, she couldn't, she wouldn't. Geoffrey!" she clutched at him. She turned to Reggie. "Mr. Fortune, it must be true. She loves Peggy. She wouldn't do anything, let anything—would she, Geoffrey? You know!"

Again Barham swallowed. "I have nothing against Miss Courtenay. Understand that, Fortune."

"Yes. Your child was injured in a way that might have killed her. Miss Courtenay was alone with her. Miss Courtenay gave a false account of what happened. But you don't know why. I shall have to go on with the case."

"Of course you'll go on with it," Barham growled. "Do what you like. Stay as long as you want. Give you a free hand."

"Yes. You had better. I'll see Miss Courtenay now. Alone. Where is she?"

Barham turned to his wife. "Fanny's lying down,"

she answered. "Oh, Mr. Fortune, she's terribly distressed. Shall I go and tell her first?"

"No. Just have me shown to her room."

"I'll take you myself. Oh, do please be gentle with her."

Mrs. Barham led him up the marble staircase, on by a humble dark flight that rose to the second storey, and then down a darker corridor. She tapped at a door, called "Fanny, Fanny dear." There was no answer. She opened it and peered in and whispered. "Oh, she's asleep, Mr. Fortune."

Reggie went into the room. Fanny Courtenay lay on the bed, in her clothes, breathing noisily. Her mouth was a little open, her sallow face damp and congested, with a purple mottling. Reggie bent close to it, felt her pulse, her body. . . . He rose and contemplated on the table by the bed an empty glass which had held milk and a bottle of aspirin tablets half full.

"She's only asleep, is she?" Mrs. Barham whispered.

"Oh yes. That's all."

"She looks so strange. I suppose she's taken a lot of aspirin."

"Yes. That is indicated." Reggie wandered away round the room, a pleasant little place with panelled walls painted white and blue. Other decorations were less comfortable. On the mantelpiece was a coloured photograph of a Crucifixion of crude horror, on the dressing table a Madonna languished sentimentality. He glanced back at Fanny Courtenay's lumpish shape and moved to the door. "We'll let her sleep, Mrs. Barham."

"She must want it," Mrs. Barham went out with him. "Poor Fanny! She was in such a dreadful state."

"Was she? Excitable woman?"

Mrs. Barham hesitated. "Well, I don't know. I suppose she is in a way. She's generally so quiet and subdued, she's always been very religious, you know. But every now and then she has a sort of nerve storm, one can't tell what it's about, just weird, and she'll be perfectly sweet after. Really she's a dear, you know. I can't understand."

"Nor do I. We'll have a nurse with her to-night."

"Mr. Fortune, what do you really believe about Peggy?"

"I don't believe anything, Mrs. Barham. I'm going to know."

They came into the library again, and she ran to her husband to tell him Fanny didn't wake, looked so strange.

"Yes. Wants a nurse," said Reggie.

Barham gave him a sullen look. "Whatever's necessary for her."

Reggie took Netherby out. "She's had too much aspirin," he said softly. "And a spot of a narcotic too. Nurses who know that game, please."

"Very well. I may say I am not altogether surprised, Mr. Fortune."

"Wise man," Reggie drawled. "Don't give much away, do you?"

The excitement of the house did not impair the quality of a dinner of admirable simplicity. Reggie admired and wondered. It was not what he feared from the Barham taste as displayed to him. But only he ate and drank as things deserved. The Barhams swallowed little though they played with food and wine to be hospitable and did their best with talk, Mrs. Barham in a flow of inconsequent chatter, Barham labouring on the story of his life, as bound to enthral a stranger.

When Reggie went wearily to bed, he confessed to himself that they had put up a decent show. Not a glimpse of distrust of each other, not a taste of bitterness on the Courtenay woman. He had it out of them that she was a poor relation, with no home of her own, but they slurred it over quickly and put the subject away. Rather sticky in talk of the child, Barham very sticky, Mrs. Barham choking and breaking off, to come again with hopes Peggy really would be all right.

He looked into Fanny Courtenay's room, found her still asleep and a grim nurse knitting by a night light. At her he raised his eyebrows and she shook her head. "Nothing, sir."

Early in the morning he was down to telephone. As he hung up he saw Fanny Courtenay loitering in the hall close behind him. "Oh. Were you going to ring up the hospital, Miss Courtenay? Needn't trouble. Peggy's had a good night."

"Who are you?" a husky voice rose high.

"My name's Fortune. I'm in charge of the case."

She stared at him, distress and fear in shrunken eyes, then looked down and sidled towards the telephone. "I want to speak to Peggy."

"But you can't. She wouldn't hear. She's still unconscious."

"Is she—oh, is she——"

"No, she's not going to die. With care."

"Ah!" It was a quivering gasp of pain. She turned her back on him and her shoulders heaved. She moved unsteadily away. Reggie checked her.

"Don't! I must go to her."

"Not now. No. I want you, Miss Courtenay." Her heavy face, pallid and blotched, confronted him with a show of patient misery. "Did you sleep well?" She nodded. "Use much aspirin?" She shook her head. "I want you to take me where Peggy fell."

Her mouth came open, she made a queer, snuffling noise. She flushed dark.

"You know, don't you?"

"Of course I do."

Reggie made a gesture to the door and she obeyed it, going slowly in front of him.

"Hallo!" Barham called from the staircase. "What are you doing, Fanny? You ought to be in bed. Didn't the nurse——" He saw Reggie. "Fortune!"

"Good morning. Miss Courtenay felt fit and came down. Going to show me how your daughter crashed."

Fanny Courtenay looked from one man to the other and shrank away.

"Now?" Barham exclaimed. "Going now? You haven't had breakfast."

"No. Shan't be long. Shall we, Miss Courtenay?" She shook her head, she made haste out of the house.

Reggie did not trouble to catch her up till she had gone through a gate from the gardens to the park. "This is the way you took her yesterday? And brought

her back? Oh yes. Often go into the park with her?"
Fanny Courtenay only answered by nods. She was in
breathless haste. "What do you do together?"

"Play."

"Oh yes. Doin' that yesterday?"

"Peggy was running about. Picking——" she stammered. "Making daisy chains."

"Well, well. Did she run after daisies?"

"She just ran." Fanny Courtenay stopped, breathing hard, and looked about her. "It was here—
no, further on——" she stumbled forwards. "Just
here."

Reggie surveyed the level ground on which they
stood, the slope to the glade out of which Aaron
Smith had climbed and found her with the child.
"Here?" he murmured. "Oh no." He swung round
on her and she flushed and shook. "Why do you say
that?"

"It was, it was," she cried. "She fell running down
here." She pointed to the slope.

"No. You brought her here after she'd fallen.
Where did she fall?"

"I've told you," the husky voice fell low. Her
dull eyes stared at him full.

"Yes. Pity you don't tell the truth. The child might
have been killed. She may be lame for life. And
you—you know how it happened. But you won't
say. Too bad. However. Where's the tree she was
climbing?"

Fanny Courtenay stared at him in the fascination
of fear. "There aren't any trees, you see there aren't.
She wasn't climbing. She was running."

Reggie gave a short, hard laugh. "Doin' your worst, aren't you? Rather bad. Beech bark on her shoes and her clothes. How did she get that?"

"Oh, scrambling about, she always does."

"Not here. No trees here. As you were sayin'," he strode on to the nearest of the park's great beech trees which rose a quarter of a mile away. Fanny Courtenay slunk after him.

The trees came down to the edge of the higher ground above the glade where it divided, one branch going on to the opal glitter of the Pavon Pool, another turning upward. Among the trees, Reggie beat to and fro. They were old and huge, they made so dense a belt that only a few bluebells broke through the brown carpet of dead leaves and nutshells. But the belt was narrow. Beyond it stretched a bare, green slope. There in a sunlit dimple stood the oriental summer-house.

Reggie had worked to the farther verge of the trees when he stopped suddenly and turned on his heel. Fanny Courtenay was picking up something from the ground. He grasped her wrist. "Thanks very much." He extracted from her fingers a yellow ball made of cowslips. "Not wise, Miss Courtenay. I had seen it. I left it to find out what you'd do. And you were going to hide it. Why?"

She would not look at him. "I only wondered what it was," she muttered.

"Oh no. You knew. It's the cowslip ball Peggy made yesterday. You caught yourself up and stopped when you were going to tell me she was picking cowslips, and said she made daisy chains. Why?

Because what she did make was a ball of cowslips, and you were afraid I should find it here. Why do you try to cheat me? You can't. Why do you want to hide how she was really smashed? Not kind to her, what? And you won't. What was done here? Why was it done?"

"Oh!" she gave a long moaning cry. "It wasn't here. She fell. I've told you. I've told you. You're all wrong. You're cruel. Leave me alone." She stumbled away, breaking from walk to run and run to walk.

Reggie kept her in sight till she went into the house, then he turned off to the garage and talked to his chauffeur, Sam, in a long, quiet colloquy.

When he came through the hall, seeking at last his breakfast, Barham met him with a scowl. "What the devil have you been doing to Miss Courtenay? She came back in a horrible state, half fainting and crying herself to pieces; we couldn't get any sense out of her."

"Sorry about that. Where is she?"

"We just got her up to her room. She——"

"Day nurse come?"

"Yes, my wife and the nurse are with her."

"That's all right. May I have some food now?"

"Well, of course." Barham led the way to the breakfast room. "Here you are." Reggie made a deliberate inspection of the dishes on the sideboard. "I want to know what's upset her, Fortune."

"You would, yes." Reggie sat down to stewed kidneys. "Well, she showed me the scene of the alleged accident. Told me I was cruel not to believe in it. And I didn't get any sense out of her either."

"You don't believe her?"

"I never did," said Reggie with his mouth full. "Nor did you. Now I know."

Barham took a step nearer. "How do you mean, you know? Have you found out someone—something different?"

Munching on, Reggie looked up at him and mumbled, "Results merely negative."

"You've driven Miss Courtenay half crazy."

"Do you think so?" Reggie took marmalade.

"Well, she is. I never saw a woman in such a state. She's not answerable for her actions. She ought to have a mental specialist. I'm getting Stafford Nene down."

"Stafford Nene?" Reggie began to peel a pear. "Well, well."

"You know him?"

"Oh yes. Quite well. But what made you pick Stafford Nene?"

"I have been to him myself," said Barham stiffly.

"Have you?" Reggie stood up. "Interesting to hear his opinion of this case. Tell him I said so. I'll be back this evening." He was out of the room before Barham could say anything more.

As he came into the park again, his chauffeur, Sam, met him. "I got the old bloke easy, sir. 'Appy to oblige, as you might say. 'E don't utter much, but 'e 'as no use for the lady."

Aaron Smith stood waiting where he had found Fanny Courtenay carrying the child. He looked Reggie up and down and touched his cap. "This be the place, sir. When I come up here, Miss was carrying little missy, like dead she were, and Miss a muck o' sweat."

"Oh yes. Why did you come up here?"

"I were going down along to the pool. I see some of the herd coursing across beyond there so I came to see for why."

"The deer had been frightened? Behind where Miss Courtenay was when you met her. Behind the beeches there?"

"Ay. They come from there, sir." Aaron's shrewd eyes gave him more respect.

"Thanks. Notice anything else?"

Aaron frowned and scratched his head. "The peacocks was squawking," he said slowly.

"Peacocks. Oh. Where are the peacocks? Where the deer came from?"

"No. The peacocks keep above the pool yonder." Aaron pointed far to the right of the beeches.

"I see. Well, well. Not usual for anybody to be in the park frightening deer or peacocks?"

"Eh, no!" Aaron was shocked. "'Tis private. Mr. Barham be strict on that."

"Is he? Yes. And when you met Miss Courtenay, was she pleased to see you?"

"She were not. I axed for to carry little missy myself. She wouldn't have it. She told me to be off to the house and tell 'em missy had a fall here."

"So you went. Before you went—did you happen to see Miss Peggy's head?"

"Ay, all bruised, her little forehead, poor dear. And beech mast in her hair."

Over Reggie's face came a small, benign smile. "Anything else occur to you?"

Aaron stared hard at him. "I didn't like it, sir."

"No. Heard of any other fellow seeing anything?"

"I have not, sir."

"Thanks very much. You did mighty well, Aaron. That's all now."

Aaron touched his cap again and trudged off to his birds of the Pavon Pool.

Reggie, with Sam at his heels, went on fast to the beeches. Where the cowslip ball had lain at the further verge of the wood he stopped and pored over the brown carpet of dead leaf and nutshell. "See it, Sam?" he murmured.

"This stuff on the ground, sir? Is this what the old bloke meant by beech mast?"

"Yes. Quite good, our Aaron. Scientific observer. Unlike the medical man. He only saw brown dust on the child. What else do you see?"

"It's been mucked about there," Sam pointed.

"As you say. Beech mast recently disturbed. Bumped and furrowed. Two or three fair hairs in it." He collected them and looked up at a huge old tree close by, branches of which spread from the trunk not far above the ground, in close array. "Easy tree for a child to get into, what? Even a small child."

"That's right," Sam agreed. "Any kid would want to have a go, swinging and such. Like so many steps, these 'ere branches."

"As you say. And somebody did have a go." Reggie was looking at scrapes on the grey bark.

"Or a kid might go after them new green leaves high up," Sam assisted him. "Pretty, ain't they? And all the rest of the old tree being bare, they'd kind of lure her."

"Yes, you have a mind, Sam. I dare say they did." Reggie gazed up through the leafless boughs. A twig here and there was broken. "Somebody fell, too."

"There you are. The poor little kid went up and slipped and crashed," Sam was pleased with himself.

"You think so? Somebody bigger than the child went up too. Look. There's the child's scrape on the first bough and the next. But bigger scrapes also. Much bigger. Heavy weight did them."

"I'd say it was. That goes all right, sir. The kid climbed up and wouldn't come down. The lady got cross and funky, went after her, made a muck of it and the kid took a toss. So the lady's afraid to own up how it happened."

"Quite good. Yes." Reggie climbed from bough to bough, following the scratches. The going was easy, the scratches went high.

"Coo! Naughty, eh?" said Sam from below. "Kid climbed away from the lady."

Reggie found himself at the last of the big scratches. But the bough above was scraped. He pored over the marks and found tiny scraps of skin, threads of brown wool. He detached them and put them away and looked down. "Thirty feet of fall. So that is that," he murmured, but his round face was puckered and plaintive. He turned and looked out from the wood to the open green slope, where deer were feeding, where the oriental summer house stood.

It was built of red and grey stone in a checkered pattern from the ground to the spike of its onion dome, but the walls were pierced by arches one above the other, the lower row latticed. From his perch on the bough he could see into it through the open upper arches, which let sunlight fall upon long chairs with many cushions and a mound of garden mattresses.

He looked away to the right. Beyond the shoulder of the slope lay the glitter of the Pavon Pool, and above it he could make out the splendid flaunt of peacocks.

He swung himself down. From the ground it was impossible to see the inside of the summer-house. The latticed arches forbade.

"Come on, Sam," he said sharply, and to the summer-house they came. The door was locked. He scrambled up the lattice of the lower arches to the open arcade above, dropped down inside and wandered about, peering, sniffing. In the hollows of a cushion of one of the long chairs were grains of white powder. He scraped them into an envelope. He put one on his tongue. "Oh. Like that!" His lip twisted. He hunted the place through again and found a scrap of tarred grit before he climbed out.

"Now we'll see the peacocks, Sam," he announced.

"Thank you, sir," said Sam, who has a chauffeur's contempt for walking highly developed, but will suffer much for Reggie.

Some half mile brought them past the deer to the peacocks' parade ground. At their coming neither the deer moved nor the peacocks screamed. "Quiet enough to-day," said Sam with a leer. "That's awkward, ain't it?"

Reggie did not answer, but he broke into a run and deer fled, the peacocks screeched indignation.

"Coo!" Sam chuckled. "That ain't half neat," and trotted after him. As a chauffeur, Sam is apt to be surprised when others show intelligence.

Reggie kept ahead, going straight and hard till the red stone of the park wall was in sight. Then he slowed and turned off into a hollow. "Lor' love a duck!" Sam muttered. For Reggie was picking cowslips. But as soon as he had a handful, he went on to a ladder stile over the wall. There Sam joined him. "You reckon some parties did a bunk when the child crashed, sir? Nipping off here?"

Reggie sat down on the top of the stile. "How do you think of these things, Sam?" he asked plaintively surveying the landscape. "Run away and get the car. Go by the road. Time yourself."

Sam breathed hard, climbed past him and departed with reproach in every line of his back.

Reggie also dropped into the tarred road. On the other side was open ground, turf and thicket. He wandered about. Not far from the stile he found tyre marks across the chalk mud of the road edge. A car had been driven on to the turf and stopped behind a mass of thorn and gorse. . . .

He was back on the road. Sam arrived. "Half an hour's walk, sir," he complained.

"That'll do. Come and have a look here." Reggie exhibited the car tracks. "What do you say?"

"Long wheel base. Not a heavyweight. One of these smarty sports cars," Sam pronounced with contempt.

"Yes, I think so. Anything like that in the garage?"

"Not a bit. Mr. Barham's cars are all class."

"All right. Ranchester Hospital now."

Reggie sat at the back of the car silent, his eyes closed. But when they stopped he did not get out at once, he leaned forward and talked softly to Sam's ear. Sam listened, staring straight in front of him and his perky face grew impish. "I get it, sir. You leave it to me."

Dr. Netherby was sent for. Dr. Netherby appeared with importance. He had been expecting Mr. Fortune. He was very glad to say that the child had recovered consciousness. Her condition was quite satisfactory. She——

"Told you anything?" Reggie broke in.

"Not of her injuries, Mr. Fortune. You will understand that I have not pressed her. But——"

"Very wise. I'll see her."

"If you please. Her talk is quite rational. But she does not seem aware of her condition."

"Like that. Yes," Reggie came into her room. Blue eyes looked up at him dim and bewildered. "I'm just another doctor, Peggy. Your father wanted me to see how you were."

"Father," she said. "It does hurt me. My leg hurts."

"I know. It won't for long."

"Why do I be here? Why aren't I at home?"

"Just to get you well quick. You did have a tumble, didn't you?"

"Did I? I didn't mean to. I don't bemember."

"It was only yesterday."

"Was it? What is yesterday?"

"Tuesday morning. You were out in the park, weren't you?"

"Yes, with Cousin Fanny. Where is Cousin Fanny?"

"She's at home, too. Like father and mother."

The child's brow puckered. "They didn't go with me. They don't play in the park."

Reggie put on the bed the bunch of cowslips he had picked.

She lifted her head a little. "Pretties," she smiled at them.

"Do you pick cowslips?"

"Yes, and primroses and bluebells, there's lots now, it's lovely times."

"I brought these for you." Reggie began to make the cowslips into a ball. "Do you ever do this?"

"Oo! Course I do," the blue eyes gleamed. "Let me." The little scratched fingers toiled with them. "I did do a cowslip ball yesterday."

"Fancy that! What made you leave it behind?"

"Oh!" The corners of her mouth turned down. "I don't bemember. It will be lost." She looked at Reggie, eyes big and full of tears.

"Doesn't matter, Peggy. Not a bit. Here's another. And lots more cowslips waiting for you."

"But I didn't ought pick flowers and drop them. Cousin Fanny doesn't like."

"That's all right. She won't bother you."

"It was a nice ball," said Peggy sorrowfully. "I didn't mean to leave it."

"Never mind. Let's make this better," Reggie helped her. . . .

Netherby followed him out. "That was a very subtle test, Mr. Fortune," he said gloomily.

"Oh, my dear chap! Quite simple. Quite conclusive."

"Undoubtedly conclusive," Netherby mourned. "She has no recollection whatever of how she was injured. The concussion has wiped out of her mind all that happened just before. I have met more than one case of the same kind."

"Yes. They often go this way."

"Exactly. One cannot say it is unexpected. But it is profoundly disappointing."

"I wouldn't say that. No. Best way it could be. She don't know what was done to her. Nor why it was. I had to make sure she didn't. But I don't want her to. Not a nice case, Netherby. Mustn't let her people see her."

Netherby's solemn eyes consulted him with apprehension. "You are in charge of the case, Mr. Fortune."

"Yes. That is so. Good-bye."

Reggie went off to the best of the Ranchester hotels. An hour later Sam joined him. After a colloquy he shut himself up in a telephone box and was there some time. He lunched at the hotel, sat dozing in the lounge, was called to the telephone and again held a long conversation.

So it was late in the afternoon before Sam brought him back to Wyburn Park.

As he was asking the butler where the Barhams were, they appeared. "I expected you back before this, Fortune," Barham growled at him. "What's kept you?"

"Oh, Mr. Fortune, how is Peggy?" Mrs. Barham cried.

Barham went on. "Netherby told me she'd come round, but he said we couldn't see her. You'd forbidden any visitors. What do you mean by that?"

Reggie's eyebrows went up. "What I said. Child mustn't be distressed."

"But I shouldn't distress her, Mr. Fortune," Mrs. Barham appealed.

"What has she told you?" Barham growled.

"Nothing. She doesn't remember anything. Stafford Nene come?"

"Yes, he has. He has examined Miss Courtenay. He wants to talk to you." Barham strode back into the drawing-room. A man with a venerable head of white hair above a dapper figure stood expectant.

"Ah, Fortune," he spoke with reproving condescension. "You have been detained. How is the little girl?"

"Makin' a fair recovery." Reggie turned to Barham. "Where shall I take him? Library?" Barham scowled and nodded.

Dr. Stafford Nene made it clear that he contemned Reggie's manner. "If Mrs. Barham will excuse us," he made her a courtly bow and undulated out.

"Well?" Reggie asked, shutting the library door behind them. "What did you make of Miss Courtenay?"

"It is well that Mr. Barham called me in, Fortune. The poor lady presents a very difficult problem."

THIS IS MR. FORTUNE

"For the Barhams?"

"No, no, no. Your methods are too brusque, Fortune. Pray sit down. I must tell you that I found Miss Courtenay in a state of profound and violent psychic agitation. The immediate cause was undoubtedly your action this morning in requiring her to reconstruct her conduct with the unfortunate child. I appreciate your anxiety to discover that. But I must deplore your treatment of her. You may take it from me, Fortune, that she will never yield to pressure of that kind."

"Your mistake. I know what she did."

Nene smoothed his white locks. "That is to say you have formed your opinion."

"No, it isn't. Statement of fact. I found the evidence. No possible doubt."

"I am not to contest your facts," said Nene recovering his tone of condescension. "What I require you to consider is that this case is fundamentally psychological."

"My dear Nene! They all are," Reggie smiled.

"Pray permit me. You are taking it as a case of crime. Now——"

"Oh yes. It is."

Nene made a reproving noise. "Allow me. I quite understand that you have convinced yourself Miss Courtenay told a false story of the manner in which the child was hurt, that she is herself responsible. I compliment you on your acumen. It may interest you to know that I had formed a similar conclusion from my analysis of Miss Courtenay's state. But that is only the husk of the case, Fortune. We know nothing

Matter for me. I have the evidence, Barham. Convince any jury." He related his discoveries in the beech wood. "You see? Peggy went up that tree just over the summer-house. Wouldn't come down. Miss Courtenay couldn't bear her bein' up there—went after her— crash. And then Miss Courtenay set herself to hide where they'd been."

"Why?" Barham scowled.

"But it's impossible," Mrs. Barham cried. "Fanny climb a tree!" She broke into shrill laughter.

"Tree quite easy to climb. Unfortunately, Barham. Your six-year-old child got up. Miss Courtenay had to go after."

"Fanny!" Mrs. Barham exclaimed. "It's mad!"

"Pray allow me," Nene took charge of the conversation. "You have asked a question, Mr. Barham. Why? Mrs. Barham has answered you. It was mad. I am not to be taken as using that term in a legal sense——"

"No, you can't," Reggie interrupted. "So you say disassociated personality—repressed, frustrated, childless woman—gettin' her own back on happy wife and child. As you were sayin'. Nice theory, convenient theory. Hushes things up. Only it isn't true."

"I cannot tolerate this, Fortune," Nene stood up. "You must be aware——"

"I'm here for the child," Reggie snapped. "Barham! You said you'd consulted Nene before. About Miss Courtenay? Expectin' her thwarted nature would leap to violence? Givin' him your reasons?"

Barham gulped and grew red. Mrs. Barham drew back, her bright eyes dilated, staring at him.

"Fortune!" Nene's voice rose booming. "Do you dare to suggest that I have been improperly influenced?"

"No. Deluded," Reggie drawled. "When did you go to that summer-house last, Barham?"

Barham made an inarticulate exclamation, and then roared, "I never go there. What the devil has the summer-house got to do with it?"

"I wonder," Reggie gave him a small, mirthless smile. "What about the summer-house, Nene? You didn't ask Miss Courtenay that? No. Not concerned with the facts of the case. Only with a theory." He crossed the room and rang the bell.

"I was not aware of the existence of the summer-house," Nene said, biting his words with contemptuous precision. "Do I understand you to suggest that——"

"That you're assistin' to conceal the truth? Yes." The butler came in and Reggie turned to him. "Has the Criminal Investigation Department rung me up yet?"

The butler was shocked. "No, sir. There has been no call for you."

"Quite sure?" said Reggie, and went out.

What he said to the telephone in the hall was little. The butler, loitering about the backstairs, heard only the name of Superintendent Bell. "Fortune speakin' from Wyburn Park," murmurs of approval and assent, then "One of my longer shots, Bell," and a chuckle. But the telephone said a great deal to him.

Long before it finished Stafford Nene passed upstairs with majestic importance. A moment or two later Barham came out of the drawing-room, hesitated, glared at Reggie and went into the library, slamming the door.

When Reggie at last said good-bye to the telephone, he made haste out of the house. His chauffeur, Sam, lounging by the garage in contemplation of the sunset, was given some careful instructions and vanished.

Reggie came in again, came up to his own room on the first floor, seeing no one, and sat down by the open window, leaving the door open. The house was quiet but for a faint sound of talk borne through the window from above. Fanny Courtenay's husky voice rose high. Reggie stood up. He heard a door shut, movement, the thud of a fall, then, as he made for the stairs, scurrying footsteps, a scream, an outcry.

On the narrow upper stairway it was almost dark. He stumbled upon a body which was Nene's. Close above, two clamorous women swayed, Fanny Courtenay with her nurse clutching at her. "How was it, nurse?" Reggie asked.

"I couldn't tell you, Mr. Fortune. Dr. Nene told me to leave Miss Courtenay to him, so I went to my own room, then I heard a noise—and this——"

"Oh yes. Get Miss Courtenay back to bed." Servants came up the stairs behind him. "Switch the lights on!" He knelt down by Nene.

The light showed blood spreading along his neck,

a bodkin on the landing. Reggie reached for that and picked it up in his handkerchief, Nene moved and groaned. "The woman——"

"Keep still." Reggie bent over his wound.

Barham's heavy tread approached. "What the devil are you all doing?" he roared. "What's this, Fortune?"

"The woman ran after me," Nene said. "She sprang upon me."

"If you please!" A sharp cockney voice called. "Mr. Fortune!"

"Right. Take Dr. Nene to his room, some of you. Give him a drop of iodine for his cut. That'll do." Reggie came down through the servants to his chauffeur. "Well?"

"Gone away, sir. Gone walking," Sam told him.

"Get on," said Reggie, thrust an arm through Barham's and swung him downstairs after Sam.

"What are you doing?" Barham growled.

Reggie whispered to him. "Goin' to find Mrs. Barham. Do you know where she is?"

"She's lying down in her room."

"Oh no. She's gone out. She's gone away."

Barham broke from him and dashed along the corridor below, flung open a door, looked into a room, and cried out and ran back after Reggie and Sam, to catch them up at the door where Reggie's car stood waiting.

"She has gone," he muttered.

"I know." Reggie thrust him into the car and jumped in beside Sam. "Step on it."

The car shot into speed along the drive, checked for a right angle turn to the road and surged through the twilight. "Slow," Reggie murmured. In the shadows ahead was a woman. Sam held the car to a walking pace. She was lost in the curves of the road between the park wall and the thickets on the other side, she was seen again, she vanished altogether. "Now," said Reggie. Sam nodded. The car rushed on to the place by the ladder stile in the park wall where they had found the wheel marks of another car, and stopped.

Reggie sprang out, looked about a moment, listened, called "Barham!" and turned into the thicket. There was another car there, a woman talking to a man in it. "Headlights, Sam," he called.

The headlights blazed and their spreading beam fell on Mrs. Barham, her face haggard in the white glare; on a little exquisite of a man. "Mr. Brendon, I believe," said Reggie. As Barham plunged forward, she screamed. "Come, David, come." She scrambled into the car and it shot forward out to the road, knocking Barham down.

Reggie helped him up. "Want to go after 'em? Very well. Hoot, Sam."

The horn of his car blared thrice through the twilight as Barham and he came back to it. "Go ahead." Sam sent the car in pursuit like a comet. Its headlights discovered the low, unlit sports car ahead. They raced on through the darkening dusk. The gong of a police car sounded. Its lights glimmered on the other side of the road and drew out. The sports car swerved, tried to cram past and its tail swung out and it skidded, turned round and rolled over with a roar.

"Golly!" Sam muttered, as he slowed to a stop behind it and his headlights steadied on the wreck. "What a do!"

Two policemen in uniform ran across the road. As Reggie and Barham got out a man in plain clothes confronted them. "You gentlemen saw that car's driving?" he asked. "I'd like to have your names. It's a bad case."

"As you say. I'm Reginald Fortune. Refer to Scotland Yard for me."

"I beg pardon, sir."

"Come on. Come along, Sam." Reggie made for the wreck.

The crumpled car was upside down. They forced a door open and dragged out to the turf at the roadside bodies helpless, bleeding and dumb. Reggie knelt by the woman's side.

"Sorry, Barham," he looked up. "No use. No help. She's gone."

Barham gazing down at her blood-stained face, groaned and broke out in oaths at Brendon. "What about him?"

"He's breathing all right," said the plain clothes man, who was searching Brendon's pockets. "Ah!" he pulled out a gold box, like a small cigarette case, and opened it. "Snow, or I miss my guess. What do you think, Mr. Fortune?"

Reggie looked at it, tasted a grain of it. "Yes, as you say. Cocaine."

"Oh God!" Barham roared. "That—that——" He made a stride towards Brendon's body.

"My dear chap!" Reggie took his arm and drew him away.

.   .   .   .   .

Superintendent Bell, staying late at Scotland Yard, received another call from Mr. Fortune. "Long shot came off. Heard from your man? Not bad, your man. Yes, woman dead. Brendon, toss up. Rotten with drugs."

"Pity about the lady," Bell grunted.

"You think so? I do not. The best way, Bell. She was too far gone. Body and soul. No chance for her here. Only do more damage alive."

Bell breathed hard. "Had you got this sort of end in your mind?"

"Oh no. Not my job. Only to eliminate her some-how. The child was in my mind—Fanny Courtenay —and at the last, Barham."

"Ah. You worked it very clever," Bell said slowly.

"My dear chap!" Reggie laughed. "Oh, my dear chap! Never less. Never knew what I was doin' till the end. Only didn't believe anybody. Only believed evidence. And took the simple obvious action. Fanny Courtenay had dope in her, but no dope in her room. Somebody had been in that locked summer-house with cocaine. Somebody had parked a cheap sports car on the road close by—Sam found out a fellow had stayed at the house, with such a car—your Mr. David Brendon. Put it up to you. You told me Brendon was a bad egg; Brendon had his car out at the relevant

M<small>F</small>

time. And I passed it to you Brendon should be watched for dealing in drugs; meanwhile making it clear to the Barhams I knew there had been queer doings in the summer-house. That broke Mrs. Barham. She'd been on the 'phone to Brendon. She had him comin' down to settle what they'd do. And they settled. With your police car on to 'em. Simple, straight bit of work. But quite well done. Congratulations. Good night. End of a perfect day."

.   .   .   .   .

He slept late. He came upon Barham and Nene in the library, Nene with a foulard scarf flowing round his bandaged neck over a dressing-gown of black and silver, more of the inspired sage than ever, lecturing Barham's gloomy silence.

"Oh no! Not like that, Nene," Reggie protested. "Not now."

Barham swung round. "He's telling me he's convinced Miss Courtenay attacked him last night."

"Well, well. Faithful fellow, aren't you, Nene? Won't desert the dear old theory. It wasn't Miss Courtenay struck you. Only Miss Courtenay's bodkin. I found it. No finger marks on it. And Miss Courtenay's hands were bare. You see? Think again, Nene." Reggie turned to Barham. "When you consulted him first, what was the case put to him? Miss Courtenay had been behavin' queer, Mrs. Barham was worried about her?"

"My wife went to Nene," Barham said.

"I thought so. And Nene instructed you Miss Courtenay was a wretched woman, gone bad with starved emotions and repressions and all the rest of it. As per the dear old theory. Standin' no nonsense from facts. A hard life don't always make people devils, Nene. You hadn't noticed that. So last night you went up to analyse Miss Courtenay once again. But by then Mrs. Barham couldn't trust your stuff any more. She had to make some evidence Miss Courtenay was mad. You packed the nurse off and drove Miss Courtenay wild. Gave Mrs. Barham her chance. And she took it, feelin' quite sure you'd swear blind Miss Courtenay tried to murder you. But you can't now."

"I—I resent this, Fortune," Nene stammered.

"You resent?" Reggie laughed. "Well, well."

Nene recovered his preaching voice. "Miss Courtenay has lied throughout. You admit yourself that she injured the child. Now I am expected to believe——"

"The truth. Yes. New experience, what? Miss Courtenay isn't a devil, as you tried to make her. Sort of saint."

A sneer spread over Nene's imposing face. "Indeed? You will——"

"Get out!" Barham roared, starting up. "Get out of the place." Nene pushed back his chair and fled.

"Understand now, Barham?" Reggie said gently.

"Brendon was in the summer-house with my wife," Barham muttered looking away.

"Yes. Bringin' her cocaine. Miss Courtenay saw 'em go in. The child went climbing the tree. She might have seen right into the summer-house from up there. Miss Courtenay couldn't bear it, went after her, got hold of her to make her come down and she struggled and fell. And then—Miss Courtenay wouldn't tell the truth, because she wouldn't give your wife away. I'm afraid she was rather fond of her, Barham."

"God! I always thought she was," Barham groaned. "And Peggy—she'd give her soul for Peggy."

"As you say. Probably thinkin' she has." Reggie put a hand on his shoulder. "My dear chap! Well. I'll go and see her."

Fanny Courtenay lay pallid, staring with dull eyes at the opening door. As she saw Reggie she shrank down on her pillow and shook.

"Not like that. No." Reggie waved the nurse out. "Rather a bad night. A better day. You're free now. Mr. Barham knows. Mrs. Barham's gone with Brendon."

She gave a long, tremulous cry and hid her face.

"You did your best. You couldn't stop that. But Peggy doesn't know what happened. You saved her from knowing—except that her mother's gone. Not so bad."

"With that man?"

"Yes. No help. He'd made her so, hadn't he? He drove off with her and his car crashed."

"She's dead?"

"As he drove her away."

"Oh," she sobbed. "It is hard. I did try. And now——
Oh, I ought to have done better somehow."

"No. That won't be the judgment," Reggie smiled. "My dear lady, you're so greedy, you saints. Want to save everybody."

"I—a saint!"

"Yes. Didn't you know? I suppose you won't—in this world. However. Try. Just for a change. Make things easier for the rest of us."

.   .   .   .   .

When he returned to his marionette theatre he gave his Mephistopheles the dapper waist and the white hair of Stafford Nene.

V

THE BURNT TOUT

THE BURNT TOUT

THE DAY AFTER he pronounced sentence of death in the burnt tout case Sir Maule Trask came upon Mr. Fortune eating a muffin in a club. Trask has earned awe as the hardest sceptic of evidence on the bench, the bane of expert witnesses and policemen. But he stopped by Reggie Fortune's chair and his frog-like eyes blinked and twinkled. "That should have given you satisfaction, Fortune," he croaked.

Mr. Fortune looked up at him over an evening paper. "Satisfied you? Great is truth, what?"

"In the right hands. I do not recall a case more difficult for the police. The facts were perverted by a brain of singular subtlety. I have never had evidence of a police investigation so sagaciously directed."

"Quite good, wasn't it?" Mr. Fortune sighed. "Not by me, though."

"You will permit me to give the credit to a controlling intelligence not always present."

"Thanks very much," said Mr. Fortune drearily.

"A sad story," the judge nodded. "I have not been unaffected myself."

Mr. Fortune watched him out of sight and read the paper again. Like all the others that day, it printed a leader to acclaim the triumph of justice in the burnt tout case, and assured the public that they could now depend on the police, armed with the unerring skill of modern science, to catch every murderer and right every wrong.

"Grrh!" said Mr. Fortune, and went to sleep wondering if old Trask meant anything—didn't matter what he meant—couldn't do anything. . . .

Mr. Fortune was introduced to the case on an October dawn in a by-way of the suburbs.

The night before, a railwayman coming home from the Barnham coal sidings saw flames break out of a window. Among miles of neat criss-cross streets, the mess of the railway yards, the concert of their shunting and of the perpetual lorries on one of the busiest trunk roads, have preserved from rebuilding some of the narrow lanes, some of the ramshackle cottages which served Barnham when it was a scattered village outside London.

Cherrywood Lane has a dust cart depot now where the wood was. The blank wall of that confronts some half dozen cottages, each in a patch of garden. It was one of these which the railwayman found on fire. He ran to it shouting, and hammered at the door, but no answer came. To break in was impossible. The whole of the ground floor was ablaze.

He said afterwards that the neighbours were a ruddy long time turning out to the row he made. But the clatter of the coal yards and the roar of the high road have produced a lack of attention to noise among those who sleep in Cherrywood Lane. Some of them did appear at last and went off to ring the fire alarm. Even then no policeman had arrived.

The fire brigade were not quick. They came promptly the nearest way, up Carter's Lane, which is at the back of the Cherrywood Lane cottage gardens. But there the fire escape ran over a man and had to stop, holding up the engine. When they got him from under the wheels they found that he was dead and a policeman. By the time they put the fire out the cottage consisted of four windowless walls and a roof surrounding charred and stinking chaos.

In the misty chill of dawn Mr. Fortune, muffled to the eyes, emerged from his house and got into a police car. It went off like a shell from a gun and flung him upon the bosom of Inspector Underwood. "My only aunt!" he gasped. "What's happened to the police? How did you come to know cars could move?"

"Sorry, sir," Underwood arranged him tenderly in the corner. "Very sorry to drag you out at this nasty time. But there's no doubt it's a case for you. And you always like us to get you in at the start."

"Me?" All that could be seen of Mr. Fortune's face, a pink nose and two sunken eyes, exhibited disgust. "I never like bein' got in to any case. Even at a civilised hour. Why this unnatural zeal? What makes the police throw fits in the dead o' night over the fire brigade findin' a corpse in a burnt out house? Who is the illustrious defunct?"

"We don't know," said Underwood. "Thought to be the resident."

"To-day's great thought. Where does it hurt you?"

"If so, name of Smith, Joseph Smith. Nothing else known about him."

Mr. Fortune made a sorrowful noise and closed his eyes. "Oh, what a futile web they weave, policemen trying to deceive," he murmured.

"It's the truth, Mr. Fortune," said Underwood earnestly. "We haven't any line on Smith at all. But there was a constable killed too."

"Oh!" Mr. Fortune's eyes opened again. "That's what stung the force. Very proper. You appeal to my better nature. Granted. I have a heart when awake. Yes, I also am a policeman. Up to me. Poor beggar. How was he killed? In Smith's fire?"

"No, sir. Run over by the fire escape."

"My dear chap!" Mr. Fortune sat up. "What are you giving me?"

"I'm asking you, sir. This constable had a beat which covered the lane Smith lived in. The alarm of fire was given about midnight, by the neighbours, not by the constable; nothing seen or heard of him. But the escape and the engines coming up the road at the back of Smith's house ran over him there. Being there, he must have seen the fire, he ought to have got on to it, blown his whistle, knocked up Smith, called the brigade. Why didn't he? Why did he just hang about and get under the escape?"

"I haven't the slightest idea," Mr. Fortune murmured. "The mind is impotent. Dead when picked up?"

"Absolutely. Smashed."

"Well, well. Man of good reputation?"

"One of the best."

"Poor beggar. You never know, do you? In our trade."

"I don't understand you, Mr. Fortune." Underwood stiffened.

"Oh, my dear chap. Possibilities unlimited. We may limit 'em when we do some work on him. Friend of our Mr. Smith, by any chance?"

"It's not likely," said Underwood.

"You think not? No. Certain lack of interest in Mr. Smith does appear. I wonder."

"Are you suggesting——" Underwood exploded and was stopped.

"Not me, no. You said he didn't do his duty."

"I just gave you the facts," Underwood muttered, and sank into glum silence.

The car swung round from the noisy high road into the narrows of Cherrywood Lane, drew up at the burnt cottage. Mr. Fortune alighted in slow time, contemplating it, then stood still and surveyed its shabby neighbours. "Not all modern conveniences, what?" he murmured. "Not everybody's money. Shy old places. Out of the way yet in the way. Well, well."

Underwood bustled on to meet a begrimed officer of the fire brigade. "Anything more?"

"Nix. Come and have a look at him. That'll do for you."

"All right. Here's Mr. Fortune."

"Good luck to him. I wouldn't have his job. I've had enough with mine." The smutty face grinned [sardonically at Reggie. "Come right in, sir."

"Thanks." Reggie gazed about the trampled sodden garden. "What a mess! However. Wasn't tidy before you came. Not much of a gardener, our Mr. Smith." He ambled on, but not into the cottage; he went round it and on down the larger section of garden behind. That also was an unkempt waste of which the hoses had made a quagmire. But Reggie picked his way over it till he reached the fence at the end.

"What's the idea?" the fire brigade officer asked Underwood.

"Don't ask me." Underwood scowled at Reggie's operations.

He looked over the fence, he moved along, he stopped, he studied it closely. "I say, Underwood," he called, and Underwood squelched to his side. "If a man got over here he would be in the lane where your constable was, what?"

"The lane's at the back here, I told you."

"Yes. Look at that," Reggie pointed.

The fence was of palings, nailed together overlapping, dark and half rotten. From a cross beam, slivers of the decayed wood had been scraped away. Two of the palings were broken at the top to jagged edges.

"Somebody did get over there," Reggie murmured.

"Might be," Underwood said sullenly. "Might have been any time."

"Oh no. No. You won't look. Something on the palings. See? Bit of flesh and skin with hairs. Not long detached from owner. From back of human hand or arm. Hair's black. What is the complexion of your deceased constable?"

"I couldn't tell you," Underwood growled.

"Don't know much, do you? However. Knowledge is now coming in. Somebody left the premises of our

Mr. Smith by stealth last night. Palings broke as he climbed, and he tore himself before he dropped into your constable's lane."

"We don't know that," Underwood objected. "It might have been someone getting in——"

"While watched by the kind constable below. You think that?"

"Might have been a fireman, I mean. Or might have been Smith himself doing something with the fence."

"My dear chap! Full of objections, aren't you?" Reggie smiled. "The perfect collaborator." He cut off the evidence from the palings, put it away and returned to the fire brigade officer. "Did any of your men get over the fence down there?"

"No, sir. We worked from the front."

"Underwood just wanted to know," Reggie purred. "And was our friend Smith dark or fair?"

"My God! Ask me another. You have a look at what he is."

"I will. Yes. What was the cause of the fire?"

"No telling. When we got here the whole inside was a furnace. Gas blazing like hell. Pipes melted, you know, compo pipes, like most of these old places have, and all the woodwork well alight. Might have started from the chimney getting too hot, all the wood's rotten, it'd catch like tinder. We can't ever know for sure. Nothing left to work on."

"Only two corpses or so," Reggie murmured.

"Two? Oh, you mean the policeman. Yes, I can't make out what he was up to. Our chaps swear they didn't see him till the escape was on top of him. He was sort of on hands and knees in the road like looking for something."

"You think so? Same like us, Underwood. We're grovelling looking for what not. Proper policeman's position. However. On with the dance. Introduce me to our Mr. Smith."

"With pleasure," the fire brigade man said grimly, and strode into the cottage. "There you are." He turned away.

The air was pungently foul. From the broken windows grey light broke through vapour upon wet mounds of black, broken wood and plaster. In a cleared space there lay upon its back what had been a man. Much of its clothes was burnt away from the darkened flesh. The head was bald. Its face had sunk and shrivelled.

Reggie knelt down in the ashes beside it. His gloved hands passed from the head to lay more of the body bare, came back to the face and dwelt upon it, moving it. The fire brigade officer went out. . . .

"Well, well." Reggie stood up and drew off his gloves. "Our Mr. Smith was a blonde, Underwood." Underwood gulped. "Sorry to annoy you. But somebody else did use his premises last night. Nothing more from him at present. Have him taken to the mortuary. Quick as you can. The sooner it's over the sooner to sleep."

Underwood strode out, but Reggie remained, loitering about the debris, gazing up to the roof. Above the broken joists of the upper story the dank, sooty walls had two or three patches comparatively clean.

He moved to the door and beckoned the fire brigade officer. "Where would you say the fire began?" he asked.

"I told you, I can't place it. Only the gas got going somewhere."

"Rather low, what? And where was our Mr. Smith then?"

"Not so easy neither. We found him on the ground floor with the stuff from above on top of him. But you can't trust that."

"You think not? He hadn't gone to bed. Still got his clothes on."

"That's right. In his slippers though."

"Yes. His day's work was done. Wonder what it was. Notice anything about his possessions?"

The answer was a stare and a snort. "Have you?"

Reggie led him in and pointed to the clean patches on the upper wall. "Where pictures hung."

"Looks like it. What then?"

"I should like to know what the pictures were," said Reggie plaintively.

"You——" The fire brigade man felt words inadequate. He pointed at the mounds of ash and broken wood and plaster. "Find pictures in that!"

"Job of work. Yes. Go through it with a fine tooth comb. Bits of picture. Bits of anything that tells a story. Especially a bit of brass or copper. Good-bye."

He went out, and the fire brigade said things.

He walked round into the lane behind Mr. Smith's cottage. That is rather wider than Cherrywood Lane, but still less frequented. On one side are the back

Nᶠ

fences of the Cherrywood cottages, on the other
the railings of a cemetery. Path and roadway had
been washed down by the muddy water which still
oozed from Mr. Smith's garden, but a little above its
broken palings Reggie found by the gutter some
clots of blood. He frowned over them, he collected them
and wandered about and about, his round face
reproachful and bewildered, glancing continually
from the place of bloodshed to the break in the
palings. It was some way below that he stooped
and picked out of a dam of dirt in the gutter a bit of
crushed brass.

"Oh my hat!" he groaned at it and wandered
back to the cottage and petulantly demanded of the
driver of Underwood's car if Inspector Underwood
was lost.

"Here I am, sir," Underwood called from a conference with the fire brigade.

"Come on. The mortuary."

"All right," Underwood grumbled, and joined
him. "Smith's body hasn't been moved yet."

"No. Not swift, are you? But your constable's has.
Begin with him. Get on."

They drove away and Underwood complained
bitterly. "I don't know what you have in your mind,
Mr. Fortune." Reggie lay back and closed his eyes.
"I suppose you think the place was set on fire. But
what is the use of making the firemen look for
pictures?"

"My dear chap. Oh, my dear chap! Fundamental
question, why was our Mr. Smith burnt? For what
he'd done or been or got. Which might emerge from

his possessions. Lots of pictures tell a story. And pictures bein' behind glass stand a lot of heat."

"Suppose they do find bits of his family portraits?" Underwood was contemptuous. "What then?"

"I haven't the slightest idea," Reggie murmured. "Your defunct constable might have."

"You're making a dead set against him!"

"Oh no. No. Inferrin' he knew more about what happened to Mr. Smith than we do."

"I see no reason to suspect him." Underwood was truculent and resentful.

"Oh my Underwood! Only what you said. He didn't give the alarm. He didn't do his duty. However. He may have had reason. Things are not what they seem. But he may have been run over as stated, more or less, though it wasn't likely. Somebody did shed blood in the gutter."

"Of course he was run over," Underwood exclaimed.

"Yes. Somehow. But why was he crawling in the gutter? Interestin' questions. Crucial questions."

"You said yourself, he was looking for something."

"Said it could be. Yes. Do you think he was looking for this? Which also was in the gutter." Reggie held out the bit of crushed brass.

Underwood turned it over and over. "So crushed up," he muttered. "Might be a cartridge case. Is that what you make it?"

"Oh yes. Case of a revolver cartridge. But sadly smashed. By that confounded fire escape."

"And you say the constable was trying to find it? What's that mean? It's saying he shot somebody—

Smith, eh?—and was getting rid of the evidence. Where's the revolver then?"

Reggie gazed at him with a satiric smile. "My Underwood! You're saying, not me. Takin' what you say—there are draintraps in that lane. But I should say you haven't thought it out. Other questions arise. Most urgent question, was the constable dark, was the constable the fellow who left a bit of himself on Mr. Smith's fence?"

They went into the mortuary. Reggie drew back the sheet which covered the constable's body and Underwood choked an exclamation of distress. The features, the very form of the man's head, were lost in crushing wounds. "Yes, his hair is black," Reggie murmured, "And his hands——" He stopped, he moved to inspect them. Underwood watched, dismally impatient, till Reggie turned upon his fidgets a face of cold curiosity and a bitter question: "Well?"

"I can see. His hands are torn," Underwood exploded.

"Yes, that is so."

"You'll say it was him got over Smith's fence."

"No, I shan't." Reggie was shrill. "The one thing I shan't say. Hands aren't torn right. Not enough gone. Don't know any more. Don't know anything now. Find something yourself. Which don't lead to nowhere. Which hasn't been mucked up. Find somebody who can tell you what this fellow was to t'other fellow. Run away."

It has been complained that Mr. Fortune lost his temper over this case, a condition rare in him. He admits the charge with pleasure and pride. No case, he maintains, was ever so confused by perversion of evidence through the tricks of chance and the ingenuity of killers. Resentment at these operations he declares essential to sanity. He is still resentful, though passion is spent. The case is his pet example of the infernal humour of chance. But he remains dubious what he would have made of it if chance had stood out and left him to deal with the murders unadulterated.

Late on that afternoon he came languidly into the room of the chief of the Criminal Investigation Department and rang the bell and dropped into the easiest chair. "A pot of your tea," he moaned. "With water. And buttered toast. With some butter on."

"We're out of butter, Reginald," Lomas said severely, "but there's plenty of hot water for you. You've given Underwood a monumental hump. And the fire brigade want your blood."

"Well, well," Reggie wriggled himself comfortable. "Thank you for these kind words. I did want balm. Now I know I am not alive in vain. There was a painful doubt. But all is well. I do still annoy our blessed public services; I can go on. On and on and up and up. Greet the unseen with a cheer. Hooray! Not much else to greet, Lomas. Lots of that, though."

Lomas sat back. "You mean to say you haven't anything new from your post mortems?"

"Oh yes, I have. All is strange and new—but negative. Washin' out everything we had before. Isn't that nice? Yet leadin' nowhere. Thanks to the little blind devil of chance—with the co-operation of another devil or so—not blind devils—human devils." The tea arrived and he sipped it. "My only aunt! Where do you buy your tea? Why do you? A larger mystery of evil. Well, well. Takin' the constable. Underwood told you?"

"He told me you had suspicions of the constable—thought he'd done a burglary at the place, and found you were wrong when you examined him. I suppose that's what you mean by telling me you've washed out everything we had. You haven't. Only what you invented yourself. We never did suspect the constable."

"No. Loyal force, the police force."

"It would take more than some traces a fence had been climbed to make me suspicious of a constable of good record."

"Very proper. Faith before facts. Yet facts have uses. A dark man did leave bits of his hand on that fence. You only have to find him and fit them on and the case is finished. He wasn't your constable. The constable's hands haven't lost those bits. Only suffered when the fire escape ran over him. But that wasn't what killed him. Cause of death, shooting. Lead bullet entered the left of throat, lodged in spine."

"Good gad!" Lomas exclaimed.

"Yes. It is instructive. About the time of the fire a dark man left Mr. Smith's premises by the back in a hurry, met your constable and shot him. Now you know why the poor beggar didn't ring the fire alarm, why he was grovelling in the gutter when the fire escape came and hit him. Speechless. Helpless. Too bad. Must have died thinkin' the whole world was at work to do him down. The devil had some fun last night, Lomas. And he isn't finished yet." Reggie put a pill box on the table. "There's the bullet which killed your constable."

Lomas examined it and made a noise of disgust. "As you say. I can swear it's .455. I can suggest it's from a service revolver. But it's so flattened we'll never link it with any particular revolver. Can't even make out the grooves of the rifling. That's what the fire escape did, running over him. Obliterated evidence of the murderer. The devil's own chance. Further to that——" He produced another pill box. "Scrap of brass from mud in the gutter. Cartridge case. But also crushed by the fire brigade. Individual markin' of the particular revolver again destroyed. Great fun, this job. Turnin' to our Mr. Smith. Previous to cremation—probably not quite dead when his cottage began to burn—he also was shot."

"The devil he was!" Lomas exclaimed.

"Yes. Plenty of the diabolic about. Lead bullet fired into left cheek, lodged in base of skull. Also a .455 and probably from a service revolver. But mush-roomed and split. There you are." A third pill box was presented to Lomas. "So that also don't help us to the particular revolver and its owner. Another devilish comic chance. No cartridge case visible by Mr. Smith. Not chance that. The forethought of the killer. Shrewd operator, effective operator. Very good fire he managed. You may say he deserved the devil's own luck. But I resent it. I object to the order of things takin' sides with a killer. Not done, Lomas."

Lomas shrugged. "No use quarrelling with the cussedness of things."

"Oh yes. Yes. That's what I'm for. Or what are we for?"

"My dear Reginald! Keep to the facts. You put up a very queer story. Someone broke in to Smith's house, shot him, set the place on fire, got out over the back fence, shot the constable and went off. Several difficulties, aren't there?"

"It's all difficulties. Only it happened."

"The men were shot. But why should any man break into a poor place like Smith's and shoot him?"

"I didn't say he broke in. Only said he broke things gettin' out. Smith may have let him in. Why he shot Smith I haven't the slightest idea. Who was Mr. Smith that somebody needed to shoot him? Up to you."

"A very odd thing nobody heard those two shots."

"Oh no. No. Such a row from the railway and the road round there a little revolver fire wouldn't count. That was foreseen by our effective operator. You're wastin' time. Only useful question now, who was Smith and what was he? Any contribution from Underwood? Anything from the fire brigade?"

Lomas took up his telephone and talked to Superintendent Bell. "Mr. Fortune's come in. He says the constable was shot. What? Oh, Underwood's with you, is he? Bring him along."

Bell and Underwood came in, a certain grim and reproachful satisfaction on Underwood's face as he met Reggie's eye. "Yes, your constable's clear," said Reggie. "He died doing his duty. What are we doing about it?"

Bell spoke. "I was just saying to Underwood, you'd work it out so he had justice done to him, Mr. Fortune."

"Shall I? I wonder."

"Well, you have." Bell turned to Lomas. "This makes it a big affair, sir."

"Quite." Lomas made a grimace. "Go all out, Bell. Smith was shot too. Both by a .455 service revolver. How many thousand of them are there in circulation?" He pointed to Reggie's exhibits. "You'll never prove which one fired the shots. That's what Mr. Fortune's given us to work on."

"Ah!" Bell frowned over the damaged bullets and cartridge case. "Too bad."

"Not all I've given you," Reggie murmured. "Dark man with skin off his hand the operator. What dark men did our Mr. Smith know who wanted him dead? Any ideas, Underwood?"

"No, sir, I haven't, not yet. But I can tell you this. That constable told the chap on the next beat he'd seen a man and a woman hanging about Cherry-wood Lane several nights lately."

"Oh! Man with woman. Well, well. Any woman known in Mr. Smith's life?"

Underwood shook his head. "I can't get a thing about Smith's life. He came to that old cottage four years ago. Lived alone. The neighbours say he kept himself to himself. They think he was retired, he didn't seem to have any regular occupation, but he was off for the day quite a bit in the summer."

"I wonder," Reggie murmured. "Retired early in life. The corpse wasn't fifty." He turned to Bell. "Undersized man, skinny, fair, recedin' brow, not much nose, a lot of upper lip, prominent rotten teeth and a bit bandy—might have mixed with horses—and no known occupation these five years. Suggest anyone known to the police?"

"A little monkey-faced man." Bell shook his head. "There's quite a few of them about. Not enough, is it? What about his finger-prints?"

"Fingers won't print. Too burnt. Effective operator, the operator on Smith. Are we downhearted? Yes. Anything heard of the fire brigade?"

Bell gave an apologetic grin. "They're not helpful, sir. I had a few words with 'em. They've sent up a bit of stuff. They say none of it's any good, but there won't be any more. Not by them."

"Happy to annoy. Well, well. Let's try again. Where is their stuff?"

"I was just having it looked over."

"Me too." Reggie stood up. "Come on."

Lomas went with him asking, "What do you expect to find, Reginald?"

"Who Smith was."

"Out of the ashes of his furniture?"

"Yes. That is so."

"Hopeful, aren't you?"

"No. Still cling to faith in the human mind. My mind. Though much discouraged by this case."

They went into a large, bare room where two solemn men were arranging on a trestle table what looked like odds and ends from a dust bin.

"Good gad!" Lomas put up his eyeglass. "They have sent you a mixed grill, Reginald."

Reggie wandered round the table and inspected a

little collection of metal, separating bit from bit with studious care.

Lomas came to inspect the results. "One—two—three pennies," he chuckled. "Damme, is this what you asked for?"

"Yes. And two brass key holes," Reggie mumbled. "Yes, not so bad, the fire brigade." He set apart another scrap of brass, which was round and with a surface deeply calcined. "They did get it. There you are. Case of the cartridge that shot Smith. And it might be any cartridge's case. All marks burnt off."

"Brilliant!" said Lomas. "And so we flop again." He turned to the two solemn men who were piecing together broken glass and strips of charred wood. "What the deuce do you fellows think you're doing, playing jigsaw puzzles?"

"Beg pardon, sir. Our instructions pictures were wanted."

"Oh, damme, carry on." Lomas lit a cigarette.

"Sorry you're bored, Lomas," said Reggie. "This is difficult for you." He went to help the puzzle builders. "Two largish pictures, what—and other bits? Yes." He worked with them, drawing from the heap of debris fragments of scorched cardboard. Portions of picture took form—a portly frock coat, a bearded face in one.

"Magnificent, Reginald!" Lomas cried. "His Majesty King Edward VII. Now we know all. Smith was loyal to the Crown." And Underwood hardly concealed a grin. "So a bad, bold Bolshie slew him."

"Yes, we are not amused," Reggie murmured. "Think again, Lomas. Edward VII but not in state.

Edward VII but also a bit of a horse. His Majesty leading in one of his winners. So our Mr. Smith took an interest in horse racin'."

"God bless you, Reginald!" Lomas laughed. "You have a great imagination."

"No, I believe evidence," Reggie snapped. "Look at it. Smith had one other big picture. You see."

"Sky and grass!" Lomas scoffed.

"Oh, my dear chap! And legs. Legs of a horse. Obviously a race horse. And this bit—this is a jockey's leg. Now wait——" He put together small charred pieces.

"More grass," Lomas shrugged.

"As you say. And underneath—HUM—ST—19—" He drew back. "Some horse who won a big race, what?"

"Humorist!" Bell exclaimed. "Derby winner. Five or six years back."

"Thanks very much." Reggie turned to him. "There you are. Our Mr. Smith was a follower of the turf."

"Ah!" Bell's stolid face was excited. "That's what you were hinting before, sir."

"I was. Yes. From his look, his make, his bandy legs. Horsey fellow. Product of the stable."

"You have given us a line." Bell frowned, in labour with thought.

"Yes, that is so," said Reggie. "Come on." He led the way back to Lomas' room, stood before the fire and gazed at Bell. "You were going to tell me——" he asked blandly.

"I wasn't—I don't know," Bell protested.

"My dear chap! Humorist. Why did that particular Derby winner interest our Smith?"

"Humorist—he wasn't the favourite," Bell muttered. "That Derby would be good for the bookmakers. Wait a minute; Humorist's year. Something in the back of my mind. I've got it! That was the year of the big bank frauds. You remember, Mr. Lomas."

"I do not," Lomas cried. "Damme, where are we getting to? From these murders to a Derby years ago and then to a bank fraud! What's the next wild jump?"

"There's nothing wild, sir," said Bell stolidly. "It was a case of a clerk—name of Gray—Herbert Gray—forged cheques for a matter of ten thousand pounds—spent it backing horses, he said. We got him all right, and he got five years' penal servitude. His story, he was lured into betting by a chap he met in a bar, and when he lost all he had this fellow put into his head he could get it back playing tricks at the bank. You know. The dear old game. Help himself out of the big accounts just temporary, and when he won put the money back. Well, it nearly came off, so he said. He plunged on Humorist, at a good price, and the bank wouldn't have been down a penny if he'd got his winnings. But he didn't. He never could find his precious pal after Humorist won. That was what he put up for a defence. It didn't go well, this pal stuff. Gray handed us nothing much to trace the fellow—said they met in one pub and another— the fellow's name was Archer and he gave out to be in with stables and big bookies, special tips and special terms. We worked his pubs, shady places, betting dives, but we never got near anybody passing as Archer, and Gray's description was no good. So we gave up—taking it Gray had been telling the tale—inventing this pal, trying to pass for a poor fool led on and done down so his counsel could pull sob stuff—that is what the judge thought. But now look. Five or six years ago Humorist won and Gray went to gaol. Four or five years ago Joe Smith retired to live on his means in that shy cottage. He was horsey, he had something special on Humorist. Just lately Gray's time in jug was up. And here we have Smith killed and his place burnt to hide who he was." Bell looked with respectful pride from Reggie to Lomas. "I'd say Mr. Fortune's got it, sir."

Reggie's eyelids drooped. He left Lomas to answer.

"Quite good, Bell," Lomas pronounced. "Go to work. Pass the word for Herbert Gray. You'll have to check up on Smith too."

"Yes, sir. Can do, I reckon. When we put some of the old touts through it. Come on, young fellow." Bell bustled Underwood out.

Reggie leaned back against the mantelpiece looking at nothing.

"Waiting for apologies, Reginald?" Lomas smiled. "They are offered. Forgive my dull doubts. One of your best things. We should have been nowhere without you."

"You would. Yes," Reggie murmured. In a sleep-walking manner he moved to the cigar boxes, took a cigar and lit it and stood blowing smoke rings and sighed, "I wonder."

"What?" Lomas cocked a curious eyebrow. "Something more up our ingenious sleeve?"

"Oh no. No. Sound man, Bell. I should say he's right. I did get it. You're right. Must catch Gray. Must trace Smith."

"Quite. All the pieces fit, don't they?"

"The pieces? Yes. Every one. And what's the picture? Nasty queer picture."

"Devilish business," Lomas shrugged.

"As you say. Devil is obtrusive." He turned on Lomas and spoke vehemently. "Nero is an angler in the lake of darkness. Pray, innocent, and beware the foul fiend."

So all the machinery of the police was driven at high pressure to find Herbert Gray, and the underworld of racing was searched for men who could be made to remember Joe Smith, and newspapers were encouraged to scream on their top notes that two murders lay behind the mystery of the Barnham fire, and call on any creature who knew anything of Gray or Smith to stand and deliver.

From this Mr. Fortune withdrew himself and tried to forget all about it in designing a new lily garden. Several days passed. He had sat down after breakfast to paint a water colour of the effect of the working plans for his sceptical wife, when the telephone called him.

"Bell speaking, Mr. Fortune. Could you come out to Hampstead Heath at once? Car on the way for you. I'll meet you there."

"What for?" Reggie moaned. But the telephone was dumb.

The policeman who drove the car could tell no more. When he stopped it on the ridgeway across the Heath, Reggie jumped out to meet Bell with a bitter cry, "I hate you——" He stopped. Bell's massive countenance was shrunken and pallid, his eyes red. "Oh, my dear chap! You're driving yourself too hard."

"I'm all right, sir. We have to go hard on that Gray case. Now you come along here, please."

He turned off the road down a track which led across broken ground between trees and thickets of gorse and bramble. Some two hundred yards on, a little party of men stood about a bulky man who lay prone. Blood had oozed from a wound in his head. Blood stained the sand.

Reggie contemplated him a moment then gazed at Bell. "You think so? Yes, you may be right. But why—why? Oh my Lord, why are we?" He dropped on his knees by the body. . . .

When he got up, he gave Bell a look of dreary, patient sympathy, took him by the arm and led him away and spoke in his ear. "Dead quite a while. Might be twelve hours ago—or more. Cause of death, shot through left cheek bone, by a largish bullet. He died at once. Shot was fired from some distance, behind him on the left. Say from about here." He stopped at the side of the track, he wandered to and fro, in and out among the gorse. "Oh yes. As stated. Two cartridge cases recently fired." He examined them. "Cartridges of a .455 service revolver. As used for our Mr. Smith and our constable. That's what you expected?"

"I did think it looked like a revolver wound." Bell spoke with glum satisfaction. "And these cartridge cases, they have clear marks."

"Yes, indentations of striker quite definite. Easy to prove they came from a particular revolver—when you get the right one. Do you think you have got it?"

"I haven't got one at all—yet."

"Oh. Haven't got Herbert Gray either?"

"No, sir, not yet."

"Pity."

"How do you mean?"

"My Bell! If the revolver which shot Smith and the constable is the revolver which shot this fellow, pity you didn't get Gray before the deed was done."

Bell glowered. "We can't do miracles. We're working, believe me. We'll have Gray soon."

"A felt want," Reggie murmured. "Any reason to believe it was the same revolver?"

"What do you think yourself? Three murders by shooting with a revolver of the same type!"

"Does indicate the same operator. Yes. That's what you wanted me to say. I've said it. Which isn't proof. We had a reason why Gray should kill Smith—and the policeman after. Why should he kill this fellow? Who is the fellow?"

"Ah! That clinches the whole thing. This fellow —he owned a string of pubs, name of George Foat. But he made his money as a low down bookmaker, and Joe Smith was a tout of his. We'd only just dug that up. Found some old timers who knew Smith

Of

as Chatty Joe working for a street corner bookie, Flash George. That was Foat. And they both faded out after Humorist's win."

"I see, yes. With their hearts so full of glee and their pockets full of gold—out of smashing Gray's life—and so Gray drags along as soon as he can and kills 'em—that's the story. Not a nice story. And we have to hang him. Not a nice job, our job. There may be heaven, there must be hell. However. More evidence required. Send this animal, Foat, to the dead house. Good-bye. Get Gray. The sooner, the safer."

Some hours later he rang up Bell. "Fortune speaking. About the animal Foat. One bullet extracted from brain. Only one. But grooving good and clear; .455 service revolver, easy to identify. If and when found. Got it? Got Gray?"

"I have, sir," Bell boomed triumph. "Gray, I mean, not the revolver. Not yet. Gray's just being brought along."

"Congratulations. Me too," said Reggie in a hurry.

He found Bell and Underwood in conference with Lomas. "Well, well." He surveyed them. "Todgers's can do it when it chooses, what? Flowers for all. Oh, the cleverness of us. How was the man Gray when found?"

"Not passing under his own name, Mr. Fortune. He's called himself Shirley, his wife's maiden name."

"Oh, there's a wife? Jolly!"

"Yes, he was married before he went wrong. We knew that. He kept it dark. He'd married too young, you see, his bank didn't like their men to marry early.

It's a common rule, of course. But I shouldn't wonder that was one reason why Gray ran off the rails. Wanted more money somehow. When he crashed his wife was away having a baby. His counsel didn't use that at his trial. Rather queer, leaving it out of all the sob stuff he pulled about Gray being a poor young innocent led astray."

"Get on, Bell," said Lomas impatiently. "I want to deal with Gray."

But Reggie drawled. "Baby living?"

"No, sir. It died. Well, you see, taking his wife's maiden name when he came out of prison, Gray covered his tracks. She'd put Mrs. to it, she's Mrs. Shirley now and doing well, secretary to a rich woman, Lady Preston, that soap man's widow, the philanthropist. But she didn't go back on Gray. She got him a job through her employer's interest. He's been in a garage quite respectable. I don't know if we'd have traced him but for publishing his portrait and description in the papers. The porter at the flats where she lives recognized him and put us on to him. But there's more than that. Underwood's got some of Smith's neighbours swearing they've seen Gray hanging round the lane there."

"When?" Reggie asked.

"Of nights. More than one night," said Underwood. "They can't put it more definite. To my mind, that makes it better evidence, they're not swearing to him because they know we want him."

"Yes. I should say they're being honest with the facts," Reggie murmured. "So are you. And fair. Very fair, Bell."

"You notice the evidence of the neighbours fits what we had before, sir," said Underwood. "The constable who was killed told his mate he'd seen a man hanging round Smith's place."

"I had noticed, yes. That would fit. Same like everything else. But the constable said a man and a woman."

"Ah," Bell frowned. "You mean Gray's wife?"

Reggie moved in his chair. "Mean there's something that doesn't fit. At last."

"It fits well enough," said Lomas. "These people only saw Gray. But his wife may have been there to help him all the same."

"Well enough!" Reggie started up. "Oh my Lomas! You shock me. Anybody may have been there any time. No proof yet Gray was there the right time."

"Quite. We'll get it," said Lomas. "I shouldn't wonder if we get it out of him, Reginald. He ought to be here by now."

The telephone discovered that he was.

In Bell's room they sat down to examine him. Bell boomed intimidating questions. "Is your real name Herbert Gray? Why do you call yourself Shirley? You've served a five years' sentence for forgery and embezzlement, haven't you? Why didn't you report to the police when you knew you were wanted?"

But Gray would only repeat one answer. "What am I brought here for?"

Reggie watched him with dreary curiosity. He sat on the edge of his chair, he would not look at anyone

straight, or at anything for long. His dark face had
been meant to please. Well enough in a common-
place way, it invited contempt by its exhibition of
stupid, angry fear, the more unlovely for his elegance
of waved, shining black hair and spruce clothes. His
hands worked hard washing themselves.

"You're brought here to answer questions about
the murder of Joseph Smith, of Cherrywood Lane,
Barnham, on the night of October 13. And of Police
Constable Browning, also of Barnham, on the same
date," Bell went on. "I warn you anything you say
may be used in evidence."

"I have nothing to say," Gray muttered. "I know
nothing about them."

"Do you tell me you didn't know Smith? I put it
to you; Joseph Smith, passing as Chatty Joe, was a
man you used to bet with before you went to prison.
You said at your trial a man called Archer lured
you into betting and showed you how to rob the
bank." Bell passed across the table a photograph of
Smith's dead face. "Isn't that the man?"

Gray peered at it and shuddered. "That—that—
I never saw anybody like that."

"Pick it up," Reggie said sharply. "Look at
it."

Gray's hands came forward shaking, lifted it and
dropped it again. "I tell you I never saw him," he
screamed. Reggie sat back in his chair and glanced
at Bell.

But Bell was booming, "Not like that, you said.
Ah, that's after he was burnt. Where were you on the
night of the 13th?"

"At home. In bed," Gray muttered.

"Where was your wife?" Lomas snapped.

Gray's mouth came open. "My wife?" he muttered. "At Lady Preston's."

Reggie was writing. He passed the paper to Lomas and Lomas read and caressed his chin and stared at Gray.

"And other nights?" Bell was asking. "Do you tell me nobody ever saw you round Smith's place at night?"

"I wasn't there," Gray answered.

"What about last night? Did you know George Foat, the bookmaker Smith worked for?"

"I never heard of him."

"Heard of him as Flash George, eh? Where were you when George Foat was shot on Hampstead Heath?"

"When was the man shot?"

"Last night, I told you."

"No, you didn't. You're setting traps for me. I won't answer you any more. You have nothing against me. You can't have. You can't keep me here. Let me go."

Lomas put the paper with Reggie's message in front of Bell. He read it, but there was no change in the grim threat of his eyes as he stared at Gray again. "You're being kept here," he growled, "for enquiries. I give it you straight, I don't believe you've told me the truth."

"I have. I told you the truth before," Gray cried, and as he was taken out he screamed, "I'm not afraid of you."

"That wasn't true anyhow," Bell grunted, and turned on Reggie. "Eh, Mr. Fortune?"

"Oh no. No. Deadly afraid. However." Reggie tapped the paper and read from it. "'His hands not damaged.' So Gray was not the dark man who skinned his hand on Smith's fence that night. A second bit that don't fit. Crucial bit. Throws all our picture out." He met a concentration of displeasure with reproachful amusement. "Sorry to annoy. Got to break it up and try again."

"I don't agree, Reginald," said Lomas sharply. "We have evidence Gray and his wife were there. It may very well have been the woman hurt her hands."

"Oh no. No." Reggie was shocked. "Wasn't the woman. Wasn't any woman. Hairy skin. Man's skin. Man's hair. Face the nasty fact, Lomas. Our determined, effective operator wasn't Gray. It was somebody you haven't got near." He turned. "Or have you, Bell?"

"I don't follow," Bell complained. "What are you suggesting?"

"My dear chap! Nothing unkind. Shuffle the bits of the puzzle and reconsider 'em. What have we got? Gray had a mortal grudge against Smith and Foat. Gray had been looking up Smith. The picture we made was that he shot Smith for revenge, set the place on fire—knocking holes in the pipes and lighting up the gas—to hide that Smith had been murdered. Then he got out at the back and shot the constable who stopped him. Quite good. Only it wasn't Gray got out. Subsequently Foat was shot by a revolver of the sort used on Smith and the policeman.

Did look like Gray too. Though rather wild of him to go and kill again when he knew we were on to him. However. Sort of thing a desperate fellow might do. Do you think he is a desperado? No. Another little difficulty. Why did Foat go out to Hampstead Heath at night so he could be shot from the bushes conveniently?"

"Ah, that got me, Mr. Fortune," Bell broke in. "I've had some work done on it. Foat's son says he has no idea why his father went to the Heath, denies to know anything about Gray except what's been in the papers just now."

"Curiouser and curiouser. Fat publicans and bookies don't walk the Heath much, cold October nights."

"No sir. You've got to remember Foat didn't live so far away—matter of two miles—down in Kentish Town. Still, it is queer."

"Yes, I think so. Obvious explanation. Foat went to meet somebody he didn't want to meet at home. Why? Who?"

"You might say Gray got him to go out there somehow," Bell said slowly. "That's an old game, you know, sir. A woman, might be."

"Gray's wife, begad!" Lomas exclaimed.

Reggie lay back and looked through the murky window. "Yes, as you were saying," he murmured. "There are objections, Lomas. The man Foat, knowing his tout, Smith, had just been murdered, knowing there was a hue and cry for Gray, lets Mrs. Gray vamp him out to Hampstead Heath in the dark. Uncommon reckless of Foat."

"Not sound, Reginald," Lomas smiled. "He didn't know she was Gray's wife. She was passing as Mrs. Shirley. She might have passed as anybody to him. And we know she was working with Gray over Smith. Why not over Foat too?"

"Yes. It could be," Reggie mumbled.

"Excuse me, sir, I don't think so," said Underwood. "The fact is we don't really know Gray's wife was round Smith's place. I've had him identified by the neighbours but not her. Only the constable spoke to a woman. They'd not noticed one. I showed 'em a photo we snapped of her too. Nothing doing."

"Failure of observation, that's all," Lomas shrugged. "Doesn't alter the fact Gray's wife has worked in with him."

"No, sir," said Underwood without pretence of agreement. He took out his pocket-book. "Would you look at her photo?"

"What of it?" Lomas frowned.

The photograph showed a slight woman in austere clothes. Her face had been pretty but was aged and strained and acquainted with grief.

"Not the sort of woman who'd cut much ice as a vamp, to my mind," said Underwood.

Reggie drew a long breath. "God help us!" he murmured, rare words on his lips. "Well, Lomas?" he asked drearily.

"I agree," Lomas nodded. "She's nobody's lure now, poor thing. That wastrel Gray! What a life for her! He may have had another woman, though."

"He may. Yes The world is so full of a number of things, I think we should all be as happy as kings. Another woman in Gray's jolly life. Sort of woman who'd help him on from murder to murder with the hunt at his heels. Yes. She could exist. I don't believe in her till compelled. You're not bein' rational, Lomas. Fundamental rule of investigation, don't invent more theories than you have to. No need to invent a woman for the case. We have a man in it unaccounted for—man who left his skin on Smith's fence."

"Good gad! You mean he worked Foat's murder too. He knew a thing or two about Smith—why not about Foat? I believe you have it, Reginald." Lomas turned to Bell. "Try it this way. Two racing sharps murdered—by another one—a gang break up."

"Some pal of Smith and Foat?" said Bell dubiously. "Well, that might be, of course. I—— Hullo! What have you got?"

A man had come into the room with a "Beg pardon, Superintendent, I thought you'd like to have this at once." He laid on the table something wrapped in a handkerchief. "Found in Gray's office at the garage, in the waste paper basket, under some envelopes and stuff. Nothing else from the garage. Nothing to signify from Gray's flat."

Bell turned back the handkerchief. "Revolver," he said with grim satisfaction, "Service revolver, .455, old gun, been cleaned. Have you tried it for finger-prints, Naylor?"

"Yes, sir. Can't get anything."

"I thought as much," Bell grunted. "Wiped careful." His sunken eyes gleamed at Reggie. "Not too bad though, eh?"

"Oh no. No. Very good," Reggie sighed. "Very useful. Take it away. Fire three or four rounds and bring me the bullets and the cartridge cases. Get my last exhibits, Underwood." As the two went out he leaned back and contemplated Bell. "Now we should not be long," he murmured sleepily. "Where was the man Gray when arrested?"

"In the garage, sir, he'd just got back from lunch. Our men missed him at his flat and went round there after him. You see? He'd heard them asking for him, only just time to dump the gun. He was half salesman, half book-keeper; the office was the one place handy."

Underwood came back with the cartridge cases found on the Heath, the bullet taken from Foat's head and, as Reggie spread them out on a white blotting pad, Naylor brought in four bullets, four cartridge cases on a saucer.

Reggie inspected them . . . examined them through a magnifying glass . . . He looked up with a twist of a plaintive smile. "Quite conclusive, Bell. Even to the naked eye." Bell leaned across him. His finger pointed at dents in the cartridge cases on the saucer, at other dents in the cases on the blotting paper. "Isn't that nice?"

"That'll do, Naylor," Bell growled, and Naylor reluctantly departed, and Bell pored over the cartridges and the heads of Lomas and Underwood joined his.

"Yes, it will," said Reggie softly. "It has done. Marks of striker quite different. Revolver which killed Foat was not the revolver found in Gray's waste paper. One more bit which won't fit. Absolute and final destruction of our pretty picture."

"My oath!" Bell glowered at him. "And what then? Gray didn't do the murders, but he had a revolver of the right make and he only thought of getting rid of it when we were on top of him. You believe that?"

"No." Reggie smiled sadly. "Too hard, Bell. No use trying. Another possibility."

"Damme, it's clear enough, Bell," Lomas cried. "This gun was planted in Gray's office to put the murders on him. Who did that? The murderer. Who is he then? Some rascal that knew all about Gray and Smith and Foat—he was in with those two sharps—one of their gang—they'd broken him or he was afraid they would. I told you that was the line."

"You did. Yes," Reggie murmured. "Racing gang break and feud. Quite good. Now confirmed."

"Well, it is in a way," Bell said slowly. "But look. That means the fellow was in the garage where Gray was—working with him."

"Why not?" Lomas shrugged. "Go to it."

"And the other end," said Reggie. "You found people who knew Smith was Foat's tout. Why not find people who know somebody else mixed up with them?"

"You take that on, Underwood." Bell stood up. "I'm going round to the garage."

"Me too," said Reggie. "Do you mind? Like to see the people—if any."

"I can do with you, sir." Bell gave him a rueful grin. "In this case, special. What do you reckon to hand me next? Gray's a martyred saint? Never robbed the bank at all?"

"Oh, my Bell! Nerves!"

The garage was small but opulently respectable, its open front showed a few good used cars for sale and behind them a cubicle of an office. From that, as they made their way to it, a woman hurried, a man following her heavily. She was pale and distressed. The man, a fat fellow, revealed agitation. "Anything I can do, you know," he was saying. She did not answer, she scurried past them and out.

Bell confronted him. "Are you the proprietor, Mr. Walker?"

"I am." The man mopped his brow.

"That was the wife of your clerk Shirley—real name Gray—wasn't it? What was she doing here?"

"Who the hell are you?" Walker scowled. Bell showed him a card. "My Lord, more of 'em!" He lumbered back to the office calling, "Come on." He slammed the door behind them. "Want to know what the lady was doing? What do you think she was doing, poor soul? Asking what the police took her husband away for."

"How did she know we'd taken him?"

Walker's little eyes flashed. "Because I told her, see? Any ruddy objection from you, Superintendent? You send and pinch a good man of mine. Why wouldn't I let his wife know? What's the game?"

"A good man," Bell repeated. "You know Gray's record?"

"I did not. Only knew him as Shirley. But he's made good with me."

"Cool off. You've heard what he had in his waste paper basket here?"

"I know what your chaps took out of it."

"Ever seen that revolver before, Mr. Walker?"

Walker looked ugly. "Come again. I haven't seen that one. And I haven't seen any ruddy revolver since I was demobbed. Anything else you'd like to know?"

"Yes. How do you suppose the revolver got into the waste paper basket in this office?"

"Search me!" Walker's little eyes were cunning.

"Ever had anything to do with racing, Mr. Walker?"

"Not me. Mug's game."

"Some of your employees perhaps?"

"Look here, I've had enough." Walker banged the table. "I'm well known, I am. And my chaps are straight; I've had 'em all for years. Long before Gray came. I'm not going to have you throw mud at them or me, see?"

"You've nothing to be afraid of——"

"Afraid, my foot!" Walker laughed.

"——if you're straight with me. Who uses this office except Gray and you and your people?"

"Nobody uses it but Gray and me. Anybody might come in, customers, travellers, dam' all."

"I see. Has anybody been in to-day?"

Again the cunning look gleamed in Walker's eyes. "Yes, there has, Superintendent. A very queer customer. Do you happen to know anything about him?"

"What do you mean?"

"Just came into my head you might. Of course you wouldn't send anybody to play tricks here before your chaps came official, would you?"

"You take it I did not." Bell glowered at him. "Well?"

"Well, it's funny, that's all. While Gray had gone home to lunch, a chap did come into the office. The man in charge outside asked him what he wanted, and he told the tale his car had been stolen and he'd been rung up by us to say a car of his had been left in our yard and what about it. He gave the name of Raper, car a Watkin six. My man went to the yard to enquire. No such car there, no car left at all. The chap cursed and quit quick. How about it, Superintendent? Just after that funny stuff your blokes come along and pinch Gray and they find a revolver in the waste paper here all nice and handy for 'em. What a game!"

"Go and get this man of yours," Bell growled, and as Walker lumbered off, turned on Reggie. "If it's true——"

"As he was sayin'," Reggie answered. "Then what a game!"

Walker brought his man, who told the same story, described Raper as a beefy, flash gent, but could add nothing more.

Next morning Mrs. Fortune's tea had just come to her bedside when the telephone in the room began to ring. Reggie sat up with a jerk and an exceeding bitter cry and grabbed the receiver. "Speakin', yes, confound you."

"We have that Raper's car, sir," said the voice of Bell. "Found abandoned out St. Alban's way. Broken down."

"Oh! Raper is real. Well, well. What about him?"

"Enquiries proceeding, sir. About the car. There's some stains on the inside, might be blood. Would you go out and have a look at it?"

"I will. I must." Reggie rang off and sprang out of bed. "The Gray case, Joan."

"That poor woman," said Mrs. Fortune.

"Oh yes. And poor me," Reggie answered as he fled.

A bright young Inspector drove him away expounding the efficiency of the police force. "We sent out a general warning for a Watkin six. A patrol remembered seeing one on a bit of waste ground beside the river Colne yesterday morning with nobody in it or near, and they found it still there last night—licence in the name of E. Garnet Raper. They couldn't move it. So I went out. Carburettor choked with sand. Very dusty, off the road there. I gave the car the once over with a flash light. No damage, but I found what looks like marks of blood inside."

"I wonder." Reggie's face was without expression. "Good work. Very good work. Yes. Why off the road? Why by a river?"

"Chap who drove it there wanted to stop where he wouldn't be noticed for a bit."

"That is indicated." Reggie closed his eyes. . . .

"Here we are." The Inspector drove off the high

road into an unfenced lane with deep sandy ruts. It led over waste land to a ford in the river which the high road crossed by a bridge. Near the water stood Raper's car, guarded by a policeman.

The Inspector opened its door and demonstrated. "You see, dark stains on the carpet there, and here in the crinkles of the leather a sort of purple smear."

"Yes. As you say. Provisionally blood. Some days old. Easy to verify." Reggie turned away. "Car has stood some time."

"I should say it was left here night before last."

"So should I." Reggie gazed at him. "And why here, young fellow?"

"To be out of the way while he saw what was inside. Then he couldn't start it and had to quit."

"Yes. Not bad. Why didn't he have it fetched?"

"He'd stolen it, he daren't."

"Might be the reason. Might be another." Reggie wandered away towards the river. It made a wide expanse of shallow water set about with rushes except at the ford. "What's that?" he pointed. Lying on a tuft of rushes was a revolver.

"Good Lord!" the Inspector gasped. "Of course it was dark when I examined the car, Mr. Fortune. I had no chance to see the gun." He plunged at it. . . .

In Bell's room a dark, full-bodied man, whose too smart clothes seemed too tight, sat before Lomas and Bell and Underwood when Reggie opened the door.

"Your statement is, you never had any acquaintance with Smith or Foat," Bell was saying. "You were a

Pf

bookmaker, weren't you? My information is you ran Foat."

Lomas' eye met Reggie's. "This is Mr. Garnet Raper, Fortune."

"Oh yes, I see." Reggie sat down and wrote for Lomas to read.

Raper had answered Bell in the husky voice of the ring. "Your information's a lie then."

"Foat's son says his father had a telephone message from you after Smith was murdered. The day his father was murdered. Why should he lie?"

As Raper's tan gloved hand took out a flaring silk handkerchief and wiped his mouth, Reggie looked up at him. "It's all wrong anyhow," he answered. "I never did. Somebody's doing the dirty on me."

"Take off your gloves, Raper," said Reggie.

Raper took no notice. Raper went on talking in a hoarse hurry. "A fake call, if my name was used. A ruddy fake. Some swine's leading you up the garden, to hide himself. I'm a well known man and never anything against me. I——"

"Why don't you take your gloves off?" Reggie asked plaintively. "Because your hand's hurt? Where was it hurt? On Smith's fence?"

Raper swore at him. "No, it wasn't. I scratched it on the door of my car."

"There is blood in your car. Yes. Skin of hand on the fence though."

"Not mine. I take my oath it's not," Raper roared. "Have you found my car? My car was stolen."

"Was it? Where from?"

Raper swallowed. "Outside my house. Day before yesterday."

"Oh. But you didn't inform the police. Well, well."

"Your car has been found, Raper," said Lomas. "So has your revolver."

"Where? I don't know what you mean. I never had a revolver."

"Service revolver taken out of the water beside your car. That revolver was used to shoot Foat. Any explanation?"

"It's all a fake," Raper gasped. "My car was stolen, I tell you. You're planting things on me, you——"

"Take him away, Bell," Lomas said sharply, and, cursing them all, Raper was hustled out.

Reggie rose wearily. "I shall have to see his beastly hands," he moaned. . . .

A little while afterwards he came into Lomas' room. "Yes. Back of right hand flayed as required. So that is that." He lit a cigar and sank into the easiest chair. "You'll hang him all right."

"Many thanks." Lomas chuckled. "Very neat work, Reginald."

"It is. Yes." Reggie's eyes were almost closed. "Better dead, isn't he? Nasty bit of work. That poor devil Gray! He has been through it. I take it this fat brute was the power behind the scenes at Gray's ruin—planned the whole ramp. Not the first time we've had hints of a brain in the background when a young fool who could get at big money was led on to bet. Gray came out and looked for Smith, the only one of the rogues he knew. I suppose Smith rounded on Raper, a good chance to squeeze him. Raper got the wind up—Gray and Smith between 'em could land him in gaol for a long term. So he wiped out Smith —and had to kill the constable to get away. Foat wouldn't like that—and Gray was still at large. If Foat and Gray came together they could hang him. Foat also had to go. Raper fixed up a meeting at night on the Heath to talk things over without anyone knowing they met, shot him there, drove out to the Colne and threw the gun in the water. Then the luck turned— about time, too, he'd had it all his own way over Smith and the constable."

"Devilish lucky. Yes," Reggie murmured.

"Quite. But the carburettor getting clogged was deuced lucky for us. If he hadn't had to leave his car there by the water it's long odds we'd never have got him. If the gun had ever been found, he could have sworn it wasn't his, or it had been stolen."

"As you say," Reggie sighed. "Extraordinary luck."

Lomas raised a startled eyebrow. "What's the matter? It's all right about the gun, isn't it?"

"Oh yes. Absolutely. Revolver found by car, revolver which killed Foat. Cartridge and bullet marks identical."

"That settles Raper. And on top of it we have him planting another gun on the wretched Gray. Dam' clever, that effort to cover the breakdown of his car at the waterside. But it leaves him with no defence at all."

"None any good, no." Reggie's eyes opened to a

steady, gloomy gaze. "You can see what he's going to say. Gray shot Foat. Gray stole his car, made a sham breakdown by the river and left the gun there half in the water to be found when the car was found."

"Who's going to believe that?" Lomas chuckled.

"Nobody. Not a soul," said Reggie. "That is the humour of it. Something else he'll say: if he was guilty, if he did come to plant a gun in Gray's office, he wouldn't have given himself away using his own name, pretending a 'phone message that his stolen car was there."

"I don't mind." Lomas laughed. "Do you think a jury would fall for it?"

"No. Not a nice case, Lomas."

Lomas stared at him. "Why this oracular melancholy? What is in your wonderful mind? Do you want to throw everything down again?"

"Not me." Reggie squirmed. "No, I do not." He sat up. "However. I must give it you. No doubt Raper shot Smith. And the policeman. His hand was hurt in that murder. But then? We've heard somebody else was watching Smith—suppose Raper lost his revolver there—over a scrap with the policeman— somebody picked it up—having spotted Raper's car —knew then that Raper was the man behind Smith— and watched him—caught Foat and him on the Heath —shot at 'em—two cartridges fired there, you know— killed Foat—went off with Raper's car—left it by the river with a spot of sand in the carburettor and the revolver handy—'phoned Raper his stolen car was at the garage—and dumped another service revolver in Gray's waste paper—thus making a case to hang Raper and wiping out the whole gang. Well?"

"Good gad!" Lomas sat back with a jerk. "You make my flesh creep, Reginald. A great story. Sorry, but I can't buy it. You didn't happen to think it plausible, did you?"

"No. Contrariwise," Reggie murmured. "That's the beauty of it."

"Quite. The pure romance. Your somebody, your mighty subtle, desperate, revengeful killer—that's the wretched Gray. Do you see him in the part?"

Reggie shook his head, blew smoke rings and through them watched Lomas with closing eyes.

"I think not!" Lomas chuckled. "His poor little wife then? Nobody else. Likely isn't it? And good strong evidence against her!"

"Not a scrap. I said so." Reggie stood up. "But plenty to hang Raper. There you are. Good-bye."

His wife came in upon him as he dressed for dinner. "Oh, Reggie, is there anything about that poor woman?"

Reggie tied his tie. "Mrs. Gray? Oh yes. She's all right. Her husband's cleared. They've got another man."

"I'm so glad." She gazed at the solemn face reflected in the glass. "Aren't you?"

"Yes. Yes," Reggie murmured.

"She's had such a sad life. You know she lost her baby when her husband was put in prison. Lady

Preston was talking to me. She'll never be able to have another."

"Oh, I didn't know that," Reggie said slowly. "God help her."

"Well, you have," Mrs. Fortune said.

VI

THE KEY OF THE DOOR

THE KEY OF THE DOOR

"Y ES, I HAVE heard that he was seen kissing her in the car," Mr. Fortune answered, and looked at the big man in the dock: "Evidence credible and probable. She had then been dead some time."

Half an hour later he left the court with the Chief of the Criminal Investigation Department. "That's all right. They'll hang him," he remarked. "Which is inadequate. However. Best we can do in this world. Come to lunch. Joan's at home."

That was, of course, the famous case of the master of foxhounds. Mr. Fortune's next case is not so well known. But he found it far more satisfactory.

They had reached the strawberries. Lomas, who was the worse for wear over a struggle to put backbone into the Public Prosecutor, had been tempted by Mrs. Fortune to the sprightly cynical gossip which he considers his strong suit. Reggie, in silent bliss, applied brown sherry to a second portion of cream and the parlourmaid presented to him a visiting card.

It bore the name of Dr. John Mayce, and an address in Staplehurst, which is a suburb of opulence. "Mayce?" he murmured. "Oh ah." and finished his cream and rose. "Sorry. One of my spiritual children, Lomas. Fellow with too much conscience."

"Natural reaction against father's ways," said Lomas. "Don't worry, Reginald. He will be about normal."

"No. Ought to have worked with you. He thinks everything's his fault," said Reggie, and lit a cigar. "There, but for the grace of God, I might have been. He's a general practitioner, lucky beggar. He does some good."

John Mayce had worked at pathology under Reggie until persuaded that he shouldn't. He came into Reggie's consulting-room looking the older man by years but with the flurry of nervous youth. "My dear Johnny," Reggie smiled. "You haven't altered a bit. How are things?"

"Thank you very much. I'm ashamed to trouble you, Mr. Fortune, I've really no right at all. I ought to be able to deal with the matter myself, but I don't feel adequate, I must ask for your advice."

"Good fellow." Reggie pushed him into one easy chair and dropped into another. "Go ahead."

Mayce went deviously. He must admit that he could not excuse himself. He had been careless, culpably negligent. One should always lock up a car before leaving it. The police were perfectly right to take that point. He could only say that he had had a long day, and the car was left in the quietest place and only for a little while. Of course that was no real defence, worse than none, for his case contained dangerous drugs. He——

"Oh, it's the case that was stolen," Reggie interrupted. "Well, well. You don't happen to think you're unique? World is full of doctors whose cases have been pinched. What were the awful contents of your one?"

Mayce stammered through a list . . . dressings . . . syringe . . . bottles . . . ampoules of strychnine, morphine, strophanthin. . . .

"Yes. Usual emergency outfit. Sounds frightful to the laity. Not to us. Why worry, Johnny? Police worryin' you?"

"Not at all. They were inclined to take it very lightly, Mr. Fortune. I realise that my own tendency is to be too anxious——"

"You have noticed it?" Reggie murmured.

"—— but I can't help feeling gravely disturbed. I only bought my practice in Staplehurst two years ago. I was assured I should find a very pleasant social circle. For a time that seemed to be true. But I have become aware of a great deal of ill will."

"To you?"

"Not at all. People have been most kind. I mean that in the common life of the place there is distrust and hostility, sometimes quite bitter."

"Cliques which are spiteful. My dear Johnny! Life is like that. Imperfect world, this world. However, one school for scandal doesn't often steal a box o' poison to teach the other school where it gets off. Any reason to think some of your people did?"

"I could not say so," Mayce wrung his nervous hands. "I can't be sure that my anxiety is justified."

"My dear chap! Oh, my dear chap," Reggie sighed. "You've come to find out. What are your facts?"

Mayce looked at him uncomfortably. "It is so diffi-cult to be definite. I don't feel that I have their confidence except medically, they don't really let me know them. They are exclusive."

"The usual rich suburb. I've had some. Born and bred in a briar patch. Go on. Who hates who?"

"I am not to say that! But I can't ignore a marked division, it is largely a matter of income, but questions of personality are involved. For example, one of my patients, Mr. William Dean; he is a wealthy man, he has been a generous benefactor to the district, he is much looked up to, his daughter's charming, and yet sometimes I find a most unpleasant tone about him." Mayce stopped for a minute. "On the other hand, the society in which Mr. Dean is a leader does show a marked dislike of some people in other circles." Again he stopped.

"Who?" Reggie asked.

"Of course it is only a personal impression," said Mayce in a hurry. "I was thinking of two ladies who conduct a kindergarten school, Mrs. Boyd and her daughter."

Through a minute of silence Reggie gazed at Mayce's embarrassed distress. "Are you telling me all you know, Johnny?" he murmured.

"Yes, really, absolutely everything—about the people. I hadn't come to the circumstances of the theft from my car. I had left it in Green Walk, that is a very quiet by-way with a few large houses. I was visiting Mrs. Wayland, a regular call, and it was a dark evening, but when I found the case had been stolen I had a recollection that as I went in I saw a woman hurrying along under the trees."

"Oh. Like anybody you know?"

Mayce shook his head vehemently—he hadn't noticed at all—he hadn't thought—the police said they couldn't follow it up, it was too vague.

"Well, well," Reggie murmured. "Any reason to think the ladies Boyd might go as far as to poison Dean—or Dean them?"

"None in the world. I had never imagined such a thing. It is a horrible idea."

"Not nice, no."

"I feel it's preposterous, Mr. Fortune."

"Yes. That is the natural feeling. Yet you came to me, Johnny."

"Well, you see," Mayce's restless hands twisted. "I had been so disturbed by the bad feeling——"

"Sensitive, aren't you?"

"I'm afraid I am"; Mayce gazed at him with miserable appealing eyes. "And I can't disguise from myself that I have been sadly in fault."

"My dear chap. Oh, my dear chap!" Reggie started up. "Good thing you are sensitive. Or we'd have been nowhere. But now you're overdoin' it. About your patients. Are you givin' any of 'em drugs that were in the stolen case?"

Mayce was bewildered. "Why, it was an emergency case. But actually I have given Mr. Dean strophanthin from time to time. He has a dilated heart."

"Has he? Well, well. I should like to have a look at these people, Johnny. Any social gathering imminent in your happy suburb? Any place where the dear things get together?"

After some confusion of mind, Mayce was brought

to remember that Staplehurst had a tennis club, that a great many people went there on Saturday afternoon and that he was a member and could introduce Mr. Fortune. It was obvious that he did not enjoy the prospect, but he spluttered gratitude.

You see now one more proof of the earnestness of mind which some people fail to observe in Reggie. For this festivity he deprived himself of the long week-end in his Cotswold garden where his lilies were at their best. He also amazed Lomas by demanding the latest on the Staplehurst robbery to which the Criminal Investigation Department had given no attention whatever. On Friday evening Lomas rang him up. "Your Staplehurst stuff. Nothing doing. Nothing to work on. The usual woolly-minded doctor left his things in his car for anybody to steal, and it was so. Quite professional, Reginald. What do you expect?"

"I haven't the slightest idea. And you? Anything known to the police about people in Staplehurst?"

"Nothing to know. It's one of the heavens of the smug."

"Yes, so I've heard. He's not woolly-minded, my Dr. Mayce. Not for people. Very sensitive mind."

"Do you mean to say he thinks the drugs were stolen to use in Staplehurst?"

"He's afraid. Lot of conscience. As I was sayin'. Pupil of mine."

"Good gad! Case of mixed drugs stolen from a doctor to poison someone in his own district? Is it likely?"

"No. Don't remember it ever bein' done. However. Man is an advancer."

"Does he suspect anyone?"

"I wonder. Very conscientious fellow, Johnny Mayce."

"Confound you! Have you a definite suspicion?"

"Not me. No. The mind is blank. Same like the police mind. But active. That's where we differ. Good-bye."

Behold him on Saturday afternoon driving his car into Staplehurst. He did not go straight to Mayce's house, he turned into the leafy shade of Green Walk and stopped there for some time. It was quiet as a cemetery. The few houses hid themselves behind palings and shrubberies. In the avenue of limes it would be easy for anyone to lurk and vanish. But a most unpromising place for a car thief to choose—unless he knew that a car would be left there worth robbing.

These conclusions Reggie did not confide to Mayce, who gave him alternate spasms of chatter and silence as they drove to the tennis club. With a shamefaced manner Mayce conducted him through a thin stream of members and whispered depreciation. A lot of courts, more than they ever wanted, rather a sin with so many poorer clubs overcrowded. All the land was their own—some of the wealthy people snapped up that top stretch to keep another club out, and built the new pavilion there, absurdly luxurious place. Reggie gazed at strident red brick contorted with many bulges, like a parody of bad Elizabethan, with a green glass roof poking out over a terrace. That seemed to

Q F

be the holy of holies. There coteries of mature people sat and gossiped.

Though Mayce was nearly useless as a social guide, in a little while Reggie had sat down to chat with two old ladies. It is a section of humanity for which he has a flair. They are all apt to tell him stories—he says they feel motherly, his wife says he can be the tamest of cats—and he is singularly successful in choosing those who tell the best.

From Miss Abercromby and Lady Jones he learnt much without asking a question which they noticed. Very agreeable, indeed, but not quite in the old way, of course things had changed, tennis was so serious now. The tournaments used to be quite festive, every-one was pleasant, now they were like a battle. Mr. Dean had made the club a wonderful place. Oh, Mr. Dean was the president.

Reggie's eyes were directed towards a man who sat alone, in a cluster of people standing, to watch the game on the first court. There was a lot of him, body and neck and face, he sagged, he was florid.

Mr. Dean used to be such a good player, a wonderful athlete, poor man, a great mountaineer. No, he never played now, his heart, of course. The nice old heads nodded and sighed. That was his daughter Rosemary playing in the final of the mixed doubles with Peter Wayland. Of course he'd come to watch her. Didn't they make a good pair?

Reggie had no difficulty in agreeing that they did. Rosemary Dean was not on her father's scale; she had a pleasant little old-fashioned figure and a pretty face which showed neither heat nor excitement though she was as fast as the sturdy Amazon against her and not much less powerful. Quite easy to look at. And the man wasn't bad. Bit of a scowl when he was going all out. Rather a jaw on him. No beauty, but he had a good smile when he missed—or she did.

The old ladies talked on. Staplehurst upper circles, it was not difficult to infer, had determined that Rosemary Dean and Peter Wayland were to play a mixed double through life, not so easy to be sure what the old ladies thought about it. Rosemary and Peter were plainly the two great catches of the suburb. There seemed to be nothing which the old ladies wanted to say against either. Peter, since they were old ladies, was naturally the favourite, but, like nice old ladies, they approved the pretty girl, and purred at the vision of her marriage. It emerged that she was Dean's only child. Reggie felt in vain after a vague elusive hint that this was not a state to be desired. They stopped talking.

"Oh, my dear, there's Sophy Boyd," Lady Jones exclaimed.

"Why, so it is," said Miss Abercromby, and then they talked fast about nothing.

But they still watched a girl who had come up from the lower courts to see the last set of Rosemary and Peter. She stood alone, a mass of black hair low on her neck glistening in the sunshine. She watched the game with grave attention, but her dark face betrayed no sign of interest in its fortune. Rosemary and Peter were winning all the way. They won, and in the clapping she clapped a little, she turned and walked away, a smile set on her straight lips. People stopped her and spoke to her. It was made clear that she had kind friends, quite clear that she did not want them just then. The last Reggie saw of her was a blaze of pride in her eyes. She vanished into the pavilion.

Peter and Rosemary came up, both of them being genial to the beaten Amazon and her dumpy partner, who bore it well. The pavilion received them also. Tea and other drinks came out of it. Dean lumbered alone to a table and consumed a whisky and soda while people flocked about him and talked till Rosemary made her way through them and took him away.

He went slowly. "Where's the young man gone?" he grumbled.

"Peter? Do you want him? He's dining with us, you know."

"Is he? Humph."

A little while after Peter came out and added himself to the noisiest set of tea tables, and it appeared that Peter Wayland had many friends of all sorts.

Reggie remarked on that to Mayce. "Of course, yes, very popular, he's so easy-going," said Mayce; "he takes nothing seriously."

"Like that?" Reggie murmured, contemplating Peter's careless joviality. "Rather vacuous, yes. Playing the fool. I wonder. Don't care if it snows. Good, ugly face though. Touch of the bulldog breed, what?"

"I'm afraid not," Mayce shook his head.

"Well, well. Never believe faces." Reggie walked away with him. "Quite interestin', Johnny. I should say you may be right. What do you know about Miss Sophia Boyd?"

Mayce gave him a startled look. "Nothing in the least against her," he spoke in a whisper. "I ought to say I have the greatest respect for her. I believe she is a thoroughly good woman. They have quite a hard struggle, she and her mother, their school is not very prosperous, but I am sure they do excellent work with the children."

"My dear chap!" Reggie purred. "Any scandal about her?"

Mayce flushed. "I thought I told you there was unpleasant talk."

"You did, yes. Anything to do with our Peter Wayland?"

"I have never heard that," Mayce cried. "I don't think it would be said to me, Mr. Fortune."

"No. I suppose not. However. About her huntin' for a husband?"

"There are sneers of that sort," said Mayce angrily. "You know what they're worth."

"As you say. Well, well. All this bein' thus, watch it, Johnny. And let me know if anything comes to you. Good-bye."

That night something did come and Mayce let him know at once. "Is that you, Mr. Fortune? This is Mayce here, John Mayce, of Staplehurst. Peter Wayland has been stabbed, he was found close by his house in the dusk, he has lost a great deal of blood, could you possibly——"

"I could," Reggie interrupted. "Where is he? At his own place? All right. Half an hour."

He found Peter on the borderland of unconsciousness. High in the muscular back near the spine was a small wound. Reggie spent some time on that. He was a long time over pulse and heart. . . .

When he conferred with Mayce in another room his round face told of nothing but curiosity. "Well, Johnny. Wound made by very narrow weapon, short weapon. Didn't get very far. Missed the spine good and well. Nasty wound, shouldn't be dangerous. In itself. You were sayin' you gave him a shot of strychnine. What did you think of his heart? Rather slow, what?" Mayce said something about loss of blood. "Yes. There is that. I should say he's had a dose of a cardiac drug. Say strophanthin."

Mayce turned white and swayed.

"My dear Johnny! Hold up. Can be dealt with." He gave directions. . . . "Tough young fellow. You'll get him through. Have you told the police about him?"

"Yes, I mean no. They'd been called when I got here. There's a detective waiting to see you."

"All right. Run away. Send him in."

A young and brisk Inspector introduced himself. "And what are you going to tell me?" Reggie asked.

"I'd like to know if I've found what he was stabbed with, sir." He produced a bradawl. "It's like a thing from a child's tool box, but it's all bloody to the handle and it was lying by the tree just where Mr. Wayland bled."

"Is that so? Yes, probably was the weapon used. I had expected something like this."

"Would it kill a man, sir? And from the back?"

"It could, yes. I don't think it will."

"I'm glad to hear that. But it beats me how a big, strong chap like Mr. Wayland could be set on by anybody with nothing more than that thing—and bring it off too, lay him out and get away with it!"

"Circumstances not normal, no," Reggie murmured. "Have you anything more about 'em?"

"Mr. Wayland was down at the tennis club this afternoon. I'm told he didn't leave till seven or so. Just after eight a lad found him lying under the trees close by, asked him if he was ill and couldn't understand what he said, tried to get him up, and found there was a lot of blood on him and ran for help to the next house. That's all the evidence I have so far."

"Scene of crime, please," said Reggie.

They went out to a night of haze and low cloud. The Inspector flashed a torch between the big lime trees and its light found a patch which shone sticky. "There you are, sir."

"Oh yes. Blood—about the right measure. Right condition for alleged time. Between seven and eight. Darkish twilight before eight to-night. Lots of cover here." Reggie took the torch and swept its beam about.

"All tarred, path and road," the Inspector told him. "No chance of any traces."

But Reggie went on plying the torch. "How would he come from the tennis club?"

"This way, sir. This is the short cut."

They turned from the Green Walk into a passage way between palings. The torch discovered a mess.

"Oh, yes," Reggie murmured and stopped and bent over it.

"Somebody been sick," the Inspector announced. "Ah, you mean Mr. Wayland was drunk—that's why he didn't resist!" . . .

Next morning Lomas looked up from papers to see Reggie come into his room and sink into the easiest chair. "Well, well," Reggie smiled. "Not likely, as we were sayin'. Only it's happened. Original as far as known."

"Don't be so infernally oracular. Are you talking about this fellow at Staplehurst?"

"Wake up. Case of mixed drugs stolen from doctor to poison someone in his own district—which hasn't been done before—not to notice."

"Good gad! Was the fellow poisoned before he was stabbed?"

"Oh yes. Not after. We didn't do it. Not Mayce nor me."

"Damme, that makes a determined crime of it," Lomas frowned. "But I've had a message the fellow's doing well, he's going to come through."

"He is, yes. Had a bit of luck. Had proper treatment. My treatment."

"Are you sure about the poison?"

"Oh, my Lomas!" Reggie sighed. "Heart slowed down. As from digitalin or strophanthin. Either might turn him giddy and muddle his sight, so he'd be easy to hit. Either might make him sick—especially strophanthin. Strophanthin is rapid. On the way he came, somebody had just been sick. I've found strophanthin in the stuff. So that is that. The inference is he had a dose of strophanthin at the tennis club to get him ready for stabbing. And there were ampoules of strophanthin among the drugs stolen from Mayce's car. Well?"

"Devilish clever," said Lomas.

"Subtle mind, yes. Spiteful mind. Takin' any action?"

"I'm told he has no idea how he was hurt or who did it."

"So he says. Good fellow. But probably telling the truth."

"You think he should know—he has reason to know?"

Reggie answered with a dreamy smile: "Not bad, Lomas. Crucial questions. Questions I've been puttin' to myself. Incline to answer in the negative. Simple mind, his mind."

"You believe you know all about it?"

"Nohow. Contrariwise. Don't know the fundamental things. Evidence not adequate. How it was done—yes. Who did it—no. Why—no. Take it another way. From the primary questions. Who had the opportunity? Who had a motive? Question number one. Anybody might have given him a shot of strophanthin who had the stuff and was in the club pavilion when he had a drink there. He drank cider cup. His known habit. Just the stuff to cover the taste of the dope. Somebody who knew his habits indicated. But everybody in the club knows him. About the stabbing—by somebody shorter than him. Most people are, male and female. Anybody could get hold of a little bradawl like the one that stabbed him and plenty drive it into him. However. Strophanthin isn't so easy to get. Mayce's drugs were stolen from his car outside the Wayland's house, close to where our Peter was stabbed. And Mayce saw a woman lurking about there just before the drugs vanished. General conclusion, look for the woman."

"I agree," Lomas nodded. "The whole thing has a feminine touch."

"You feel that? Yes. So did I. Could you say why?"

"Because this toy of a bradawl was the weapon. It's not much bigger than a bodkin. A man out to kill would have used something more lethal."

"Might have been lethal. However. It wasn't. Sound argument, your argument. And yet—why such a small bradawl. Lots of bigger tools with points about."

"Out with it, Reginald," Lomas smiled. "What is the brilliant theory?"

"Isn't a theory," Reggie mumbled. "Only a nasty fact. Miss Sophia Boyd and mamma keep a kindergarten school. Teachin' handicraft. Little tools for little children. Sad but true."

Lomas made a grimace. "Not too strong though."

"As you say. Only a pointer. But it does point. Now about the drug. Strophanthin is a bit out of the way. Not often chosen by a poisoner. But anybody who'd had to do with heart disease might know how it worked. Mayce has given it to William Dean, the big noise in Staplehurst, who has an only daughter, Rosemary. She and our Peter are the two catches of the place. Public opinion is sure they're as good as married. And I saw 'em doin' a star turn together at this tennis club, very jolly. That's just before Peter was doped and stabbed. Rather bafflin'. The bradawl does point to Sophia. The drug might point to Rosemary or Dean. Not so good. However. Lots of people know a bit about drugs now. Unfortunately. Lots of people have toyed with a little bradawl. Finally, combination of poison with stabbing is curious. Don't often get both the dagger and the bowl."

"Quite," Lomas nodded. "But in spite of the combination, the victim wasn't killed. Not an efficient murderer."

"Not actually efficient, no. Though so determined. I've wondered about that. Might have been efficient if our Peter hadn't had the right treatment. As I was sayin'. However. The methods were more subtle than sure. That's all about question one—who had the opportunity. Question two—who had a motive? Johnny Mayce reported bad blood about. I found queer undertones. Mayce says Dean's circle have a down on Sophy Boyd and mamma, but there are those who back the Boyds. Nice old ladies let out to me they didn't like Dean, but they pity him. No reason given. While breathing the voice of Eden over Rosemary's marriage to Peter. Same nice old ladies feel there's something not quite nice about Sophia. Don't leave Rosemary much motive for crime. Well, passin' to facts: Sophia came to see Peter and Rosemary cut a dash in the tennis tournament. All alone and aloof. With a riddle of a handsome face. Went off into the pavilion when they'd won, lookin' a flame of pride."

"Into the pavilion," Lomas repeated. "That's where the man would go for his drink."

"As you say. He did. So did Rosemary. But I didn't see Sophia after. Rosemary emerged and went home with father, leavin' Peter behind. Father asked where he'd got to, and she said no matter, he was dinin' with 'em. Then Peter came out and joined the merry throng, very jovial. In which state I left him. My mistake. Didn't think anything was bein' done then. I have no imagination."

Lomas chuckled. "Your fixed delusion. If you had any more——! You've taken a lot of pains with this, Reginald. You——"

"Yes, I have. But not enough. Why don't you do a little work? Asked you that before Mayce's dope was used on Peter. You said nothing to work on. Your gross error. However. Police principle, never look for thief till horse is stolen. Horse now gone. One horse. I've recovered him. Which is not good enough. Better shut the stable door."

"What do you suggest? On your facts it looks the common case of the young man with two women after him, attacked by the one he's turned down. The Dean girl seems to be his choice—she's his partner in a tournament; they win while the other damsel looks on in a temper. That puts the motive of jealousy on her and leaves Miss Dean without any. I dare say you're right. But you have no definite evidence."

"Tell me not what too well I know. I am right. And we're nowhere. You're a good judge, Lomas. Which is a mercy. However. Not the only need. Action required—get the evidence—subtle and determined crime—as you were sayin'—operator still at large. Well?"

Lomas lit a cigarette. "Do you expect another attack on Wayland?"

"Not till he's out again. He will be soon."

"He might be able to give us a line."

"You think so?" Reggie smiled. "He says he don't know how it happened. I believe him. He's not officially engaged to Rosemary Dean. If you expect him to say the other girl was so sweet on him she tried to murder him, you miss your guess. Simple, clean fellow. He hasn't thought of anything like that. If you put it to him, you'd hear where you got off."

"Very helpful, Reginald. What do you suggest?"

"A little work," Reggie murmured. "Quiet, unobtrusive work. The obvious—who was handy in the pavilion when Peter Wayland swigged his cider cup, where were Sophia and mother and Rosemary and Dean when Peter was walking home."

Lomas smiled. "You don't trust Burt?"

"The bright young divisional Inspector? Oh yes. Quite smart on the job."

"We are much relieved," said Lomas. "Well, Burt's got all that. Miss Boyd was there or thereabouts when Wayland had his drink. Both the girls were at home, according to the servants, when he was stabbed. And old Dean and Mrs. Boyd with 'em. Isn't that useful?"

"Obvious answer to the obvious. However. Must verify. Anything more by our Burt?"

"What can he do?"

"Oh, my Lomas! Lots. The background, the obscure and nasty background. What's the scandal in Staplehurst? Why the bad blood? Why are the Deans set up against the Boyds? Why do nice old ladies pity the great William Dean like a miserable sinner? Why do they jump and go dumb when they see Sophia Boyd come where he is and his daughter?"

"Good gad! That's more than obvious. It's what you've given me already. Dean has bad health. His daughter and Wayland make a good match and people believe the Boyd girl after him. And all that works out in suburban gossip and scandal."

"Yes. Also in a nasty crime. Dig up the origins. Dig up the past of the Boyds and the Deans. This didn't begin yesterday, Lomas."

"Well, we can try," Lomas shrugged. "It's the devil of a job tracking scandal down. Hunting for a black cat in a dark room."

"As you say. Sorry for Burt. However."

After the case was finished, Reggie sought to comfort Inspector Burt with praise for the digging of him and his men. "We dug like beavers." Burt shook a disconsolate head. "But it wasn't the digging that did it, sir."

"Oh yes. Yes. Operative factor," Reggie smiled. "Induced the fatal action."

In a week they had dug up nothing which by any ingenuity could be made of use. Peter Wayland, well on the way to recovery, maintained in stolid bewilderment that he couldn't think of anybody who would want to murder him, couldn't understand a dam' thing about it, stubbornly declined to believe that he had been poisoned at the tennis club. Rosemary came to see his mother often, saw him as soon as he was visible. Dean called. Mrs. Boyd called, but not Sophia. Peter was taken away by his mother to convalescence at Eastbourne.

Some days after that the telephone roused Reggie from the chair in which he smoked his after breakfast pipe. "Lomas here," said the telephone, "Will you tell me what you expected next at Staplehurst?"

"No. Can't. Possibilities incalculable. Expected more trouble. And evidence. With luck. Found any?"

"I like your modesty. Very wise. We have only the trouble."

"Clever of you. Well?"

"Rosemary Dean has disappeared. Her father informed the police this morning. He says he expected her in to dinner last night, but thought nothing of it when she didn't come; she often made up a party with friends for a country run in the summer. He went to bed early, got up and found she hadn't come back. That's all he knows. The last he saw of her was at lunch yesterday. The servants say they don't know when she left the house. None of her particular friends he can think of have seen her. Pleasant little problem, what?"

"Yes. Curious and interestin'. Rather cool about it, father Dean. Didn't worry too much about only daughter. Some men don't. Quite plausible story, his story. However. Takin' it she is gone, anything from the bright young Burt?"

"Damme, he's only just been informed."

"Just going to begin, same like Mr. Snodgrass. Was he surprised?"

"Don't be superior. So were you."

"Oh no. No. I didn't say that. More trouble was clearly indicated. Doing anything with it?"

"What's in your mind?"

"I wonder. Ideas hoverin'. Look up the invalid, Peter, at Eastbourne."

"Good gad, do you think she's gone to him?"

"Many possibilities. As I was sayin'. Our Peter is a factor. Better check him up. Where is the bright Burt? Right. I'll go and see him."

Inspector Burt was at the headquarters of his division, for which he apologised. He had men working every line there was; he thought it best to stay put and keep all the strings in his hand.

"My dear chap!" Reggie purred. "Quite sound. Directin' intelligence should direct. What have you?"

"The Boyds went away last night. It was the end of term at their school yesterday. The place is all shut up. I haven't got their address yet——" He was interrupted by the telephone. "Yes. Speaking. Thank you very much." He turned to Reggie with a frown. "That was the Yard telling me Mr. Wayland and his mother are still at Eastbourne together alone, haven't been away from their hotel. I never supposed they had."

"No. Nor did I. But we wanted to know."

"Did you think he'd gone off with Miss Dean?"

"One of the possibilities. Not probable possibility. She might have gone to him. Rather more probable.

However. She hasn't. Now we want to know all the more where the Boyds are."

"I haven't forgotten that," Burt answered sharply. "I——" Again the telephone rang. He wrote as he listened. "And here it is! Mrs. Boyd told the post office to forward letters to a boarding house at East-bourne."

"Fancy that," Reggie murmured. "Check it, though." And Burt rang up the boarding house.

While he was at it, one of his men came in, hot and important. "Half a minute," Burt muttered, still listening. "Thank you. Now then!"

"About the Boyds' school, sir. They had the regular sort of do for a school breaking up yesterday, you know, song and dance by the children with parents and pupils there. Miss Dean went. I've got that quite hard. Several people saw her talking to Mrs. Boyd and daughter. The show finished about four. I can't find anybody who saw her go away. The Boyds cleared out and left last night, there's no one in the place and it's locked up."

"You wait," Burt waved him out. "That's funny stuff, Mr. Fortune."

"Yes. Curiouser and curiouser," Reggie murmured.

"This Eastbourne house says the Boyds did go there, arrived about nine-thirty last night, but they went out after breakfast this morning. I think I'm justified in getting into their school."

"Absolutely," Reggie agreed with enthusiasm. "Good man. Let's go to it."

They went. The energy of Burt discovered a window which could be entered, his men went through it and

Rf

opened the back door. They searched the place, a rambling old house, all its rooms but three given up to the children, all neat and innocent, not a door in them locked. But at last, in the gloom of the basement, behind the stairs, they came upon a door which would not yield at the turn of the handle.

"Hullo!" Burt exclaimed and flashed his torch on it and they saw a keyhole without a key. He put his back against the opposite wall and drove a foot at the lock.

With a rending of aged wood the door flew open and stopped with a jerk. His torch light showed the pegs and umbrella racks and boot rails of a cloak room. The door had hit against a woman who lay behind it. She moaned with difficult breath, she moved as if she were fighting pain, but she seemed neither to see nor hear them. She was lying upon her face. The torch searched it. It was white and smeared with dirt and it twitched.

"My God! She is Miss Dean, is she?" Burt cried.

"Oh yes." Reggie took the torch and knelt beside her. . . . He scribbled on a card. "Go to a chemist for that, quick. 'Phone for an ambulance, Burt." He studied her pulse again, laid her more easily and stood up and went out.

Burt met him with the breathless question. "She's been poisoned too, has she, Mr. Fortune?"

"Yes. Same like Peter Wayland. Heart feeble and jumpy. Other symptoms same, but more so. I should say the same dope. Strophanthin again. Only we have her at a later stage."

"My Lord! Later!" Burt muttered. "That stuff,

it'd make her go giddy blind, like Wayland, and helpless, then she was shoved in here and locked up and left to die. Devilish, isn't it?"

"As you say."

"Can you save her, Mr. Fortune?"

"Don't promise. I'll try." Reggie swept the torch light about the doorway and floor of the dark passage. It fell upon a key. "Well, well," he sighed and picked it up in his handkerchief and delicately tried it in the lock. It turned. "The key of this door," he murmured.

"That's queer," said Burt. "They must have dropped it when they went off—they would be in a funking hurry to quit."

"Natural condition, yes," Reggie mumbled. He took out the key and examined it in the torchlight before he wrapped it in his handkerchief and pocketed it. "May be useful."

"Finger-prints?" Burt frowned. "But the Boyds' prints might be on it anyhow. They wouldn't be evidence."

"As you say. However. Try everything." He studied the door again.

Heavy steps thudded downstairs, the detective arrived breathless with several chemist's packets. Reggie took them and went back to Rosemary . . .

The ambulance came and she was carried upstairs. "To her own house," said Reggie. "She may be sick on the way. I want that. . . ."

Some time afterwards he came out of Rosemary's bedroom with Mayce and turned into a sitting-room and asked: "What do you say, Johnny?"

Mayce stared distress. "I suppose it is strophanthin again. That's ghastly. Oh, I am a fool! It's all my fault. If I'd only locked the car——'"

"My dear chap! Oh, my dear chap! Too much conscience. If it hadn't been your drugs, it would have been somebody else's drugs. Determined person planned this game. Thoughtful person. Lots of resource. Matter of fact, you spoilt the operator's fun, bringin' me in. Well. Forgettin' ourselves, like good doctors, what about the patient?"

"Do you think you'll bring her through, Mr. Fortune?"

"Through this, yes. I should say it's passin' off. Wouldn't you?"

"I hope so. But her breathing is bad."

"As you say. Heart not so bad." Reggie turned and looked out of the window. "Pleasant old garden." He looked down upon a broad stretch of crazy paving, good rose beds set in a lawn between a glow of perennial borders. "Well. Dose of cardiac drug, provisionally strophanthin, taken some time ago, probably yesterday. You agree? Yes. Come and tell Burt. Have to see the anxious father too."

They found Burt in a sombre smoking-room and Rosemary's father with him. Both showed signs of temper. Burt sprang up. "I won't ask you anything more now, Mr. Dean. I have business with these gentlemen."

"That be damned," said Dean thickly, and turned his bulk to scowl at Mayce. "How is she? What do you say?"

"Miss Dean is not conscious yet, sir," Mayce wrung

his hands, "But I am glad to tell you that Mr. Fortune thinks her condition hopeful."

"Mr. Fortune?" Dean's tone was not flattering as he transferred his scowl to Reggie.

"How do you do?" Reggie murmured. "Don't be hasty with Mr. Dean, Burt. There are one or two things." He sat down. "Rather a difficult case, Mr. Dean. I have to tell you there's no doubt your daughter has been poisoned. What did she have for lunch yesterday?"

Dean's heavy, florid face became greyish. "Poisoned?" he muttered. "What poison?"

"Not certainly identified. Will be. Probably one of the drugs commonly used in medicine for the heart. Do you have any lyin' about the house?"

Dean turned on Mayce. "What is it you give me for my heart?"

"I have given you strophanthin at times," said Mayce nervously. "I have never left any dangerous quantity in your hands."

"There you are." Dean glowered at Reggie.

"Oh yes. Yes. I was askin' what did Miss Dean have for lunch yesterday."

"I don't know"—Reggie's eyebrows went up— "bit of fish, I suppose, bit of cold meat and salad."

"And she drank?"

"Doesn't drink anything at lunch. Lemonade. Coffee."

"Oh! And you?"

"Whisky and soda."

"She seemed well when she went out?"

"Perfectly fit when I saw her last. Same as usual."

"She didn't tell you she was going to the entertainment at this school?"

"No, she didn't say a word about it," Dean frowned.

"You're surprised she went?"

"I never thought of her going there. I don't know why she did."

"Well, well. The children's school of the place, isn't it? Quite a show—quite a crowd does go, what? Why shouldn't Miss Dean go?" None of these questions Dean answered with anything but a scowl. "By the way, was Miss Dean there as a child?"

Dean flushed again. "That's years and years ago," he said hoarsely. "It's a kindergarten. Rosemary's twenty-five—twenty-six, I mean."

"I thought she was about that," Reggie murmured. "Thank you."

But Burt, who had been fidgeting for a chance, struck in. "I have to ask you, Mr. Dean—is there any sort of feeling between the Boyds and your daughter and you?"

"I have nothing against Mrs. Boyd," Dean spoke loudly.

"And what about your daughter and her daughter?"

"I don't know Miss Boyd," Dean growled.

"You know of the attempt to murder Mr. Peter Wayland. Do you see no connection between that and the poisoning of your daughter?"

"Yes—I mean I don't—there may be—how can I tell—you haven't found who stabbed him, have you? D'ye expect me to do your job?"

"I expect you to give the police all the assistance in your power, Mr. Dean," said Burt. "I advise you to."

"I have." Dean lay back in his chair sweating.

"You don't want to add anything?"

Dean shook his head. "Well, well." Reggie stood up. "I shall be seein' Miss Dean again. Good-bye."

"You'll see me again, sir," said Burt.

Outside on the pavement Reggie loitered and looked back. A wall surrounded the garden. The house was of mellow red brick, too high for its base, but with an agreeable eighteenth century dignity. "Not a bad old place," he murmured. "Have the Deans been here long?"

"Donkey's years," Burt answered impatiently. "Are you off, Dr. Mayce? Let me know anything fresh about the lady." He put Mayce into his car.

"There won't be to-day," said Reggie. "I'll be out in the morning, Johnny." As Mayce drove off he turned with a twist of a smile to Burt. "And what is it you don't want Mayce to hear?"

"What did you make of Dean, Mr. Fortune?"

"Wouldn't give much for his heart."

Burt's sharp eyes twinkled. "Meaning he's heartless?"

"You're so swift. Didn't mean that. Meant medically, not morally. Excess of heart, got too big, done too much." Reggie moved to his own car.

"That was one of my points." Burt followed him.

"Only one?" Reggie murmured. "Can I drop you?"

"If you don't mind going back by the station, Mr. Fortune." Burt got in and they drove away. "About his heart disease—would he have much of this strophan-thin to play with?"

"You heard what Mayce said. Not given by Mayce. You may believe that. But don't forget what we began with. Strophanthin stolen from Mayce. And Dean would know the effect. Sharp slowing of the heart from a proper dose. Danger from more."

"That's what I was after." Burt nodded satisfaction.

"So I gathered. Happy to oblige. And then?"

"Did you like the way Dean answered?"

"Not much, no. Not all the truth. Not all he knew."

"I should say it wasn't. And besides that, he don't seem to me to have any feeling for the girl."

"Not a gush, no," Reggie murmured. "I wonder."

"He took her disappearance very casual, and now that we've found her, he don't like it."

"You think not? What is the theory? He poisoned her at lunch?"

"Would that work medically?"

"Oh yes. It could be. Doped her lemonade or her coffee. Time factor uncertain. But then? The girl was locked up in the school. Very difficult to connect that with Dean."

"I see it is. But you asked him about the lunch yourself, Mr. Fortune."

"Always try everything. Wanted to see his reactions."

"You got results all right. We left him in a sweating funk."

"Mind not at ease, no. May be on his own account."

"I should say so," Burt laughed.

"Yes. One of the possibilities. Several reasons why Dean might be afraid. No certainty. Marked anxiety in Dean to know nothing about the Boyds. Curious and interestin'. Next experiment for you—get the Boyds back and hear how they take things."

"We'll get 'em," said Burt. "But we want Miss Dean's story too."

"Oh yes. Won't have it to-day though. Do the work that's nearest. Get the Boyds. And anything about the Boyds. Or the Deans. Which you haven't yet. Hence these tears." . . .

But the Boyds supplied no information that day. They did not come back to their boarding house at Eastbourne till nightfall. The detective who met them then obtained only expressions of surprise at the discovery of Rosemary in their school, of absolute ignorance how she came to be locked up there.

In the morning they were brought back to assist Inspector Burt's investigations, unprotesting except by objections that they did not see how they could.

Reggie strolled into Burt's room as he opened fire and contemplated the effect in dreamy silence.

Woman worth seeing, Mrs. Boyd. Beautifully still and calm. Looked as if she'd been through fires and forgiven 'em. All passion spent. Not life, though. Grey and lined and past fifty, a handsome creature. Compelling, tranquil eyes. She knew, she was sure of herself.

Yes, Sophia got her make from mother. Same dark, austere style. But passion wasn't burnt out of her.

Eyes a blaze of a black glow. Blood up. Tense and fierce.

The crisp voice of Burt went through formalities about finding Rosemary and wanting information, and they offered none; they looked through him. "I tried to find you ladies before," he sharpened his tone. "Where were you all day yesterday?"

Sophia was beginning to answer when her mother said quietly: "We were out on the downs, Inspector."

"You didn't expect any enquiries? You went away leaving your school shut up with Miss Dean locked in the cloak room. Didn't you go over the building before you left?"

"I did," said Mrs. Boyd. "But it didn't occur to me to look into the cloak room. I am sorry. I can't conceive how Rosemary was locked up there."

"Were you and your daughter on good terms with her?"

"Yes," said Mrs. Boyd. "We always invite Rosemary to our school parties, and she came."

"I have to ask you whether there has been any cause of quarrel between Miss Dean and your daughter."

Sophia answered that quickly. "None at all."

Burt turned on her. "You're aware, Miss Boyd, a murderous attack was made on Mr. Peter Wayland. Now we have an attempt to murder Miss Dean in your school. You know them both, don't you? Can you think of anyone who was at your school entertainment who might have a motive for murdering them?"

"You believe someone tried to kill Rosemary?" Sophia cried.

"I do. I have reason." Burt leaned forward, staring at her.

"The same who stabbed Mr. Wayland?" she said slowly, and her eyes met his with contempt. "That's mad."

"Can't you imagine——" Burt began.

"Oh no. No," Reggie interrupted. "Not like that. Miss Boyd, how long have you known Miss Dean?"

"Twenty years, I suppose."

"Well, well." He studied her dreamily. "Very small girls together. Did Miss Dean come to your school?"

"Yes, when I was a child too."

"You would be," Reggie murmured, and turned to her mother. "Relations with any others of the Dean family, Mrs. Boyd?"

For the first time her calm was shaken. A moment passed before she answered. "There is only Mr. Dean. I have known Mr. Dean for many years."

"And has Mr. Dean ever been in your school?" Reggie purred.

"I don't remember." She hesitated. "Not for a long time."

"When was the last time?"

"I couldn't possibly say. Not since his son died."

"Oh! There was a son once. At your school?"

"Yes."

"Died while there?"

"Not at the school," Mrs. Boyd said quickly. "He died at home. It was an accident. He fell out of the window of his room."

"Well, well. How old?"

Mother and daughter looked at each other. "Gerry was nine," said Sophia. "It was six years ago." She looked at Reggie and the glow in her eyes was shadowed.

"Yes. Sad world," Reggie murmured. "That's all now, thank you."

"You'll be staying in London, please," Burt asserted himself. "You may be wanted."

"We shall be at home." Mrs. Boyd rose, and Reggie opened the door for them.

He came back filling a pipe. "I don't understand what you were working at, Mr. Fortune," Burt complained.

"My dear chap! Oh, my dear chap!" Reggie sat down and lit the pipe. "Diggin' up the hidden treasure of the past. Which you hadn't dug."

"I don't see that you've got anything—a kid fell out of window. What's the good of that?"

"Apparently irrelevant fact," Reggie mumbled, and blew a smoke ring. "I wonder."

"It seemed to me that I had the line all right. This girl, Sophia Boyd, she's hot stuff, if I ever met it."

"Don't know your experience. However. There is power in our Sophia. Girl of interest."

"Interest! She is interested. And passionate, isn't she? There's the motive, jealousy."

"Yes, you may be right," Reggie's eyelids drooped.

And Burt went on triumphantly. "Nothing else, is there? Wayland's the big catch of the place, Wayland fell for the other girl, so Miss Boyd set herself to murder him, and when she missed him went for—— Hallo, what's the matter?" He turned to answer a knock at the door.

"Beg pardon, sir," one of his men came in. "That Mr. Wayland's here asking for you, making quite a fuss."

Reggie put one smoke ring through another. "Actions and reactions," he murmured.

"Bring him along," said Burt. "He's tumbled to it, eh, Mr. Fortune, now the Boyd has gone for his girl, he wants her blood. He——"

Wayland strode in. His plain countenance was red; it seemed to have more jaw than ever. "Why did you bring Mrs. Boyd and Miss Boyd up here?" he demanded.

"Good morning, Mr. Wayland," Burt was suave. "I take it you've heard what was done to Miss Dean?"

"I've heard she was found locked up in the school. I don't know a dam' thing about that. Nor does Miss Boyd, nor her mother. Where are they? What the devil have you done with them?"

"Those ladies have gone home for the present, Mr. Wayland. Now——"

"Well for you they have," Wayland glowered at him. "For the present be damned. Don't you try bullying them any more. If you don't know when you've made a beast of yourself, I'll teach you. You're not up against women, you're up against me. I'm going to marry Miss Boyd."

"Well, well," Reggie sighed. "Have you told her so, Wayland?"

"Of course I have"; Wayland's flush deepened. "Umpteen times. It's all settled now."

"I see. Congratulations."

"Thanks," Wayland's scowl lightened for him. "That's all I have to say to you, Inspector. Good day." He swung out.

And Burt gave forth a sullen protest. "Why didn't the girl tell us she was engaged to him?"

"My dear chap!" Reggie smiled sadly. "Oh, my dear chap. She don't know she is. Been holdin' him off. As stated. Now our Peter means to take her. Since he was attacked, since the Rosemary was attacked. Got him going. Actions and reactions. I should say he'll have Sophia. Lots of power in our Peter, too."

Burt pondered and pushed back his chair. "Well I have to own I don't see why the fellow should be lying. And if we must take what he says, it turns down my idea jealousy was the motive. Then where are we?"

"I wonder," Reggie murmured.

"The Boyd girl had nothing to be jealous about. She's out. The Dean girl might be jealous enough, she might have tried to murder Wayland. But herself —that won't work at all."

"Not obviously, no. However. Take a broader view. Not the only tragedy in the Dean family, this tragedy. I'm going on to see Rosemary. You'd better come too."

They called for Mayce, and Mayce and Reggie examined Rosemary, found her better, well enough to talk, let the nurse arrange her and sit her up and introduced Burt.

"This is the Detective Inspector who's going to find out how it all happened," said Reggie.

She smiled, she shuddered. "Oh dear, it's so horrible. Inspector Burt?" She gave a little frown at him. "Have I met you somewhere?"

"I was investigating the attack on Mr. Wayland," said Burt.

She drew a deep breath, her blue eyes enlarged. "I remember. Mrs. Wayland told me. Is Peter all right?"

"He seems to be." Burt put some sarcasm into his tone. "I understand he's got engaged to Miss Boyd."

Rosemary smiled all over her face. "At last! Bless them! What a time they've been!"

"Have they?" Burt did not trouble to conceal his amazement. "You're not surprised, Miss Dean?"

"Why no. Everybody knew they would, except themselves, poor dears."

"Well, that's very nice," said Burt. "But it doesn't help me with your case. I hear you've told the doctors you have no recollection what happened to you?"

"No, really I haven't. I've tried to think, but it's all blank."

"Just tell me the last thing you do remember," Burt suggested, and she gave him a bewildered stare. "I mean about the party at the school."

Her smooth brow puckered. "It was so close," she said slowly. "I felt faint. I went out, I went to sit down in one of the little class rooms and everything went round and round."

"You were dizzy," said Mayce. "After that you don't remember anything more?"

"No, I can't, not till I woke up here."

"Did you have anything to eat or drink at the school?"

"There was tea."

"When?" Reggie asked.

"I don't know the time. After we'd seen the first little play, before the last one, the *Hiawatha*."

"And when did you feel faint?"

"While they were doing *Hiawatha*."

"Who gave you tea?"

"I didn't have tea. I had lemonade. Sophy gave it me."

"Remember anything about that?"

"No, how could I?" She looked distressed and pushed back her hair. "It was still lemonade. It wasn't very sweet."

"Oh. And then the children acted a bit of *Hiawatha* and you felt faint and went to another room?"

"Yes. I told you."

"Well, well. Some drug actin' on the heart was put into you——"

"I was poisoned?" she cried.

"Poisonous drug, yes. Question is when. At the school or before you went to the school."

"Before? I was here. I had lunch with father. And then—why, but I was shut up in the school, wasn't I?"

"That is so. Your father didn't go with you?"

"Of course not"; she laughed a little. "Father wouldn't."

"He's not keen on the school?"

"Why, men don't go to the school parties unless they have children there."

"I suppose not. He used to go when your brother Gerry was there?"

"Gerry?" she gasped, she put her hand to her eyes and it trembled. "Oh, don't. Poor Gerry! Why do you talk about him?"

"He died when he was at the school, didn't he? Could you tell me anything about that?"

"No, no, he just fell out of his window here. It was dreadful. He was only nine. Darling!" she sobbed.

"Must have been rather a shock," Reggie murmured. "Nothing to do with the school. But your father hasn't been there since?"

"I don't know," she spoke through tears. "I couldn't remember," she lay back on her pillows, turning her face away.

"You might try." Reggie turned away. "Won't ask you any more now."

Outside in the corridor, "Send the nurse back to her, Johnny," he said to Mayce. "Sorry and all that. Had to be done. Come on, Burt." He went downstairs fast. The parlourmaid met them. "Mr. Dean in?" Mr. Dean would not be back till lunch. "Were you here six years ago? No? Is there anyone in the house who was?"

"Mrs. Shove, sir, the housekeeper."

"I want to talk to her."

S<small>F</small>

They were put into the morning-room and Mrs. Shove arrived, a fat woman conscious of her importance but with shrewd little eyes. "If you please, sir," she announced herself to Reggie, who was looking out of the window at a corner of the garden.

"Oh yes. Were you in the house when the small boy Gerry was killed?"

Mrs. Shove put back her head. "I was, sir," she gulped.

"Just come back from the kindergarten school, had he?"

She took a moment before she answered with a gasp. "That's right, sir. It was the end of the term."

"He fell from a window?"

"Yes, sir. He was climbing out and he fell right down."

"Oh. Climbing. Where was his room?"

"Up at the top of the house, sir. It had been the nursery always and he had it still, though he'd begun to get a big boy."

"I see. Climbing out of a window on the top floor. Why did he?"

"That wasn't rightly known, sir. How can you tell with boys? They will do things."

"As you say. However. Was the door locked?"

Mrs. Shove blinked. "You've heard all about it, sir."

"No. Never heard that before," Reggie smiled awry. "Well, it was locked. Who did that? Who had the key of the door?"

"He'd locked himself in, sir. It was like this: Master Gerry was a daring boy and a regular monkey to climb, he loved it. He'd got it in him, as you might say, his father was always off to the mountains in his young days. And then Master Gerry had been reading those tales from history they give the children in schools nowadays, wonderful escapes from prisons and castles and towers and such. He had a book of 'em. Well, he must have tried to do such himself. One evening we heard a crash, and we ran out and found him lying right under his window mixed up with an old rope, and he never spoke nor moved again. The doctor said he must have died at once, his neck was broke, poor child. You see, he'd locked the door on himself so he could be like a prisoner escaping out of his prison, climbing down a rope, and it came down with him."

"Too bad," Reggie murmured. "Thanks very much. I want to have a look at his room."

"Sir?" Mrs. Shove was much shocked. "I couldn't do it, sir, Mr. Dean not being here to say. Nor I couldn't anyhow. Master Gerry's room has been kep' locked ever since, and Mr. Dean has the key."

"I see. Yes. Of course you can't do anything. We'll wait for Mr. Dean. Smoke a pipe in the garden. Let me know as soon as he comes in."

"I will, sir," said Mrs. Shove sternly disapproving, and put them into the garden.

Reggie wandered to a seat in the shade and lit his pipe, and through the smoke gazed up at the house.

"Well, I ought to have got that, Mr. Fortune," said Burt gloomily. "It does give us a reason for Dean's grouse against the Boyds. They put ideas into the poor kid's head that killed him. I've only been in the division eighteen months. I never heard of this child's death. That's no real excuse, I should have dug it out. Six years back and never a police matter, just an accident—I don't wonder the old stagers didn't hand it to me, but it's a bad break not getting it from any of the local gossips we worked."

"My dear chap!" Reggie condoled. "Oh no. What we have from our Mrs. Shove is the version of the Dean household. All the fault of the Boyd school. Probably wasn't put at the inquest. Inference, not evidence. Probably a general hush up. Friends of the Deans wouldn't make a lot of noise over a queer accident in the Dean home. Friends of the Boyds wouldn't want any nasty talk about the school. But feeling would rankle and fester. That's the way these things work. Sad world, difficult world."

"It is a queer story," said Burt. "But you do get boys doing these crazy tricks—boys try what hanging feels like and hang themselves, boys tie themselves up, or lock themselves up and never get clear—lots of cases."

"As you say. Weird animal, the human boy. Lopsided. Incompetent to manage his brain. Not improbable Gerry Dean would try to do a prison-breaking stunt. Our Mrs. Shove gave beautiful reasons. I should say they were partly true. Hence these tears. Well,

well." Reggie pointed his pipe at a top window, across half of which were horizontal bars. "That's the nursery; I suppose that's Gerry's room. Forty feet and more, what? And a clear fall to the crazy paving." He rose in slow time and wandered across the garden and looked up at the window and inspected the stones with dreamy melancholy eyes. . . .

Dean lumbered out of the house breathing hard, did not see them at first and called in a thick voice: "Mr. Fortune!" then made haste to them. "What do you want?" he panted. "What are you doing there?"

"When was this pavin' laid down?" Reggie drawled.

Dean swallowed. "Years ago."

"Six years or seven? Well, well. Nice little saxifrages in the stones now. I did want to speak to you again. About your daughter."

Dean gave a jerk of surprise. "Why, is she worse?"

"Oh no, no. Curious case, her case. Poison used was strophanthin. Soon as we found her I gave her an emetic. Had an analysis. Strophanthin present. But not very much. Shouldn't have made her as bad as she seemed to be. Don't understand her statement. Says she felt faint in the school and don't remember anything more. Can't account for complete unconsciousness from so small a quantity."

"I don't know what you mean," Dean answered slowly. "She must have been helpless and unconscious. She was put into a room and locked up there."

"Room was locked, yes. Key of the door not in the

keyhole. On the floor outside. Here it is," he pulled out a box. "You see?"

"I see it," Dean looked from the key to Reggie's face which told him nothing. "Well?"

"Six years ago"—Reggie drawled—"when your son fell down on these stones—from his window up there —his room was locked. Where was the key of the door?"

"Inside the room," Dean muttered, staring at him.

"Oh yes. It would be. In the lock?"

"We had to break the door open. The key fell on the floor."

"It could be," Reggie murmured. "We have to see that room now. The key, please."

Dean's mouth came open, but for a moment he made no sound. Then he muttered, "I'll get it," and lurched away.

They had to wait for him on the first landing. He emerged from a room wiping his mouth; he held out to Reggie a bedroom door key of the common kind. Reggie examined it closely. "Now the door," he murmured.

Dean went up fast for all his weight, and stopped and pointed. "That's Gerry's room."

"One moment." Reggie knelt down, turned up the edge of the carpet and ran his finger along the bottom of the door. He rose and turned the key in the lock and Burt and he went in. Dean stopped on the threshold.

The air was stale. Sunshine fell upon dingy curtains and faded paint and paper. But the room still waited for a child, and was ready, bed made up, washing things, toilet things, as a child had left them, in disorder. A small cricket bat, small pads and white boots in a bundle lay dumped by a cupboard, a school blazer on the floor. Among the chaos of small boy treasures on the table a book was open.

"Kept all just as he left it," Reggie sighed. "Only shut the window."

Dean muttered something, strode across the room and pushed up the sash. A rush of fresh wind came in.

Reggie was inspecting the book. The open page depicted, with colours dimmed by dust, a hero in gorgeously fantastic costume climbing down a rope which hung from a little barred window high up in one of the towers of a nightmare of a castle. The book's title was *Famous Escapes of History*, but it was not austerely historic. It had improved upon Joseph's adventures in the pit, taken Casanova's word for all his miracles on the prison roof, it gave Dumas's account of the way the Duc de Beaufort got out of the castle of Vincennes.

"Well, well," Reggie turned pages which were still stuck together by their gilt edges. "Not much read. Where did Gerry get this volume?"

"He'd heard the cursed stories at school," Dean answered fiercely. "He must have bought the book with his own pocket money. I didn't give it him. He was too crazy about climbing as it was."

"Oh yes." Reggie wandered away to the window.

"Wouldn't use this book in any school. Origin of book unknown. Easy to get out over these nursery bars when you're nine. Origin of rope?"

"What? The rope he fell with? It was an old Alpine rope of mine put away in the box room with my climbing kit."

"Fell with rope, yes. Didn't drop off it. Fell a long way. What was the explanation?"

"He'd tied a loop at one end. He must have put that round something in the room and it slipped off as soon as the strain of his weight came."

"Oh. A loop. Loop which remained tied after fall?"

"Well, of course," Dean said quickly. "Have you never heard of a loop slipping off a rock?"

"Yes. No rocks here. He'd put his loop round what? Bit of the furniture. Any of it out of place when you broke the door open?"

"The bed. The bed wasn't straight. Gerry must have put the loop round a leg of it, just round"— Dean stammered in his hurry to explain—"silly, reckless thing to do, but he had these crazy stories in his head, you don't expect a boy to be careful. Then at the jerk of his weight the loop was dragged off under the castor."

"You believe that?" Reggie sighed. "Oh no. No. That wasn't the way. Rope from loop round leg of bed must go up to get over the window sill. Strain of boy's weight would pull the loop upwards, not off. Bed would then move, might be dragged against the window and jam there and tilt. But it was only just out of the straight when you broke in. Loop didn't slip off." He stopped, he looked into Dean's bloodshot eyes for a long moment and then asked: "Who was in the house when the boy fell?"

"I was at the office," Dean muttered. "The servants."

"Yes. As Mrs. Shove said. Where was your daughter?"

"She, she'd gone out before, gone to tennis."

"Oh." Reggie walked to the door and beckoned to him, and he came unsteadily. Reggie drew him outside, shut and locked the door, then took out the key and pushed it underneath. "You see? Goes quite easily. Pity. Let us in, Burt."

Burt opened the door for them, and Reggie took the key again. "Like that, Dean. Somebody could have been inside helpin' Gerry, though you did find the door locked and the key on the floor inside. Somebody who helped the loop slip. No evidence on the key now that it was put under the door. But the key of the school cloak room, where Miss Dean was locked up, we found that on the floor outside." He opened its box again and displayed it. "Look. On these rings of the stem, specks of grey stuff. Which are old wood. Came from the bottom of the cloak room door. This key was pushed underneath it. From inside. Why? So we should think the door was locked from the outside."

Dean swayed and put his hand to his chest.

"Sorry," said Reggie. "Had to show you. That's as far as we can take it now."

"Take it, you haven't taken it," Dean spoke, panting, running the words together. "Get out." He lurched across the room and slammed the window down and turned, holding by the sill, his face flushed dark and distorted with rage, and made a violent gesture. "Get out of my house."

Reggie moved to the door. "I shall be seeing you again, sir," said Burt. "Your daughter, too," and incoherent noises of fury came from Dean as they left him.

Burt followed Reggie in silence downstairs and out and to his car. "Take you anywhere?" Reggie murmured.

"If you don't mind, the station." Burt got in beside him. "I say, Mr. Fortune, you might have given me that about the bit of wood on the cloak room key."

"My dear chap! Always suspected that key. Which I indicated. Only determined it was decayed wood last night. Even so, not evidence, by itself. Didn't become conclusive till we heard of the other case of a key of a door in Miss Dean's life."

"I don't see how we can make it conclusive now. Your case is all theory. I can't imagine any way to prove she played tricks with the rope and killed the boy."

"Do you doubt it?" Reggie sighed. "Oh, my Burt! Motive, jealousy. As you were sayin'. Jealous of father's fondness for only son. Never heard of a sister killin' for that before? Jealous of Peter Wayland and our Sophia. First effort, murderous attack on Peter, arranged to look like Sophia's work. Didn't come off. Contrariwise, produced enquiries by the active and intelligent Inspector Burt into the past of the Deans and Boyds. Very uncomfortable for Miss Dean. Second effort, clear herself and damn Sophia, by fakin' an attempt to murder Miss Dean which only the Boyds could have made. Ingenious effort, but with error of judgement. Underrated our simple minds. Not a sound judge of people, Rosemary Dean. Misunderstood Peter's pleasant nature. Never thought that loadin' suspicion on Sophia would rouse up Peter to take the girl by storm. Nasty jar for her, hearin' she'd made the match by doin' her damnedest to stop it. Courageous creature, though. Resourceful creature. Took the shock well, didn't she? However. Not really a nice girl."

"If this is the truth of it, she's a devil," said Burt. "But where's the proof of any charge we could make? I don't see how to handle it, Mr. Fortune. I'll have to consult headquarters. Will you——"

"Me?" Reggie was hurt. "My dear chap! Not me, no. I've finished. All facts clear. Passed to you for action. I want my lunch." He glanced at the clock in the car. "Oh my hat!" The car arrived at the police station in a rush. "Go to it. Confer with the higher powers. Tell 'em all."

He drove away to lunch at that one of his clubs where everybody is nobody in particular and they eat like their grandfathers. With salmon and a braised duck he restored himself, he sat long over a bottle of Musigny and greengages; after a glass of Marc in the library he let his cigar out and slept till some eccentric came to get a book.

It was late in the afternoon when, vague but benign,

he drifted into the room of the Chief of the Criminal Investigation Department. Lomas put up his eyeglass for a piercing stare. "My dear old thing!" Reggie murmured, collapsed into his favourite chair and sat on the small of his back. "Higher intelligence embarrassed?"

"Where have you been?" Lomas snapped. "I've had them trying to get you for hours."

"Thank heaven. The world is too much with us."

"Why did you cut out?"

"Oh, my Lomas! No more in it for me."

"What do you suppose is going to happen now?" Lomas frowned.

"I wonder." Reggie's eyelids drooped. "Matter for the higher powers. Well?"

"Dean's killed his daughter," said Lomas. "A little while after you left, Reginald. He sent her nurse out of the room. When the nurse came back and knocked she could get no answer, she went in and found the girl with pillows piled on her face, dead. The man had strangled her and he was lying across her, collapsed. They say his condition's hopeless."

"Oh yes," Reggie nodded. "It would be. Speakin' physically. Heart couldn't stand up to work like that. Done too much. Borne too much. That was fundamental."

"Good gad!" Lomas exclaimed. "You knew his heart was rotten and you drove him to it and left him!"

"Drove? Not me, no. The girl drove. Who was safe while she lived? We couldn't put her out of action. Not a chance of a case against her. I left Dean, yes. Left him to choose. He chose well. She can't kill any more. And he's gone to his boy. Best we could do for 'em. Not too bad. I have my uses. Alterations and repairs by R. Fortune."